Thank You!
Hope You Enjoy It

THE HIKE

(Formerly Titled Pacific Crest)

Searchlight Nevada
Winter 2014

CHARLES LEONARD HILL

ISBN-13: 978-0-9905232-1-5

DEDICATION

Dedicated to Dave Smith for replacing my legal pad and pen with a real computer. To my son, Charlie (technical advice on computers and *hacking*) and my son, Mike for taking me up on the crazy idea of hiking over 100 miles of the Pacific Crest Trail with 60 pound packs. To my daughter, Kelly who got all the attractive genes in the family, and my son, Joe who always thought it would be cool to have a writer for a Dad.

To Irene VosBurgh at Red Reef Publishing for many hours of help in bringing this book to initial print.

And, to Irene Parker, my soul mate who supported me, literally, while I wrote this book.

After my family, readers are my favorite people. If you have any feedback or comments feel free to email me at clh@charliehillbooks.com, I read them all. Please don't send forwards or attachments, because they get deleted out of self-defense.

CHAPTER ONE

Early summer 1990. . .

In the Sierra Nevada Mountains at more than ten thousand feet the air tasted antiseptic, clean, with no soot or smog. There was just too damned little of it. Breathing at this altitude had become a conscious motion. Too fast or too shallow meant becoming dizzy. It had to be deep and controlled. Hell . . . a cough made stars appear and just standing up too fast could make a guy pass out altogether. Max felt the giddy desire for a cigarette. The view, Christ . . . was forever. He noted his surroundings and thought what a great spot to come back to someday . . . but of course he never would.

Max, Shawn and Nolan hiked up a gradual incline past gnarled stumps of ageless fir trees and up to the rock-strewn plateau. They wasted no oxygen on small talk.

When one of them saw something of particular interest he would merely nod or grunt until the others noticed.

Small birds darted from scrub pine and brush, revealing themselves for only a glimpse before disappearing again, and then flying full speed into the next bush. *How do they do that?* he thought. High above them, larger birds of prey circled in lazy arcs, wings motionless, held aloft on air currents swept up from the valleys below.

They heard the steady drone of a single engine airplane several minutes before catching sight of it. The consistent buzz changed abruptly to a sharp, metallic cough. Max turned his sunburned, sweaty face toward the sky, covering his squinting eyes with his gloved hand. He waited to get a glimpse of the plane.

Its engine gave one last rattle, dying a quick death. Coming over the tree lined ridge and bearing right at them, the plane caught Max and the others by surprise.

"Heads up." shouted Max as he scrambled for the cover of the rocky ledge below the trail.

Max saw the pilot's determined face glaring at his instrument panel. He saw him struggle with the yoke in a frantic effort to bring the red and white plane back into the sky.

The crash unfolded before them like an episode of a stunt movie. There were no spectacular explosions or pyrotechnics that follow the most incidental collision in action films . . . just a terrible rending of metal and plastic as the small Cessna ripped between two rock outcroppings and slammed into the hillside.

Max reacted quickly. Unstrapping his pack and letting it fall to the ground, he stood up and tried to run to the wreckage. His legs protested after hiking the trail at a steady pace with sixty pounds on his back. He moved like an astronaut on the moon in a stiff-legged, near out-of-control gait to the downed airplane. He could smell fuel and another sharp, pungent odor. He couldn't immediately identify it, but it made him think of Southeast Asia . . . he thought he'd stopped remembering.

The pilot appeared to be in his mid-thirties. His red hair was made even redder with the blood that still pumped from above his ear where a six inch piece of steel tubing extruded like some kind of attachment for his headphones.

Even as Max reached for what was left of the mangled door and tore it open, he knew this man was not going to see another day. Max pulled on the pilot's collar as Nolan and Shawn crab-walked down to the plane in the same painful style as Max had. They froze in their tracks at what they saw.

"Help me get him out of this plane before we have a fire, will ya?" said Max. There was no real reason to hurry on the pilot's behalf as his blood flow slowed to an ebb.

The pilot seemed heavier since he was now dead weight. Real dead. Max grabbed the pilot's arms and pulled him free of the plane as Nolan and Shawn took his feet. They dragged him clear of the wreckage and laid him against a weathered stump of a long ago fallen pine. Odd-looking large black flies appeared from nowhere. Attracted by the smell of blood, they began to congregate on the pilot's neck and face, beginning a new life cycle, with Man back at the bottom of the food chain.

"Let's check the plane. Maybe we can find something that'll tell us who this guy is," Shawn said. "Hey, there's an emergency locator device on these planes that should have some kind of rescue attempt starting soon."

They returned to the wrecked plane and peered inside. The instrument panel was covered in blood that was turning to a dark thick jelly. Behind the pilot's twisted seat were scattered several flight maps and a large, formidable, and expensive metal suitcase. Max took the maps and the suitcase from the plane and put them down near the pilot's body.

"Let's see where the hell this guy came from, or

maybe where he was headed." Taking the flight maps, he spread them out on the ground. They were not new; the markings indicated a few short hops and one long route. A trip taken more than once judging from the worn creases that caused the maps to fold easily in a particular fashion.

The maps showed most of Arizona, Nevada and California. Notations indicated a flight plan from an unmarked airstrip just north of Nogales on the Arizona/Mexico border. From there it headed across the Huachuca Mountains, over desolate parts of the Mojave Desert, then up the Sierra Nevada Mountain range crossing the Pacific Crest Trail, where they were hiking. The flight plan continued up the Sierras and turned west above Susanville to an airstrip near the town of Bieber. This would put the planned destination in northeast California on the edge of the Modoc National Forest about a hundred miles east of Mount Shasta.

"Awfully strange flight path if you ask me," drawled Nolan. "Not one I'd choose unless I didn't want to be seen much. Let's see what there is in this suitcase."

Max turned the case around and tried the latch. It was locked but had been loosened by the impact. Max took a knife from a sheath inside his boot and pried up the clasp until it separated with a satisfying *pop*.

"Guess maybe we shouldn't be doing this but I'm way too curious to wait for permission. Besides, I think we'd always be wondering if we didn't."

It wasn't a big surprise that the case contained money, but the amount was definitely a shock. The case was large by any standards and it was full. There was nothing inside the case but money. Lots of it.

"I always prided myself on my honesty, you know, where if I got too much change from a cashier I'd return it . . . but this is a different matter altogether," said Max.

"What are you saying?" asked Shawn. "Aren't they going to be looking for this guy soon?"

"Who? His partners? I get the feeling this fellah

had bad partners and if the police get their hands on this money it's going to be marked exhibit A." Max paused for a moment. "Let's hike down the trail . . . somewhere away from here. If we can shift just a little weight out of my pack I think I can carry this thing for a short while."

Shawn tied Max's sleeping bag and cushion to his pack-frame and carried his water bottles in his hand. Nolan took the tent and Max's food bag. Max slipped his pack on and smiled. "This is more like it," he said. "I feel like I could jog."

Shawn chuckled and held up the suitcase. "Don't forget this." The suitcase was bulky and heavy. Max tried carrying the case first in one hand, then in the other. He finally opted to hold the case to his chest. He grinned at the others and started up the trail.

The three hiked in silence for about thirty minutes, each lost in his own thoughts. Max had no trouble figuring out what to do with the money. He made his decision in the first five seconds or so after seeing what the suitcase held. This was a gift. It had dropped in their laps and now it belonged to them. He would just have to let Shawn and Nolan arrive at the same decision. If they didn't . . . well, it wouldn't make any difference. This money didn't belong to anyone who deserved or needed it more than they did.

Max harbored no misconceptions about money. It wouldn't change his life. He already lived comfortably. He did what he wanted, when he wanted and with the people he chose to do it with. The real important things in his life . . . health, happiness, etc., responded more to his attitude about them than to his bankroll. This view of money had come from once having more wealth than he needed and then losing it all. He had learned from the experience . . . going from no disposable income to a multi-digit bank balance didn't necessarily mean there wouldn't be any real problems to face; just as being broke didn't mean he couldn't have a good time. Right now his only concern was putting as much distance as possible between the crash site and his group. Max looked back at the others as he cleared a rocky outcropping and started down a gradual decline.

It was several minutes later when Shawn cleared the same outcropping and looked down the trail at Max's receding back. Shawn was in his early thirties and newly engaged to a girl named Marlene who ran cocktails at The High Way House, a restaurant and bar combination outside Sacramento. This month long excursion was the source of several arguments and a real shouting match the night before the hike began. She called it . . . oh yeah, "A waste of time, male bonding bunch of crap with a couple of tree hugging granola eating . . . etc." How would she react now?

Nolan, on the other hand, realized this was what he had fantasized about many times. He'd be standing on some street, waiting for a light change or a bus, when a car would careen around the corner. A bag would be thrown out and land at his feet. The car would speed on as police cruisers chased after it and he would be left standing there with a bag of money . . . Most fantasies went along similar lines. Always, he would figure out how to keep from being found out by the police or the crooks. He would wind up with the money without anyone else knowing about it. He felt an uncomfortable twinge thinking about Rhonda. He wished there were some easy way to keep her from finding out he had the money at all. No chance of that.

It was now close to one in the afternoon and the sun beat on them, drawing strength from them almost as fast as the exertion of climbing at this altitude. The trail began a series of switch-backs up an almost bare hillside. Forward progress was tough as ground changed to loose shale. The trail took up total concentration. Rocks the size of clenched fists with sharp angles littered the trail. Real ankle-breakers. The two or three foot area in front of them became their universe, rolling under them in a continuous motion. If they stopped and looked at a fixed point in the sky, it caused the clouds to appear as if they were falling away from them . . . sucking them into some kind of vortex.

Max began to breathe heavy in John Phillips Souza rhythms to keep his pace up. It worked okay unless it became an unfortunate mind choice, some unwanted tune stuck in a loop in his brain. " . . . You're every woman in the world to me . . . "No. No. Think military damn it. ". . . give me your left, your right your left. Give me your left, your right, your left . . . You're everything to me. My midnight fantasy . . . "No, damn it. Try harder. "Ain't no use in looking back, Jody's getting all the crack." That's better.

The three of them climbed in silence, pushing hard, knowing they had to get to some type of cover. Max topped the crest of a hill and waited for the others to come up the trail.

Shawn walked up next to Max and stopped. "Let's rest for a minute. I think we should talk."

"About what?" asked Nolan, slipping off his pack and reaching for his water bottle. "We already know what we're going to do. It don't take a brain surgeon to realize we've been given a gift here. All we have to do now is figure out how keep it."

Max looked from one face to the other, both showing the eager signs of acceptance of their newfound wealth. "No problem keeping this money if we just use our heads. Right now there's a search starting . . . a plane as new as that would have a working Emergency Locator Transmitter activated by the crash. The Civil Air Patrol is going to jump all over this. Let's get off this marked trail as soon as we can and head for civilization. Where's the nearest town of any size close to us, Shawn?"

After studying the geological maps he carried, Shawn got a fix on their location. "Looks like Lone Pine is our best bet . . . it's a ways. Once we get to this road here," he pointed at the map showing the dark line leading into the foothills, "we might be able to hitch a ride. Unless someone has a better idea we can be off this mountain and on our way home by tomorrow afternoon."

"Well, we best get moving then, it looks to be just a couple of miles up the trail to decent tree cover." Max put his pack on and picked up the suitcase. "After that we can take a break. Let's haul ass."

The going was much easier now with the trail sloping down across a treeless plain toward the welcome edge of the forest. It was sparse and scattered but it looked good. They felt naked and exposed out in the flat. The best place to be right now was somewhere else.

They began to move down the slope to the relative safety of the tree line. The pace picked up considerably at the sound of a small airplane, but as they hurried into the trees the plane passed well to the east. They hiked for another ten minutes to a spot where the trail cut back and the ground was granite. Max climbed up a rock outcropping with difficulty. Panting from the weight of the suitcase, he looked back to make sure he could not see the trail. Rocks and trees shielded them from anyone coming up the trail. His hands and arms were starting to ache from the weight of the suitcase.

"Man!" panted Shawn as he bent over while inhaling deep lungs full of air. "Haven't kept up a pace like that since the Army."

"I don't think the Army can pay you like the payday we got here today. No way," Max exclaimed. "Okay guys, let's figure out where we can get off this trail as quick as we can without losing time. Show us where we are again Shawn and the fastest way out of these mountains."

"Looks pretty simple, Max." Shawn replaced the top to his water bottle and gestured ahead of them with the map he was holding. "We can head northeast at the tip of that meadow up ahead and I'd guess there's good campsites to be found if we stay parallel to this ridge. There are occasional flat clearings and a couple of brooks showing on the map in case we need more water. As long as we keep those peaks there over our left shoulder we'll be in great shape."

"It'll be rough going off the trail," said Max, "so we had better stay within sight of each other. We sure don't want to get separated." Max looked at the topo map again. "This looks reasonably passable after the meadow. There should be deer trails to follow and they should take us water to water all the way down to the road. Right now we need to make some changes in our packs if we want to pick up the pace."

"How so?" asked Shawn around a mouthful of candy bar.

Max began to take things out of his pack and spread them on the ground. "Let's start by lightening the load we're carrying." He took his food bag back from Nolan. "If we're going to be out of here by tomorrow afternoon then we sure don't need eight days of food." He dumped out the bag and kept only some of the candy bars and trail mix. Then he took out the small gas stove. "We don't need to cook either."

Shawn took out his food and set aside just enough for a full day, with nothing that required cooking. Then he piled up his clothing, holding up a pair of worn Long Johns. "Do you think we'll be able to afford new duds to replace these?"

They laughed and went to work, taking out everything except what they would need that night; food, all their clothes except what they had on, the ground cushions for under their sleeping bags, pots, silverware, cups, most of the first aid gear except powder and band aids, the wetsuit booties for around the campsite, even the tent got tossed. When they were finished the weight of each pack was down to almost nothing.

"What about the suitcase?" asked Shawn.

"That's easy. I'm beginning to feel a little like Fred C. Dobbs in *The treasure of the Sierra Madre* anyway. We need to count this down in rough fashion now, split it up between us, and get out of here. That way each of us will be responsible for our own shit."

"Sounds good to me," Nolan said, "but we should get it down about how we're not going to run home and start flashing hundreds around, buying all kinds of extemporaneous crap, quit our jobs, and start wearing silk. I'm going to have enough trouble keeping Rhonda from spending it all at the mall once she finds out."

They gathered around the suitcase and squatted, each trying to remain aloof about the money. Shawn picked up one of the banded stacks. "How's about we just go to the closest airport and give it all to the Hare Krishnas."

"Sure. Just buy our way right into Nirvana," Max muttered as he began stacking banded wedges of bills next to his gear. "We're going to have to hurry, there's a lot to count. It might not be too bad, I think each packet is marked . . . Let's just check some at random to see if they jibe."

The amounts matched on the first few stacks so they began to separate the money into three piles. Max took the empty suitcase and set it aside. "I'll really miss lugging that heavy thing around."

"This is great," said Shawn as the three of them looked at the money stacked in front of their packs. "They could make a beer commercial out of this, for sure. Wouldn't be any more bizarre than the situations they try to sell us on now, right? Like all the great looking babes pawing at those nerds on TV just because they're drinking long necks. This looks like more fun to me, no shit."

"Okay now." Max said as he finished stuffing his pack with money. "Carrying this is going to make each step a whole lot easier." Max stood up and stretched his legs. "Now we need to hide this stuff." He pointed at the gear scattered around them. "Make sure there is nothing that will identify you like underwear with you name sewn on. Bring that stuff over here." He walked over to a depression next to a pine tree near several good sized rocks. They worked at the ground with sticks and hands until the depression was large enough to put the suitcase in. They opened it so the polished metal was against the ground. Then, they threw the gear in, covered the pile as best they could with dirt and pine needles and pulled the loose rocks down on top of the pile. It would be safe unless a bear decided it was food.

Satisfied with their work, Max and the others walked back to where the packs were. "Ready?" Max looked from face to face. "There's one other thing I want to do before we go." He took out a small roll of Duct tape he had wrapped around a pencil to use for repairing gear. Then he took out his version of rain gear; three green plastic garbage bags. He used one of them to cover each of their packs and taped them on. Now, instead of the bright colors of the packs showing, they looked more like their surroundings. "This way we should be pretty tough to spot from the air."

"It's a good thing no other hikers have seen us yet." Shawn said as he put on his pack.

"Good luck for us." Max replied. "Judging from the boot tracks we've been following, there are two hikers almost a day ahead of us. Other than the guy who passed us two days ago we might not meet anyone hiking from north to south."

"Why not?"

"Because the directions in the books all read from south to north since that's the only way to do the whole three thousand miles in one stretch." Max almost bounced under the lighter load of the pack. "It's not going to matter to us anymore. We're getting off the trail now. All we're going to meet up with till we get to civilization is deer and bear."

They began to hike again and Nolan chuckled, giddy with the lighter weight of the money. "After all the grief Rhonda gave me about going on this trip . . . I wish she was here and I could see her face."

CHAPTER TWO

Rhonda stood in the kitchen, wearing a burgundy wool dress with a business jacket. The dark color highlighted her olive skin and almond eyes. She wore a pink tinged white carnation, picked from the window box and pinned to the lapel of her jacket just above the nametag that said "Foothills Realty." She parted the curtains and tilted her head slightly to the open window. "Is this better?" she asked.

"Yes, much." Marlene snapped the shutter on the Pentax twice. "Now let's get one of you sitting at the table with an open briefcase in front of you, talking on the phone." Marlene pulled the chair away from the table so Rhonda could sit down. "Smile like you've just closed a deal and you're telling the new home owners all about it."

Rhonda sat down, arranged the open leather briefcase in front of her, reached for the phone, when it rang.

"Hello."

"Great," said Marlene, as she took the picture.

"How realistic can you get?"

Rhonda gave Marlene a professional smile as she talked into the phone. "No, I don't care to learn more about the future price of rare coins."

"Here, hold this pen while you talk." Marlene handed her a ballpoint pen. Rhonda acted like she was taking notes.

"Yes," Rhonda tilted her head and pointed to the bottom of the real estate listing form in front of her. Marlene took another picture and gave her a thumbs-up sign. Rhonda spoke into the phone. "You're probably right; I could be washed away financially if I pass up this opportunity. Can you hold on for a minute?" Rhonda laid the phone down.

"What do you think?" Rhonda asked.

"With these pictures on your flyers, no one will ever suspect you don't know what you're doing."

"Great. That's the look I'm going for. I really appreciate this, Marlene."

"No problem. I'm happy to do it for you. Thanks for picking me up and taking me shopping with you. There's nothing I like more than spending other people's money for them. By the way . . . the outfit looks great on you."

"You mean it's a *power outfit*?"

"Absolutely. Blitz Krieg. The art of the deal." They grinned together. Marlene changed expressions to one more serious. "Actually, I'm jealous. I wish I had the drive to learn a new profession. I just don't seem to have the initiative." Marlene put the camera back in its case as she talked. "But this way, I get a vicarious thrill out of helping you get started in your new job, kind of like a career voyeur." Marlene put the camera bag next to the phone receiver which was still off the hook.

Marlene walked into the kitchen. "Have you got the makings of a sandwich here?"

"Check the fridge. There's cold meatloaf and rye. In fact, there's stew from last night in the crock-pot."

"Well, you must be exhausted after such a grueling photo session. Let me fix us some lunch." Marlene took bread, lettuce, tomato, cheese and the left-over stew and went to work.

Marlene was blond. Nordic features with corn-silk hair cut shoulder-length framing her milk white skin and hazel eyes. She wore faded Levi's and a short sweatshirt cut below her breasts, showing lots of midriff.

Rhonda picked up the receiver and listened. She was rewarded with a dial tone and hung up. She sat at the table, watching Marlene make lunch, and thought back to the first time they met. Rhonda had just left the Sacramento County Morgue where her life had changed forever. The knock on the door had come that day as she sat down at the kitchen table for a cup of coffee. She had spent the morning shopping for Tawna's thirteenth birthday party. Oh no. It just couldn't be. It had to be a mistake. "Are you Mrs. Locklear? Do you have a daughter named Tawna? I'm Detective Andrews of the Sacramento Sheriff's Department. I'm afraid I have some bad news. There's been an accident and your daughter . . . no I'm sorry, she's not all right. She died in the emergency room. We need you to come down and identify her."

The rest of that day was like walking in a dream state, a nightmare. She looked so small and helpless lying there. How could it be so? What was she doing out of school? She was not supposed to hang around with those kids. Damn her. If only she were alive. How do I tell Nolan when he gets back?

It made perfect sense to her to stop at the High Way House. She sure didn't want to be alone. After bringing her a second drink, Marlene had to ask . . . "What's wrong? Have a fight at home?"

Rhonda smiled, then cracked. Crying was one thing but this was not in the same league at all. Racking sobs shook her frame till Marlene was sure the woman would fall to the floor. "Hey, girl . . . it's going to be okay." She set down her drink tray and motioned to Jack, the bartender, to cover for her as she put her arm around this forlorn stranger. "Go ahead, let it out. I have nothing but time."

"I just lost my little girl. I don't see how I'm going to ever tell my husband, he'll be home in a couple of hours. There's just no way I can tell him. I'm completely lost here."

Slowly rocking back and forth and crying she began to get some semblance of control. "I shouldn't be burdening you with my troubles. Leave me alone for a little bit and maybe I can get home. I'll be okay"

"Sugar, there is no reason to be alone now. I lost my brother not long ago so I know what I'm talking about. Let me get my sweetie over here and we'll help you get home. You hold on for just a minute now."

Marlene got her coat and told Jack she had to leave. Shawn, her sweetie, was early and already at the service entrance to pick her up anyway, so Marlene led Rhonda out the back door.

"Is she okay?" asked Shawn as they headed toward his Wagoneer. "What's wrong with her? Do you know this lady?"

"Give me a break will you? She's hurting bad but it's not anything a doctor is going to fix. Her daughter was killed today, and she needs someone to kind of help her through the low spots. Let's drive her home and make sure she's okay. She doesn't think she'll be able to tell her husband."

"You mean he doesn't know yet?" Shawn looked at the stranger. "Man, that's rough."

Shawn drove through the small Sierra town of Placerville. Businesses had long since closed for the evening since it was past eight at night. Small town signs like *Andrew's Feed & Supply*, *StihlSaws*, and *Down Home Help* reflected in the rain. They passed the all night restaurants and drive-thru's that catered to those headed to the Lake Tahoe casinos. During the drive Rhonda sobbed softly, while Marlene kept making sympathetic noises. She knew the content of what she said didn't matter. As long as Rhonda felt another person was there for her and she wasn't alone.

Rhonda began to talk again as they got nearer to the house. "I am just so damn mad and sad at the same time, does that sound peculiar? I mean we just had an argument over this yesterday. She insisted that though these friends of hers used drugs occasionally, it was harmless. Social use! Can you believe that? Is that like casual sex? Was I born a little too late or what? Jesus. How am I going to tell Nolan?"

"I hate to mention it but this is starting to look more like a driveway than a road, although that's not unusual in these parts. I need some directions here," said Shawn. "I know this place pretty good so just an address or street would probably get us close."

"It's on Canyon View off Big Cut road. You know where it is?"

"You bet."

As Shawn drove he tried to come up with something more substantial to say than *You be*t but nothing came to mind. It was always that way when he was near women who cried, no matter what the reason. This made him really conscious of the differences between men and women. He secretly believed they were a different species altogether. Coming up empty on the conversational end of things he concentrated on the road. Where she lived was easy to miss.

Rhonda's house, perched on the edge of a ravine, turned out to be a surprising mix of early Victorian and abandoned mining camp. To reach it Shawn drove down a narrow, steep, mud driveway left slick from the rain. The Jeep slipped a bit but came to a stop near the front door. There was no paving or cement in front of the house. As hard as the mud tried to keep their shoes, the three stepped gingerly to the door. Red mud, you could paint with it. It clung to their shoes that they took off and left just inside the entry. As Shawn walked into the living room he could see the wrapping paper and presents scattered across a worn, legless sofa. A portable tape player, a real "boom box", had been in the later stages of gift wrapping when Rhonda had gotten the knock on the door that shattered her life.

"I guess it doesn't matter anymore if the price tags are still on does it?" said Rhonda as fresh tears started down well-worn tracks from her eyes to her chin. "I think I'll be okay now. I sure do appreciate your helping to get me home."

They shifted uncomfortably for a moment, then heard a car stop outside. Rhonda looked at the door with a blank expression. "That must be Nolan now."

Nolan walked in looking puzzled. "Where's our car? Did it quit running again? That car has got to go. Is Tawna home yet?"

"Honey, sit down please. Tawna is not home. Our little girl . . . She . . ."

It didn't take a rocket scientist to figure what had happened. Nolan went to Rhonda and held her without making a sound, just rocking back and forth and looking over her shoulder. He seemed unaffected, stunned, or perhaps it was a defense mechanism. "I think we need to be alone. You folks were nice to help out but we're fine now."

"Okay. We're going to the High Way House to bring your car back for you." said Shawn. "Do you have the keys handy?"

"You don't have to do that. I can get to it in the morning. There are probably lots of things we're going to need to handle." Nolan stayed composed but Rhonda began to cry.

That was enough for Shawn. He picked up the keys from the coffee table and headed for the door. "I don't know either of you, just met in fact, but you have plenty on your minds. We'll be right back."

Neither Shawn nor Marlene said anything for most

of the trip back to the restaurant. Finally Marlene broke the silence. "They seem like nice people, I just got a wave of gratitude. I guess our problems aren't as bad as I thought. Too bad someone has to take a fall for people like me to feel better about their lives, huh?"

"God. You sound like a bumper sticker. But you're right. I had a friend who always used to spout off some quote. *I cried because I had no feet, till I met a man who had no feet either*. Or something like that. Anyway, he said he sometimes wished he had a blind man in the closet so he could look in from time to time and feel grateful. I don't mean to sound crass but I feel grateful too, even though someone had to have trouble for it to happen." Shawn pulled into the parking lot at the restaurant. "Are you going to follow me back in their car?"

"Sure. It's the red coupe over there." Marlene indicated a red Olds with custom plates . . . CUL8RQT.

It took a minute to figure that one out.

During the drive back, both came to the decision to try to become better friends with Rhonda and Nolan. Neither of them realized just how close they would be to these new friends. In the days following, through the grief of the funeral and all the messy arrangements that one doesn't think about; what to do with the clothes; the phone calls that came weeks later from a friend who *didn't know*, and the endless phrases that started with the words, I'm so sorry . . . a bond was formed between the two couples that remained stronger than most families. That had something to do with how they happened to be on this hike to begin with.

Three months later, Shawn met Max at the Racquet Club where he worked out every other day. During a heavy weights session, Max offered to help him and they became workout partners. Their schedules were the same, which is the primary prerequisite for a weight-training partner. Though Max was years older he was the stronger of the two.

"Come on, Shawn . . . my grandmother can lift more than that and she's dead three years now. Push."

The weight moved the last inch with just a minimum amount of assistance from Max, making Shawn squeeze the last remaining strength from his swollen chest muscles. The bar clanged onto the rack. "Okay . . . twenty pounds more than last time. That's plenty for today. Let's hit the showers."

"I got some bad news today," Max said as they came out of the showers. "My camping partners both got transferred to cushy jobs back east. I'm left high and dry for the hike next month."

"What hike?" asked Shawn as he toweled his hair.

"Oh, I thought I mentioned it. We were planning to hike a big chunk of the Pacific Crest Trail; it goes from Mexico to Canada across some really fantastic country. Incredible. It's like walking across the top of the world."

"So? Go anyway."

Max laughed. "No. I don't want to go alone. Three people is the ideal number." He pulled on his shoes and began to lace them up.

"How come?" asked Shawn.

"In case one gets hurt, the other two can carry him out or one can stay with him while the other one goes for help."

"Oh . . . that sounds just great." Shawn stuffed his sweaty gear into his carry bag. "Really makes me wish I was there. So what if they can't go. Why not wait and go later?"

"It's a little more involved than that. I've already sent dried food and supplies to some Post Offices along the route."

"Why?"

"So I don't have to carry a month's food on my back from the start. There's enough junk to carry as it is."

"So, have it mailed back."

"I went through a lot of trouble to get permits for the

wilderness areas I'd be going through. Also, it has to be done at a certain time of year. If you go too early there's snow and too much run-off makes for some dangerous crossings of the creeks. If you're too late in the season you can get stuck in an early storm, in which case you become a *hiker-sicle* and they find you in the spring."

All around them the noise of men acting like boys swelled as the lunch hour jocks raced to get back to their jobs. "How good of shape do you have to be in?"

"Well . . . , Max adjusted his pullover and reached for his gear bag, "you could do it; if someone is in good condition to start with they'll be okay. After about the first few miles you can settle into a pace that will work for everyone. Why do you ask? Want to try it?"

"Tell you what I'm thinking, Max," Shawn said as he tossed his towel to the counter girl who flashed him a cheery white smile, "I've got this friend who could use something like this, so just maybe it could be worked out. He's in pretty good shape physically but has been down mentally for months now. Let me talk to him and call you."

Max stored his bag in the back of his Jeep and climbed up into the driver's seat. "I'm willing to cover for most of the food, since I've already sent it off. All you'd need would be good boots, and the rest of the gear you could rent. There's still a couple of weeks to get prepped for this. It's no cake walk but it certainly would be something to remember in your old age."

Shawn watched him drive out of the parking lot, already figuring out how to sell this to Nolan. He seemed completely apathetic since Tawna's death. Nolan had confided in Shawn how he should have seen what was happening with his daughter. He felt he should have noticed she was taking drugs and ditching school. Maybe this was just what the doctor ordered.

Nolan considered Shawn's proposition for all of two minutes that evening over beers. The answer came without hesitation.

"Okay."

"Okay, what?" asked Shawn as he reached across Nolan's cigarette burned, scarred table top to get at the chips.

"Okay, I'll do it. I'll go on the hike."

"Great!" Shawn said around a mouthful of potato chips. "Let's rock. I thought you'd stall on this idea but this is gonna be fantastic. I just know it."

CHAPTER THREE

They spent the night under the stars, having sacrificed the tent for weight when they buried their gear the previous evening. One big bonus of having almost no equipment was getting ready to go in the morning. Breaking camp in the early dawn was an exercise in simplicity. Get up, take care of nature calls, stretch, eat a protein bar, slip on the pack and start hiking. They opted for a steady pace, stopping only twice to rest and remove their boots to cool off their feet. Their goal was the dark line on the map indicating a road leading into the small town of Lone Pine. For several hours they passed through some of the most beautiful scenery anyone had ever ignored. The wall of trees ended, one minute they were walking through woods, the next minute they were standing on packed dirt. It was about a car and a half wide, a little gravel, recently graded. No cars. No car sounds either. It was as though the road had been built for aesthetics rather than utility. Max looked at Shawn who already had the map out.

"Which way?"

"This way . . . and we should be seeing farms and houses soon . . . or a restaurant." Shawn folded the map as he began walking. "I'm thinking maybe a hamburger and fries."

"Yeah. With extra grease," said Nolan. "And a shake."

Max gave it some thought. "No. I'm thinking tacos, about eight of them, followed by Dos Equis beer, that's so cold I'll get a headache if I drink it too fast . . . which I intend to do."

The food conversation quickly escalated to pure fantasy, killing the clock as the road unwound behind them a step at a time.

There was no traffic on the road but twice in the next hour the sound of small planes caused them to look to the sky. They no longer felt the need to run for cover. They were a long ways from the scene of the crime, so to speak, and intended to get further away as fast as possible.

Max considered their options on putting distance behind them. "Maybe there's some kind of daily bus service out of Lone Pine . . . or even a train would do."

Shawn chuckled. "How about Lone Pine Metropolitan Airport? We could just take a 747 home."

Max laughed. "Good idea, but not likely."

"No. I'm not kidding. Look over there." He pointed at what had looked like a barn off to the left of the road.

The small air strip rose out of the grassy field looking like part of an old photograph set on the absolute stillness of the early afternoon. A faded, once bright windsock flicked its tail as the beginnings of a breeze toyed with the leaves of maple and elm trees lining the road. The sweat dried where exposed but squirmed under the straps of their packs as they stopped and considered what they were seeing.

Shawn looked at Nolan's haggard face and asked

the obvious. "What have we here?"

Max adjusted his pack. "Let's go see if there is a cup of coffee to be had here. Anybody got cash?"

"I'll cover it this time," quipped Nolan.

"No . . . I wanted to know if either of you have any normal currency. We can't pay for our damn coffee with hundred dollar bills peeled off a banded stack of hundreds or someone might be wondering why backpackers have to tote their life savings along on a hike."

"Serious cash . . . don't leave home without it," said Shawn in a terrible Karl Malden imitation. "I have about fifty bucks in normal money on me, and a couple of hundred thousand for the tip. I always was a big tipper."

"I can almost taste the coffee now," said Max. "Maybe we can get a donut."

Max led the way down a narrow, gravel road to what looked to be the main building. It stood a story and a half high constructed of grey faded clapboard with *Buster's Flying Service* painted across the front in letters two feet high. The *F* could no longer be seen, having worn off a decade or so ago. Dust swirled around them like small children welcoming home long lost uncles as the three of them walked toward *Buster's lying Service.*

Heat waves shimmered off a runway that looked like an asphalt quilt with tar stitching. A cow bell clanked a lazy cadence from somewhere out of eyesight near the end of the Quonset hut hanger.

"I'm not too sure about finding coffee here." Shawn said.

"I'm not too sure about finding people here." Replied Max as he looked through the window next to the front door. Movement caught his eye and he opened the door. "Anybody here?"

"You need something, buddy?"

The voice came from a young mechanic looking up from under the wing of an old but clean Piper Lance, a fixed gear single engine plane faster than a lot of twin engine models.

"Hoping to find a cup of coffee. Any chance of that?" asked Max in an even, flat voice.

"We don't have much of a restaurant here but I was just going to take a break if you don't mind a few minutes' wait." The mechanic wiped his hands as he motioned the three of them to an open door. "This is what we call *The Pit*. Come on and grab a seat. You fellas look a little spent."

They followed him into a room that had a worn, Naugahyde, avocado green couch at least nine-feet long as its main attraction. The mechanic began to make the coffee, dumping the remains of the last pot out an open window where nothing grew. "Pretty quiet here right now . . . everybody who should be here is flying CAP today, that's Civil Air Patrol. Someone's emergency signal went off up in the hills and they're looking for a downed airplane. Don't bother me none. I like the quiet."

Max leaned against the windowsill so he could read the mechanic's name tag. "How long does it usually take?"

"This coffee maker's pretty quick . . . just a few and it'll be done."

"No, Bob, I mean to find an airplane that's down."

"Who?" The mechanic glanced down at his nametag. "Oh, you're reading the coveralls. Actually, everyone here would be Bob. Bob used to work here and bought ten pair of these coveralls. They got delivered about a week after he missed the runway in a Mooney. We all use them. My name's Cal." He held out his hand.

Max shook it and repeated the name back to him instead of giving his own. "Cal. Pleased to meet you. What about the plane?"

"Oh. It would all depend . . . sometimes they find them right away, sometimes never. Probably quick this time. I just heard on the radio that one of the pilots saw debris and a ground search is headed to look-see."

Shawn took off his pack and sat in the middle of the couch. He sank to the floor with a grunt of surprise. "Hope I don't need to get up soon," he muttered.

"Sorry, I should have warned you. The ends are fine but the middle is a bit weak. We call that couch the *Venus Fly Trap*."

Max doubted Cal was sincere on this point, he was sure all first time visitors got the chance to bounce their butts off the floor, maybe even got sent to look for a sky hook right afterward to make the day complete. "Who around here does the flying service? Is there an air taxi out of here?"

"John handles that. He's the one what took over from Buster years ago. He just never bothered to change the sign. He should be back pretty quick. I think the search is winding down. If they have a ground search going then they're about done. So's this coffee, if you guys are ready."

All three of them were definitely ready for their first cup of real coffee in a week but tried to act calm about it, like maybe it was no big deal. Shawn did this the best since he couldn't get out of the grip of the couch anyway. "Could you grab me a cup?" he said to Max.

"No problem partner, black and sweet, coming up." Max handed Shawn a cup with *Bob* on the side in gold leaf, and wondered if *Bob* had passed up buying anything with his name on it. Probably had a set of personalized plates floating around somewhere.

"Where you guys headed?"

"We need to get up to Reno. Been hiking near here but need to get moving." Max did all he could to get eye contact with Shawn and Nolan. Please don't mention California. Max knew it would be a careless move to leave a trail home from here but he wanted to put distance between the three of them and that damned plane.

The radio came to life behind the desk where Nolan sat. Cal grabbed the mike and said "Roger copy. Clear to land on runway two four." He put down the mike, moving to the window to watch the plane land. "Here comes John now. I knew it wouldn't be long."

The small single engine airplane dipped at the end of the runway, swam in the heat waves, became whole again and touched down with a puff of white smoke from the tires. When the plane got to the hanger it spun around with a roar to end up facing the runway and cut its engine. Cal smiled. Max and the others felt they were watching a performance practiced many times.

John jumped down from the plane and walked briskly to the office carrying a worn flight bag. He entered the 'pit' and grabbed a cup of black coffee Cal held out for him. "Thanks."

"I got the Lance ready like you asked. The parts we got from Reno should have fixed the problem," Cal said. "At least you won't have to fly low enough to read the street signs to know where you're at."

"We can only hope. This is the second time around on those parts. I'll return the ones that didn't work to Reno. It'll give me a chance to try these out in good weather."

"How'd the search go?"

"Piece of cake. The plane crashed conveniently out in the open. Too bad for anyone in the plane. Who we got here for company?"

Max extended his hand to John and shook. "Hi. I'm Bill. Me and my partners have been hiking and shooting pictures near here. We heard this place served the best coffee around so we had to try a cup." Of course it could be termed a little strong . . . like mud. Hope I can still have babies, Max thought. "Are you saying you're headed to Reno today?"

"Just as soon as I make a trip to the little boys' room. Why do you want to know?"

"We were going to hike on into Lone Pine and take a bus up to Reno but if it's okay . . . we'd pay for the trip. Roughing it is starting to wear thin."

"That's a hundred apiece."

"Great."

"Cal, load them up. We leave in about five minutes."

Max liked the way people did business around here. Too bad he was never coming back. He hustled Shawn and Nolan ahead of him to get the bags in the Lance. He excused himself to the bathroom when John came out and pulled a few hundred-dollar bills free to pay with. When he came back to the plane John was already running up the engine and Cal was motioning him to get in as he held the door open. Max ducked into the plane and quickly passed his bag to Shawn who stored it behind his at the rear of the plane. Within minutes they were leaving the runway while another plane was landing.

"Getting to be a damn traffic jam around here anymore," shouted John over the howl of the engine. "Used to be you wouldn't see three planes a month." The plane climbed for a while then leveled off. The noise inside the plane dropped considerably and it was surprisingly smooth and comfortable for the rest of the flight. All three dozed off and suddenly they were landing at Cannon Airport in Reno. They taxied past the commercial terminals to Butler Aviation where John parked the plane. Max and the others got out on stiff legs from the hike and the cramped confines of the plane.

Max paid John with three one-hundred dollar bills, an act probably less conspicuous here in Reno than most places. They started to walk to the main terminal for a cab when one sped up to them. The driver jumped out and opened the trunk.

"Service with a smile. Where to?" The cab driver asked as he tossed their bags in the trunk.

"Downtown." Max glanced back at Shawn and Nolan.

Shawn remembered the last time he was in Reno. He and Marlene were just getting to know each other.

In fact, Shawn had asked her to . . . "run off to Reno with me . . ." almost as a joke, but he sure didn't hesitate when she said yes. He smiled as he thought about the fun they had acting like kids at a carnival. They had been inseparable ever since. "Drop us at the CircusCircus please."

"Sure thing, Pal."

Max flinched but didn't say anything. The cab drove past the MGM Bally's Grand and into the downtown area of Reno. The cab driver chattered on without ever taking a breath. He kept up a constant dialogue, never noticing that his remarks and questions elicited no response from the three weary, worn out men in the back seat. Max wished Shawn had said to take them to a different Casino and let them walk to the CircusCircus but it was too late to do anything about it now. They pulled up at the hotel entrance and Shawn went in to register them while Max and Nolan headed for the nearest men's room.

They walked on incredibly gaudy pink and purple carpet, past clowns making balloon animals for groups of squealing kids, a juggler, and another clown applying makeup to the face of a six year old girl who looked to be putting up with it for the sake of her ecstatic grandparents standing nearby.

Max and Nolan stood in adjoining stalls and relieved themselves. The rest room attendant eyed their dirty, unkept appearance with disdain.

"Just like peeing in the woods, huh, Max?" Nolan quipped. "I can almost hear the wind blowing through the trees."

"All I hear is a babbling brook."

Just to keep up appearances they didn't wash their hands and the attendant smiled because he really pegged the two tramps.

At the front desk Shawn stared at the most gorgeous thing he'd ever seen, at least since leaving home. The top of her blouse parted just enough for the silky full cleavage to dance in rhythm to her pen strokes. "Your name?"

"Shawn Sanders," he crooned.

He felt the tug on his groin as she reached across the counter to get a new form while her upraised hips and arched back sent him off on another fantasy. It was now a huge effort to keep the two planes of existence separated. There was the one playing in his mind where she was begging for more and the one where he was just another experienced world traveler full of mystery checking into her hotel for the night. "Credit card?"

"Of course." He handed her his MasterCard, the gold one from his credit union, and made sure she would have to brush his hand to take it. She ran an imprint of it and handed it back

"Thank you Mr. Sanders. Enjoy your stay." She smiled warmly and he returned his best David Niven grin.

"All set?" asked Max walking back to the front desk. "Let's hit the showers boys." And they walked to the elevators.

The girl at the desk, who was supplementing her grant at the University by working part time smiled at that one. Great. Three queens to a room. I knew it. She pictured the three of them in a shower and was both excited and repulsed. Mostly repulsed.

Once in the room Shawn dived for the shower as Nolan found the room service menu. "Prices are kind of high to eat in your room here. A hamburger is six bucks."

"That's because they want you to eat downstairs near the gambling tables. Down there you can get all-you-can-eat buffet for about three bucks. I think we can afford to eat from room service right?"

Nolan called down and ordered himself a steak dinner and a half bottle of house wine. "Order me a double cheeseburger with extra fries and a shake," Max said.

"What about Shawn?"

"We'll let Shawn suffer for grabbing the damn

shower." Max laughed. "It'll serve him right to watch us eat."

Food ordered, Nolan called his house and Rhonda answered on the second ring. "Hello?"

"Rhonda? This is Nolan."

"Nolan? What happened? Where are you?" Rhonda asked. "Did you have an accident? Is anyone hurt?"

"Relax. We took a detour is all. We're fine. We're in Reno."

"Reno? What are you doing there?"

"I can't tell you over the phone but I've got a huge surprise for you. What time is it?"

"About five. Why? Did you lose your watch?"

Nolan smiled. "Very funny. Can you come and pick us up?"

"When? You mean now right?"

"Of course that's what I mean. And bring Marlene if you can. Okay?"

"Sure. In fact she's here now. We went shopping together. We'll come right on up. In fact we'll bring Shawn's Wagoneer, there's more room. Can't you tell me what the surprise is?"

"No. But I will tell you we're at the CircusCircus in room 1427. How soon can you be here?"

Rhonda thought for a second. "We can be there in a couple of hours or so. Is that quick enough for you?"

"Love you too. See ya." He hung up.

The room service arrived as Shawn got out of the shower. Max paid in cash and left a ten dollar tip to insure future orders were just as quick.

"Perfect timing," said Nolan as he dug into the steak dinner while Shawn stared.

"Go ahead and order up," said Max around mouthfuls of cheeseburger.

"You spend weeks in the wilderness with someone and you think you know them." He looked over the menu and ordered a shrimp dinner, dessert and coffee.

After all three had showered, Max suggested getting new clothes. Since they had to discard almost all their gear to get the money in the packs, they had been wearing the same clothes for too long. "I'll stay here while you two go get us some new clothes. Here are my sizes. Just don't buy them in this hotel. Bright pink is not my color. And get me some sneakers too."

After they had left and he had locked the door he drank the last of the coffee and looked out over the city. The wind had picked up as evening approached. Below him people tucked their heads into it and hurried along. He noticed the clouds which formed a magnificent billowing trough overhead all the way from horizon to horizon like a huge crimson snake climbing out of the ground. He knew the name of this cloud formation caused by the winds coming from the Pacific coast, across the central valleys of California, over the Sierra Nevadas and sculpting this phenomenon. Photographers had tried to capture the scope of it for years. He also figured most of the people who lived here probably wouldn't know what you meant by *The Sierra Ridge*. . . they would think of a rock formation. At least there weren't any people on the sidewalk below looking at it now. Just another one of God's light shows gone unnoticed from familiarity.

Looking over the city as evening came and the lights stood more in contrast to the desert sky, he began to feel the weight of what had happened to them in the past two days and a touch of fear over events to come. Somewhere there were people very upset over the loss of this much money. He felt pursued. He remembered a line his mother used to say when he had done something wrong . . . *The guilty flee, when no man pursueth.*

He understood.

CHAPTER FOUR

An empty logging truck whipped up dust and pine needles as it rumbled through the small northern California town. There used to be ten trucks an hour through here but this was the only one today, and it was empty. When locals did come to town, commerce centered on the combination gas station, store, and video rental housed in a raised building on the state route. There'd be a stop sign here if the town had one.

Two middle-aged women in print dresses sat in front of the store on a wood bench next to a newspaper rack displaying both the Redding paper and a free local handout. On the side of the store were littered index cards and paper slips advertising logging trucks for sale or hire ("firm prices" fast becoming "best offer" prices), backhoe work (reasonable), houses for sale or rent, house cleaning, baby sitting or ironing done (dependable) and a yellowing Claude Dulles wanted poster next to two bumper stickers with the messages . . . "Central America is Kansas" and "Save Logging/

Wipe Your ass on a Spotted Owl."

Here everybody knew everything about each other but nobody knew anything for outsiders. After the death or wounding of the logging business the money left town. Those who stayed found other sources of livelihood. The more prudent ones saved their money during the boom years and had enough stashed away now to get by, but most were not quite so lucky or frugal.

Recently a new breed of locals had sprung up. They seemed not to work, take a lot of trips, never have company over and spent money quietly. This town was ready made for them.

Jessica tried to take her mind elsewhere, think of something, even school. She hadn't been in weeks. It bothered her to enjoy what the dark man was doing to her. It made her feel dirty and she tried not to find any pleasure in the act but she sometimes couldn't help it. He felt heavy inside her and kissed her neck while muttering soft words in Spanish. She knew he was close to being finished as he began to move faster and faster in her, becoming less gentle and more like an animal. His breath hot, and reeking of lunch. He strained, tensed, and was finished. Jessica rolled away from him and reached for a towel from the floor. She cleaned herself while he did the same but used the sheets like always.

She padded into the kitchen and pulled a root beer from the refrigerator. She turned on the radio to a rock and roll station. Her dad used to never let her drink root beer, or listen to rock and roll; said they rotted her teeth and mind. A regular damn Bible Belter he was. Boy, did he get pissed off when Armando first started to pay attention to her. He wasn't a local and not even a real American citizen. When Armando offered to pay her forty dollars to clean his house . . . well . . . Dad began a kind of hands across the border outlook. After all, that was a lot of money for a girl barely thirteen to earn and she should learn the value of a dollar.

Now her dad leased the flat acreage adjoining his own place to Armando for three times what it was worth. It got used only a few times a month when a small plane would land, and take off again, often without shutting off the engine. He always paid cash and wanted no receipts so Uncle Sam got nothing. That made Dad happy. The family did better now and they even had a little extra money at the end of the month which was a luxury around these parts. Her brothers and her sister didn't talk about her gradual move to Armando's. It was like she grew up and went off to the city or something.

She put on the coffee like Armando always wanted. The sunlight behind her showed small breasts through the thin T-shirt large enough to reach her knees.

Armando lit a cigarette, hacked and coughed, pulled on a pair of jeans and walked into the kitchen. He hummed a non-tune and grinned at Jessica. He liked having her in the middle of the day. Kind of like *siesta sex*. These stupid gringo North Americans called her young. Shit. Back home this girl would be a pro by now. Her being untouched at her age was a happy surprise, one of the few since being sent here. Sex in the mid-day was like home, coffee at mid-day was a vice he had acquired here.

Uncle Lucho sent him here because of his ability to speak English so well. Too well. Better than these stupid hill people around here. Armando liked it better here than back in the hot, bug infested, armpit of a jungle watching his uncle's soldiers avoid work all day. Here there was no work to avoid. All he had to do was be the family *banker* which consisted of meeting the plane once or twice a month, like today, and tending the storage vaults. He called them the "fish tanks."

Back home they never thought their problem would

be where to keep the money. When the family just dealt drugs there was some concern on where to put it. But, when Uncle Lucho got inside the military and started to *fight the communist hoard* the North American money really began to flow. Imagine them using him to buy the armies he already controlled! Great stuff. Now there was so much damn money they decided to ship much of it here where it wouldn't mold or mildew, a major problem at home. Plus, the government was more secure here, in case their own house of cards ever collapsed.

There was always the possibility some do-gooder would find a way to transplant IQ points into the peasants back home or the jerks here who thought they were helping world peace. Other South American governments had fallen to coups. Uncle Lucho took notice of that fact and made sure much of his money was kept in the politically stable U.S. What the hell . . . that was where the money came from anyway, what better place to hide it?

"Fix up a thermos, Jessica," said Armando as he went back to the bedroom to finish dressing. He pulled on boots, a cotton work shirt and a baseball cap with *CAT* in big yellow letters on the front. He favored this symbol of American manufacturing because his nickname with the troops back home was *El Gato*. Aviator glasses completed the look for him. He took the thermos Jessica held out, went through the door and got the black Bronco from the barn. He chirped the tires on the concrete floor he had added to the old barn and drove into the woods on a small track behind the house.

Several large Rottweilers raised a chorus of barking from the trees where they were kept chained at irregular intervals on the property. The chains were attached to special dog collars that had releases which could be triggered by a remote wireless Armando carried with him. Other remote releases were at strategic spots in the house and the vault. Armando's fantasy was some jerk teasing one of the huge dogs, staying just out of reach of their sharp teeth and powerful jaws, then Armando releasing the collar and seeing the look on the jerks face just before the Rottweiler removed both the look and the face.

He liked the dogs ever since seeing them in action back home. His uncle had calmly set two of them loose on a peasant soldier who thought to return to his village without asking first. The powerful jaws made short work of the peasant whose frantic attempts to protect himself only excited the dogs all the more. Incredibly ferocious, the dogs were not satisfied with the death of the peasant but with his complete mutilation. Armando was thrilled by the power of it all. "This will keep the dogs happy, and that crying wife and brat will remind the rest of these peons not to leave the army of Lucho," Uncle Lucho had said. He was right. The AWOL rate dropped to zero after that.

Armando put in a Ruben Blades tape and the rock station Jessica had tuned in was replaced by the sounds of salsa music. In minutes the Bronco reached the edge of the forest behind Armando's compound. It was an old clear cut area Jessica's dad kept smooth for him. Armando settled down to await the plane's arrival.

He listened in anticipation for the radio on the seat to come to life. The plane was now over two hours late and it had never failed to show up on time. Never. He checked the radio for the fourth time but knew there was nothing wrong with it. He walked to the far end of the dirt clearing and looked to the sky as if some activity on his part would speed up the process. At least it made him feel like he was doing something. "Shit, oh dear," he muttered.

He used a North American pilot for these flights.

The man hadn't gone into business for himself, had he? This was the largest delivery so far but it was also the fifth trip. If the pilot were going to go AWOL with the shipment, he would have done so before now. It just didn't seem likely the pilot had skipped out on them.

It was almost dark when Armando pulled the hand held mike from the dash. "Jessica." He waited a second. "Jes."

Jessica pushed the send button on the radio in the kitchen. " 'Lo."

"Get hold of your brother and send him back here to the landing strip right away."

" 'Kay."

What a conversationalist she is, thought Armando. He threw the mike down and resumed his pacing.

Jessica loved to tell her brother what to do and phoned her "old" house. When Russ came on the line she said, "Armando wants you out at the clearing and he means right now." She hung up smiling. Shit rolls downhill don't it? She liked it when some came to rest on her family.

Russ got to the clearing out of breath. "Here. Take this flashlight and radio. If you hear bosco, bosco, bosco, you press this button twice but don't say anything. Then hit this button here and the lights will come on. After the plane lands shut off the lights by pressing the button again. Then put everything down on the ground and go home. You understand?"

"Got it."

"Good." Armando's expression did nothing to encourage further conversation. He jumped into the Bronco and sped back to the house.

There was no way around it. Something had happened that made it impossible for the pilot to contact him, which he would have done if he had to set down with engine problems. Of course he wouldn't have left the plane with the money in it either. This was bad.

He put the call through to Uncle Lucho first. He

hated to have this conversation.

"Señor Lucho," the servant said as he held out the phone with his head bowed. "It's Armando. He says it's important." Lucho hated to be called during dinner since it was his second favorite thing to do.

"What is it?"

"It is not here yet."

Lucho had questions but a phone line was not the place to ask them. He knew only too well the possibility of eavesdropping by the North Americans. They took it so personally when someone like him got rich by selling their clambering populace the poison they desired. They also just loved to play with their high tech toys.

"Backtrack and search?" he asked.

"At dawn," was Armando's quick reply.

"Do it. This one was special my nephew. Find it." He hung up softly.

Now Armando began to sweat. His next call was to a Vietnam Veteran who flew charters from an airport at the nearby town of Bieber.

"Doug?"

"None other. Who wants to know?"

"This is Armando. Can you get free tomorrow?"

"Sure. Where to?"

"Don't know for sure. I have a flight plan to track. I'll show it to you before we leave."

"When?" asked Doug.

"First light. When do you want me there?"

Doug thought about sunrise and figured quickly. "Meet me at the hangar at six. I'll figure for all day okay?"

"That'll do, friend."

With nothing left to do, he spent the remainder of the night with little sleep and lots of worry. One thing Uncle Lucho was not noted for was a big sense of humor. He remembered his uncle's words . . . "this one was special." Armando knew it had to mean more money than usual this time. How much money was a question he hoped to find out himself. That way he would live longer.

Armando drove fast through town and out the interstate. Shit! He had stayed up till three in the morning thinking and worrying. Then he had fallen asleep on the couch and overslept. Jesus. Like he didn't have enough going against him. He screeched to a halt at the side of the hangar and trotted to the plane where Doug leaned against the Cessna 210 waiting. "You ready?" He asked.

"Sure thing," Doug replied.

They got in the plane and Armando threw his bag behind the seat. He took a flight map from an inside pocket and handed it to Doug, "Here is the flight map with the route marked. Yesterday a plane flew this course, at least it took off, but it never arrived. I want you to track it backwards and try to find it."

Doug whistled. "Did the pilot check in with air traffic or check in anywhere along this route?" Doug pointed at the highlighted line stretching almost to Mexico from where they sat warming up the engines at the end of the small runway.

"No."

"Has anyone been told to look for him?"

"No."

"Do you want me to radio this in?"

"No." Armando thought for a moment. "Look, there's a reason he didn't advertise his flight. I don't know if anyone is looking for him and I really hope no one is. I need to find this plane before anyone else does. If we do manage to do that I'll take good care of you. Okay?"

Doug made a quick decision. He looked right into Armando's eyes and read urgency and need. He felt

Armando was good to his word, at least here and now. "You got it." Doug took the map and began to taxi out to the runway. "You picked the right plane to look for him with. These high wings make it easy to see the ground."

"Thank you, my friend. I hope we are lucky today."

They took off, circled once to gain altitude and began retracing the missing plane's route. "Start looking now, pal. It wouldn't be the first time a plane went down when it was almost home. What kind of plane was it?"

"A Cessna 182 RG. It was high wing, like this, and it was red and white." Armando knew the written flight plan ended here at this airport. He also knew if the plane had, in fact, crashed real close to its' destination they would need to start searching from the clearing behind his house. "Buzz my place once before we go."

"Okay."

After they had flown over Armando's compound they settled into a routine. Doug monitored the Emergency Locator Channel of 121.5 to pick up the other plane's Locator Transmitter which would be set off if the plane had crashed. They kept their faces to the windows and searched the ground. For the next few hours, other than seeing a lot of countryside, nothing happened.

Doug began a sweeping turn. "I think I see something down in the trees, over there." He indicated where white and red debris littered an area dotted with fallen trees. Armando's heart leapt to his throat as he noticed a smoldering fire. "I'll get right down on the deck to look," said Doug. He pulled full flaps and dropped the airspeed till the stall warning horn stayed on. They came in at tree top level and entered the clearing to the upturned and frightened faces of two men and a small boy tending a fire of cleared brush. A large dog barked furiously at the plane as Doug gave it full throttle and climbed back up in the sky. They could now see the torn down red and white trailer in the area cleared for a new home.

"Bet that took a year or two off their lives." Doug laughed nervously and got back to a safer search altitude. It was now almost mid-day and both of them had strained neck muscles from looking out the windows and throbbing headaches from the constant squinting. The radio came to life and this time the chatter included the word "search." Doug turned it up and they heard cross talk from two Civil Air Patrol planes searching for an Emergency Locator going off near someplace called Lone Pine.

"Does that mean a downed plane?" asked Armando.

"Sure as shit does." Doug looked at the flight map. "We're near Lee Vining right now. If you want to take a look where they are searching I need to land and get fuel."

"Yeah, I need to look."

"Okay, we'll land at Independence, get fuel and join the hunt. At least they haven't found it yet."

By the time they refueled and got near the search area the plane had been located. "Let's go look," said Doug. It took only thirty minutes to reach the crash site. The plane hadn't burned and the tail numbers were clearly visible but Armando didn't need the plane numbers to know it was the right one. His spirits reached a new low when he heard ground searchers were nearby.

Armando slumped in the seat and thought of what he had to do. "Get me to a phone, Doug."

"Right."

Doug quickly located the small airstrip near Lone Pine and lined up to land. He had to wait till a Piper Lance took off and had cleared the runway before he could land. They taxied to the parking area next to a hanger badly in need of fresh paint. While the engine was still winding down Armando got out of the plane and walked to the small building marked "Office" where he found a mechanic with his name on his coveralls. "Do you have a phone here Bob?"

"You bet, buddy, right over there on the wall. If it's long distance, you need to use a calling card," Cal replied.

"Thanks, I will"

His uncle got on the line. Armando made his report. "It went down. I didn't get there first. I'm in a little town called Lone Pine." Armando told him.

"I understand," Uncle Lucho said softly and hung up. He drummed his fingers on his chin for a few moments. He sighed and dialed a number from memory.

It rang in the den of the split level house perched on the side of the hill overlooking San Diego. The man answering the phone had been putting the final touches on a model car for his son who stood near the window. "Yes?"

"Can you be available for a job?"

The man smiled, recognizing the voice at the other end. The last "job" Lucho had for him went very well. He had thoroughly enjoyed himself. "What is your wish, señor?"

CHAPTER FIVE

Rhonda finished packing the small canvas sport bag that passed for her "luggage" with the base necessities for the trip to Reno, namely her credit cards, a change of under garments, and the hundred dollars in "mad money" she kept stashed at the back of her top drawer. Nolan would never look but a good burglar would. She was dressed in faded jeans and a short cotton top which showed her small waist without being flashy, and had *RENO* in glitter over her left breast. Blue cotton leg warmers over aerobic tennis shoes and a blue hair ribbon completed this very attractive picture. She had achieved this stylish result without much thought and only a quick glance at the full-length mirror in her bedroom. The mirror was not her idea but was Nolan's. He used it a lot to preen himself and he never passed it without at least a look.

She called to the kitchen where Marlene was making coffee. "You got the thermos ready?"

"Of course I do, you slave driver. Next you'll have

me doing the floors and I don't even do that at home." She twisted the top of the thermos on tight and put the cups and a couple of napkins in a nylon tote bag. "Just for that I think you should drive."

"Okay," said Rhonda. "I think the Wagoneer's fun. I like being up so I can look down on the other drivers."

"You think we should bring some sandwiches?"

"No." Rhonda answered emphatically from the living room. "We should make the boys spring for dinner when we get there and we can always stop for a snack on the way if we get hungry."

"Yes. I think they should at least buy us dinner. After all, they wouldn't tell us what their surprise is or even why the hell they're in Reno when they're supposed to be out in the wilds doing that male warrior thing. Didn't Nolan tell you anything?"

"Nolan did his best to keep me in the dark," Rhonda said as she locked the front door behind her and they got in Rhonda's Olds. "Hey. Maybe they never went to the mountains at all. Maybe they just went to Reno." They chuckled at that.

"Yeah, and lost all their money and need a ride home."

Rhonda pulled in at Marlene's and they picked up the Wagoneer. Within minutes Rhonda was maneuvering the Jeep easily through the twists and turns of Highway 49 to Auburn. "I really do like driving this thing. Makes me feel less vulnerable than when I'm driving a regular car."

"Not me," said Marlene. "I hate it. I'm afraid I'll run over someone and never know it . . . maybe find a Subaru wadded up in the wheel well when I go through the car wash." Marlene turned to Rhonda. "Hey, what if the boys spent all their money at that whore house out there? What's the name of that place?"

"The Mustang Ranch." They both laughed at the thought of the *Boys* spending a week in a house of ill repute. "Actually, Nolan would have to bring a book with him. He'd be done in about two minutes then he'd have to find something to do for the rest of the week."

"It's not that bad."

"No, it's worse. Nolan hasn't been tending to business in the bedroom for quite a while. He was great when we first met but after we got married, well . . . it was like he aged or something." She turned onto the main highway to Reno and picked up speed.

"Maybe it was losing Tawna?"

Rhonda had the Jeep in the fast lane now and drove smoothly up I-80 through the foothills into the Sierras.

"No. It started to come unraveled way before that. I thought I could just let it slide and I thought I would be able to go without sex, but not having sex isn't all of it."

She slowed down for a frizzy haired man in driving an older Volvo about fifty-miles-an-hour in the fast lane. The back of the car was festooned with bumper stickers telling anyone unlucky enough to be behind him to *save* everything.

"He doesn't communicate in other ways either."

She finally went around the Volvo on the right and received a look of scorn from the other driver. Four cars followed her lead and did the same maneuver.

"I could do without sex if there was some other kind of closeness but there just isn't any."

Marlene thought Rhonda was more angry than sad. "So what do you want to do?"

They passed a van with a sticker that said "Nuke the Gay Whales for Jesus" and Rhonda smiled. "I think we're the only car in California without an opinion on something."

"Maybe it's not so bad." Marlene chuckled. "There's a guy who only has one friend." The car they were passing had a bumper sticker that said *I'm a friend of Bill W.*

They laughed and Rhonda pointed to the next one that said, *Pearl Harbor Survivor*. It was on the back of a Mitsubishi sedan.

"Oh well. I don't know how I'm going to do it but this relationship with Nolan is over. I decided two days after they left on this trip. I just have to figure out how to tell Nolan."

"You could always try the direct approach and say *it's over*." Marlene got the thermos out and poured a cup of rich black coffee. She held it out to Rhonda.

"Well, one way or another I'm not going to stay in a barren relationship. My whole upbringing was the same way and I'm not having any more of it."

They drove on in silence. Marlene put in a Stevie Nicks tape to fill the void. The rest of the drive was uneventful and they passed the time looking at the panorama afforded by the Sierra Nevada Mountains. It really was quite spectacular with sweeping views of deep wooded canyons and snow-capped peaks. The Wagoneer was high enough to afford a terrific view of Donner Lake. Every other time Rhonda had driven this road she had been in a car that sat closer to the ground and about all she had seen of Donner Lake was the guard rail.

Reno sat like a jewel in the darkness, resembling a small town in every way except the high rise hotels with their miles of lights. Rhonda took the third exit in town and drove the few blocks to the CircusCircus.

"They made some changes to this place." Marlene looked at the high-rise and parking tower that had been added since her first visit to the casino with Shawn. "Turn in here."

They drove into the parking garage and up four flights before finding a parking space. After noting the level they took the elevator down to the second floor and rode the tram to the main hotel and casino. "That's new since I was here last," said Marlene.

A group of men from some convention turned their heads in unison as they walked by and Rhonda smiled to herself. At least she wasn't over the hill or doomed to desperate measures to attract male attention. They passed through the casino area with all the clatter of the evening crowd. It was eight o'clock now and the daytime crowd with lots of kids was being replaced with a more grown up version; out for dinner and a little gambling. In the elevator Rhonda punched number fourteen and the car started its climb.

"I wonder if the boys know they're really on the thirteenth floor."

"How come," asked Marlene.

"Because they don't have a number thirteen floor, see." Rhonda pointed at the numbers where it went from number twelve to number fourteen. "They figure gamblers might be a bit superstitious so number fourteen is really the thirteenth floor."

"Let's keep that bit of trivia to ourselves, okay?" The doors opened and they walked to room 1427. "Maybe they think they're gonna get lucky."

They knocked on the door and waited. "They probably assume they're going to get lucky. You know, it could be the reason they called us. Maybe they've been here all this time and just couldn't get laid?" Rhonda smiled at the thought.

Shawn opened the door and grabbed Marlene, carrying her through the door. "Just like the first time here right?" He swung her around in a circle, nearly knocking Max over in the process.

Marlene laughed freely. "Sure it is, except there's three other people here this time. Put me down, you goof."

"Okay." Shawn obliged by dropping her unceremoniously on the bed grinning from ear to ear.

Rhonda hugged Nolan a bit more reservedly and walked to a desk attached to the wall. A print of a clown hung above it. She cleared a space in front of her by moving a tray of dishes. "I see you cleaned the place up for us. We were kind of expecting a fancy dinner." Rhonda pointed at the tray. "Does this mean you guys are going to take us out and watch us eat?"

Max observed this exchange with interest from a chair near the window. "I think you might want to order room service. There is something you need to know and it will take some time to tell."

Rhonda handed Marlene the menu. "Here, I already know what I want." She picked up the phone and dialed room service. "Hello, room service? I'd like to order a double cheeseburger with extra fries and a chocolate shake." She looked at Marlene who pointed at the menu. Rhonda wrinkled her nose at her and grimaced. "And a spinach salad with mineral water." She picked up the room key and looked at it. "This is room 1427. Thank you."

Max smiled to himself. Rhonda had a quick intelligence not to be outdone by her great looks. Maybe he was just a male chauvinist and hadn't noticed the smart part. He also realized she had ordered the same meal as he and wondered what other appetites they had in common. Better to leave that alone. Other people's relationships were hands off for him. He knew just having a relationship was hard enough without any outside interference.

Rhonda looked at the three men and raised her brows just a bit. "Well, what's the news?"

Max watched her reaction as he began to remove a few camping items from his pack. There weren't many since most had been taken out and buried in the woods to make room for the money. When he began tossing banded stacks of hundreds on the bed, both girls gasped. He kept tossing them out till his pack was empty.

Shawn paused for effect and did the same.

By the time Nolan finished emptying his pack on the bed the pile was impressive, to say the least.

Rhonda picked up one of the packs, thumbed through it and handed it to Marlene. Finally Rhonda looked up.

"Okay, we're impressed . . . flabbergasted beyond belief . . . how many people did you kill to get this?"

Shawn laughed. "Only one. And we didn't kill him. We'll start at the beginning."

Someone knocked at the door and everyone froze for a moment. "Room service." Max pulled the bed covers over the money and Nolan let the waiter in. Shawn tipped him ten dollars and asked him to take the dirty trays with him.

The room service waiter picked up the trays while stealing poorly disguised looks at the girls.

After he left, the girls ate their food while Shawn Nolan and Max took turns filling them in on what had happened. They finished telling the story at the same time the girls were done eating. "So now what?" asked Marlene.

"How much money is here?" asked Rhonda.

Max liked the latter question better. "We counted a couple of stacks at random. There are fifty hundreds in a stack and there are six hundred stacks. So that's six hundred times five thousand or . . ." he paused a bit for dramatic effect, ". . . three million dollars. A three way split would be a cool million tax-free dollars apiece."

"Unbelievable," said Marlene. "I guess now you're going to say I-told-you-so about this hike being a good idea, right?"

"I'm never going to let you forget it," laughed Shawn. "Now we should give some thought as to how to keep it without being obvious. We probably shouldn't go on any spending sprees."

"How about we sit on it for a year and then launder it?" asked Rhonda. "We could buy old coins and say we inherited them or something like that."

"Where'd you get that idea?" asked Marlene. "From the guy on the phone?" Rhonda rolled her eyes.

"Who?" asked Nolan.

Marlene continued, "Or we could say we won it gambling. At least that way we could blow some of it trying to back up the story by playing in the casinos.

That might be fun."

Max shook his head. "It's pretty odd to win this kind of money gambling unless you start with maybe a bankroll of a million or so, and then you'd still have to explain where the original bankroll came from. No, there are better ideas than that."

"Like what?" asked Rhonda.

Max looked at her for a moment and held her eyes. "If a person didn't mind staying in a tropical paradise, he could just leave the country. A lot of places don't care where you got your money."

Rhonda felt a disconcerting tug on her emotions as she listened to Max. She credited it as a reaction to all this money but felt it as an awakening of sorts when he spoke to her. It was like he wasn't doing anything else . . . wasn't thinking of anything else, but was speaking to her only. It had been a while since anyone had given her their undivided attention. "How would you get it out of the country?" she asked.

"Walk."

Marlene broke the moment by picking up one of the banded stacks and hefting it in her hand. "What if we did it this way?" She put the stack down at the end of the bed. "We could form three companies with the three groups of us here." She put another stack down with the first. "We purchase services from each other for whatever exorbitant amount we come up with. Say it's some kind of consulting fee or something. And each time we want to spend the money legally we just pay ourselves more money. Like this see." She now had three stacks of money separate from the big pile in the center. "This company "A" charges company "B" which charges company "C" . . . and the money goes in a circle. We could even write off a bunch of other expenses too and call it business."

"Won't fly," said Shawn.

"Why not?"

"Well, for one thing, taxes." He picked up a stack

of hundreds from the pile. "If company "A" makes a hundred dollars and passes it to company "B" who passes it on to company "C" then each company makes a hundred dollars right?" They nodded automatically and tried to follow him along. "So each company pays . . . say twenty-five percent on the hundred which is twenty-five dollars each times three companies . . . that comes to seventy-five dollars in taxes on the same hundred. So now we have only twenty-five of the hundred left and if we take salaries we'd be taxed again."

"Wait a minute. If the same dollar gets taxed so many times then how come the Government is broke?" asked Nolan.

"Beats me," said Shawn with a shrug. "Maybe that's why they have printing presses?" Shawn tossed the bills back on the bed. "Why don't we just say we found the damn stuff?"

Max uncoiled himself from the chair and stretched his arms. "It's okay to have this idea session to come up with some ways to handle this, but in the end, each one of us is responsible for his own money and the problems it brings." He punctuated this point by beginning to put the money into three stacks. "As long as everyone agrees there is no reason to hand this money over to the drug dealers it came from or the police or the IRS, I feel we're going to come out okay. Now let's get this counted out and separated so we can get on with our lives, okay?"

"Good enough for me," said Shawn as he spread the money out further on the bed. "Let's get started."

It took more than two hours of eye-straining counting with many mistakes and re-counts. But, in the end, they looked like bank tellers flying through the stacks. There was no argument about Max's receiving a third of the money. They counted it out and each share came to twenty three hundred dollars over a million.

Half way through the counting process Marlene went down to the coffee shop and brought back coffee for them. When the count was done they each repacked their bags.

"Anyone want to go out to gamble or whatever?" asked Shawn as he stood and stretched. No one responded to the suggestion so he looked from face to face. "Then I vote we get out of *Dodge*. What do you say?"

"Sounds good to me," said Max as he, too, stood and stretched. "Any objections? Great. Let's go."

"I'll check us out at the front desk," Shawn said.

Marlene picked up her travel bag and looked at Rhonda. "Rhonda and I will go get the car and meet you at valet parking."

"Well, I guess Nolan and I have to do the hard work." He grinned at Nolan. "How do they know we'll be there and not just walk off into the sunset?"

"Probably because you could have done so if you really wanted to," Rhonda said as she got up to leave. "I don't think you'd have gone through this much trouble just to get the money counted. Right?"

Max smiled at her and began picking up their bags. He held her eyes for just a moment and felt a jolt of electricity again. *I got to get away from this girl*, he thought.

They met at the front door fifteen minutes later, loaded up and drove out of Reno. "I bet we are leaving this town with something hardly anyone takes with them," quipped Marlene.

"What would that be?" Shawn asked.

"Money!"

They laughed as the lights of Reno receded in the rear view mirror. The general feeling was that their lives were also on a highway to a better, or at least more comfortable life.

Max laughed with the rest of them but his thoughts took an off-ramp. Life is good, isn't it? Then why can't I shake the feeling the ground is slipping under my feet? When I was five or six I remember lying in bed, peaceful, waiting for sleep to transport me magically into the next morning. Suddenly the bed seems to tilt, falling away rapidly, jolting me awake. Afterwards I waited for sleep with just a tinge of apprehension. I feel like that now.

CHAPTER SIX

He smiled as he hung up the phone. After tapping his gold Cross pen lightly on the edge of the desk he folded the single sheet of paper covered in notes. He used his own version of short hand; a mix of computer slang, numbers, and mnemonic devices virtually undecipherable and meaningless to anyone other than himself.

His son remained at the window silhouetted by the afternoon sun.

"Come over here, Tony."

He held out the finished model car, a Ferrari Testerossa, and waited for his son to take it. Tony reached for it and carefully held it up to the light.

"Thanks, Dad. It looks great."

"That's what I'm here for," he replied with a smile. "Wish my old man had been around more to help me out."

"It looks swell, Dad," said Tony as he retreated from the room before he got the rest of the pitch. He'd heard it a lot. He was glad his dad paid attention to him. His friends thought it was cool. Most of their dads were gone a lot but his dad had a job that allowed them quite a bit of time together. He really wasn't too sure what his dad did for a living. It certainly didn't require much time away from home, just a few weeks every so often.

He ran back outside where his sister and mother sat around the pool. "Look, Mom."

Susan took the model car Tony held out to her. "Wow, Tony. It looks like it wants to just drive away." She looked at her daughter sitting on the edge of the pool dangling her legs in the clear water. "Does it look like what you want to drive when you get older?"

Kelly looked at the car and wrinkled her nose. "Nah. I want a four wheel drive truck with tires so huge you need a ladder to climb up into the seat."

Tony giggled. Actually a truck like she was describing was what he would rather have too, but he would never tell his dad. Kelly had way more nerve than he did, especially when it came to Dad.

Kelly poked her little brother playfully in the bellybutton, sending him into further giggle fits till he retreated clutching the red model car and scampering off to play. "He really likes Boyle doesn't he, Mom?"

"It sure seems that way. Why? Is that so bad?" She palmed more lotion over the front of her legs and dried her hands on the monogrammed towel at her feet.

Kelly looked across the pool. She watched the palm trees, manicured evergreens, and clouds reflected in the water as they rippled and distorted each time she moved her legs. When she kept them perfectly still the picture slowly came back to focus. She wished life were the same way. "I know he takes good care of us, we certainly have enough stuff, but sometimes I miss my father. It doesn't seem fair that Tony will never even know his real dad." She looked at her mother and wondered if the passage of time would be as kind and gentle to her as it was to her mother. She looks more like my sister, Kelly thought. No wonder Boyle takes such good care of us.

"Sometimes I miss your dad too, but Tony can't possibly remember him. He died when Tony was still a baby."

Susan still remembered the argument she and Dave had the night he died. Dave kept going on and on about how he didn't trust or like this guy Boyle and how something just wasn't right about him. Susan had yelled right back, how Dave was the one who had left them and he didn't have the right anymore to tell her who to see or what to do with her life. She was single now, thank you very much.

He had stormed out of the house and drove off with a pretty impressive display of power in his custom vintage Mustang. It was the model called the Mach I, and the police said that was about how fast it was going when it left the winding road and launched itself off into the deep canyon.

The police pointed out the lack of skid marks and said it looked like he had never even touched the brakes. He also never bounced on the way down. The car was going so fast that the first impact was on the bottom of the canyon. He had died instantly.

Susan regretted the argument many times since but especially when the man from the insurance company had delivered the check for two hundred thousand dollars to the door of their modest apartment. It seemed ironic that Dave provided almost nothing financially to the family in life . . . yet was so generous in death.

Boyle walked through the sliding doors onto the pool deck. He buttoned his cotton golf shirt with the name of a local country club to which he belonged stitched above the pocket. "You want to come with me today?"

Susan twisted the top back on the lotion and got up. "Okay. I'll go get Tony. Kelly, you go change clothes."

Kelly sighed and stood up. She dried her legs and headed inside. She hated going to the old folk's home but it was just too rude to say so. Anyway, maybe there was such a thing as Karma and if she did her duty now, then someone would visit her when she got old.

Boyle drove the Cadillac up Highway I-5 through light Sunday traffic. What had started as a near cloudless sky had filled with the puffy beginnings of thunderheads. This was supposed to be a drought. A drought was what Californians called that period of time separating two flood seasons. In the typical uncharacteristic fashion of southern California weather, it began to rain.

In the back of the car a summit meeting was taking place on where the dividing line was for each half of the seat. “You always want to sit in the middle,” Kelly said. “Why can’t you just stay on your own side?”

Tony laughed at first then, with a rapid mood swing reserved for small kids and pregnant women, he began to cry.

“Why don’t you two play a game or something?” Susan suggested from the front seat.

“Okay,” said Kelly. “We’ll play window worms.”

“That’s fine. Just try to be nice to each other.”

She leaned close to Tony and told him the rules to the game in a low conspiratorial whisper. “It’s a race. See the drops of water at the top of the windows?” She pointed to the rear window. Tony nodded. “We each pick one and race them to the bottom of the glass. Are you ready?”

Tony tilted his head and looked at his sister quizzically. “How do you get them to move?”

“Simple. You tap the glass with your finger like this and they move.” She tapped the rear window and the bead of water on the top moved down an inch.

Tony grinned at her. “Okay. You say when.”

“On your mark, get set, GO.”

They each had a drop picked out and tapped the glass to start them moving. As the drops began winding their way down the window, Tony realized that if he really smacked the glass with his palm the drop went faster. By the time the drops were half way down the window they were both banging furiously on the glass and convulsing in laughter.

"Quit that right now," Susan turned and shouted, bringing the game to an abrupt end. "What's the matter with you two? Can't you do something a little quieter to pass the time?"

Kelly and Tony sat back but continued to giggle helplessly.

Susan looked over at Boyle and wished he would say something every once in a while. He was too good to the kids, at least he never disciplined them. When she mentioned his lack of discipline he said they would get plenty of flack later in life to make up for what grief he didn't give them now.

Boyle drove up the curving driveway past a double row of meticulously manicured oak trees set on perfectly tended grass. Ivy covered the lower half of each tree. A carved wood sign nestled discreetly between two of the oaks. The inscription echoed on most places designed to care for the elderly. It said . . . "Grow old along with me for the best is yet to come" . . . Boyle smiled. He couldn't agree more. The entrance to the care facility looked like the lobby of a resort Hilton hotel, only more subdued. Also there were no hookers. The image of what a hooker working the old folk's home would look like trolled across his mind.

He parked the car a short distance from the front door, the parking lot conspicuously empty. There was no doubt some California law requiring the parking lot be large enough to hold at least a half a car for each patient, or resident as they were called, to handle all the visitors they didn't get. Boyle smiled. He wondered if there had ever been a court battle over custody of the parent? Anyway, the rule meant lots of available parking.

The lobby also resembled a hotel; indoor palm trees, lots of glass and open area, and a marble desk much like a reservations desk. Behind this stood two young men who gave every appearance of just waiting for the next person to come in so they might be of some service, at which time their lives would be complete.

Susan and the two kids went to the lounge area and settled down to wait. Boyle approached the desk.

"Good afternoon, Mr. Brandt. How are you today?" asked greeting clone number one from behind the desk.

"Fine, thank you. Is Mr. Lasker here today?"

Mr. Lasker was the facility director and always wanted to chat with him. Boyle preferred to get that part of the visit out of the way. Maybe Mr. Lasker wouldn't be here today. No such luck.

"Yes he is, Mr. Brandt. Right now he is with a resident but will be around in twenty minutes or so. I'll tell him you asked for him," the other clone replied.

"I'll go on up then."

Boyle moved across the tiled lobby, past huge indoor palms planted in clay pots at least five feet across. He walked down the hallway leading to his father's room. This place cost him plenty but the result in image was calculated. Coming here once a week was an act admired by all who knew of it and was the highlight of Boyle's week. He was grinning as he opened the door to the "apartment," as they liked to call it, where an attendant was tucking a blanket around the legs of the old man in the wheelchair.

"Look who's here, Mr. Brandt," the attendant said animatedly to the old man. "Your son is here to see you."

"How has he been this week?" asked Boyle.

The attendant nearly clucked like an old mother hen. "Not much change, he just sits there. I sometimes wonder if he knows we're here."

Boyle smiled at the attendant. "Oh, he knows we're here. I can tell. Can you leave us alone for a time?"

"Sure, Mr. Brandt. Just hit the buzzer if you need anything." The attendant backed out of the door. Too bad more of his patients don't have kids like this one. Most of them never get a visitor but Mr. Brandt's son comes almost every Sunday. In fact, he seemed to enjoy the visit more than the old man.

Boyle turned, the smile slipped from his expression. "Well, Dad. How are you this week?" The old man in the wheel chair sat immobile in a pool of sunlight. The room looked more like a dormitory for a college student than a near hospital environment for an elderly patient. It had a single bed, dresser, desk and reading light. The sunlight came in via two French doors leading out onto a redwood deck.

All very attractive looking.

All very active looking.

All very wrong for an old man who couldn't move without assistance and whizzed his pants about twice a day.

Boyle moved to the wheel chair and turned it so the sunlight shone directly into the old man's eyes causing him to flinch but in a feeble fashion. "I really like to see your eyes when I talk to you. That's one of the things you taught me, Dad. Remember when you would say . . . look at me when I talk to you? . . . just one of many things I owe you for."

Boyle knelt beside the wheelchair and adjusted the old man's position so his head faced almost straight up. He looked like an eaglet waiting for food. Boyle wasn't sure if it hurt or not. He hoped so.

"Would you like to get out of here for a while?" he asked in a kind mimic.

Boyle looked around to be sure no one was in the room. The attendants had those damn tennis shoes that either squeaked like mad or were perfectly silent. Ninja nurses. An attendant had almost overheard him during one of his fireside chats with dear old Dad. It wouldn't match up with his image and he couldn't have that.

"No, you're not getting out of here this weekend but maybe next weekend, Dad." Boyle pulled out a cigarette from an inside pocket and lit it. He didn't smoke except for these little get togethers.

"Too bad I'm not interested in fucking you, huh?

Maybe that's why I got to go on as many fishing trips as I did, right?" Boyle blew on the end of the cigarette. "Too bad for you but maybe next time. I suppose young bodies are just more appealing than old ones huh?" Boyle turned as if in surprise. "What's the matter? Cat got your tongue?"

Boyle raised an eyebrow. Sweat began to form on his upper lip. He punctuated each word of his next sentence by bringing the hot end of the cigarette closer to the old man's face. "Too . . . bad . . . you . . . can't . . . tell . . . anyone . . . what . . . I . . . do . . . to . . . you . . . FUCKHEAD." Boyle's neck muscles were corded and teeth clenched as the last word was rasped out into the old man's ear. He stopped the cigarette only a fraction of an inch from the old man's eye.

The old man could not move but stared helplessly at the hot end of the cigarette. He strained with all his might to scream. A weak sound barely leaked past his lips.

Boyle relaxed and stood up straight. He smiled, sighed and patted the old man's face almost lovingly. "It'll be our secret right? No one would believe you anyway, and I'd just deny it. Who would believe a senile old man instead of an obviously loving and caring son?" He paused as if waiting for the answer.

"Of course, they would believe me first. But they would also tell me about it and then I'd really make your life tough. You know that, don't you?"

Boyle reached down and straightened up the old man's head to where it looked comfortable again. "If you let anyone else know our little secret you'll get me in trouble and you don't want to do that do you?" Boyle took one long pull on the cigarette and tossed it into the toilet. "That's because you love me isn't it?" He flushed the cigarette and walked to the door. "Gee whiz and golly. Seems just like old times. Guess what goes around comes around doesn't it?"

He backed out the door until only his head remained in the room. "You take care now you hear?" Out of the corner of his eye he could see the attendant returning to the room. "Love you, Dad. See you next week."

He timed his turn from the door and nearly collided with the attendant. He feigned surprise and stepped back. "Excuse me."

"No, excuse me, Mr. Brandt." The attendant smiled.

Boyle walked down the hall humming. Damn he felt great. He couldn't wait to get started on his next job.

CHAPTER SEVEN

Armando hung up the phone. His uncle was hard to read sometimes but there was no mistaking his mood on this one. Armando had to do something to improve his situation. Action was always a good idea. Even if he had no idea as to what course of action to take. He looked at Doug then at the mechanic. He saw the name tag. "Bob, is there a way to rent a car here?"

Cal started to correct him about his name, and then figured . . . What the hell . . . he didn't like Mexicans anyway. Especially this one, for some reason. Cal didn't think he would like him if he were white and local.

"Actually we do have a pickup truck we rent out to pilots from time to time, but it's expensive compared to renting one in town."

"What's expensive?"

Cal thought for a moment. "Eighty-five a day."

"Okay."

"Two day minimum."

Armando shrugged. "No problem Bob." He

counted out two days rental and gave it to Cal.

"You need a receipt?" asked Cal.

Armando smiled. "No, just point me to where it is and I need a map of the area."

Cal gave him a map and took him outside to the six-year old Chevy truck parked next to the hangar. It started rough but ran fine once it warmed up.

Doug hopped in after tying down the airplane and they headed into Lone Pine. "I get the feeling Bob rented you his own truck," said Doug.

"Why do you say that?"

"Cause the plates on this thing say BOB1, that's why."

On any other day it would have been funny.

They located an older cafe on the main street of Lone Pine. There wasn't much to the town but compared to where they were from it was almost metropolitan. Maybe the plates on the truck helped because they got smiles and nods from the few customers inside.

After a quick meal that probably tasted better than it was, they decided to return by air to the crash site. Armando didn't really think there was much to be gained by this action but he did not want to tell his uncle there was nothing left to do.

It was late afternoon by this time and Doug wanted to hurry or there would be no light to even see the crash site. After a quick warm-up they took off and flew in a constant climb to the east to gain altitude, then up the eastern slope of the Sierra Nevada range. Although, it was only fifteen nautical miles to the crash site they had to go from thirty-eight hundred feet to over twelve thousand feet. With the sun in his eyes Doug wanted some altitude before approaching the mountains.

There was still one plane in the area. A helicopter had already taken out the pilot's body. No doubt the FAA would soon begin to investigate the crash. Listening to the radio chatter Armando heard no mention of a suitcase, not that he expected to.

He looked over at Doug as they made a sweeping circuit of the crash area. "How many people do you think were in the search party?"

"Looks pretty crowded down there to me." Doug indicated the scene below where about a dozen or more people were walking around the downed airplane. The area was fairly open with no real tree cover to hamper a search.

Armando calculated the options. Maybe the pilot had thrown the suitcase out before the crash. Not likely, since he was probably trying to find a place to land. Taking the time to drag a heavy suitcase from the rear compartment, open the door and pitch it out wasn't plausible. Or had he hidden it after the crash? No, that didn't make sense either since his injuries had been fatal. Someone had to have found the suitcase first. Someone had his uncle's money, which meant Armando's death certificate.

But who?

"How come they found the crash site so quick?" wondered Armando out loud.

"Probably because of the trail." Doug pointed to the well-worn line leading off from the crash site in both directions. "According to the map it's called the Pacific Crest Trail. This is just a part of it. It goes from Mexico to Canada and you can see it up by Mount Shasta too. This section gets some action this time of year. That made the crash site real easy to reach."

Armando sat upright. "Are there check points or things like that for this trail?"

"I'm not that familiar with it but I would guess there are areas you would need permits, you know, for camp fires and such. In fact, I'd bet that someone would have to have some type of permit even to be in some of the areas they call the wilderness."

"Let's get back to Lone Pine. I gotta make some plans. I may want to go hiking."

Doug turned the plane back to the east. By now

the sun was setting behind them and Doug enjoyed a great sunset reflected in the cloud formation scalloped by the wind coming off the Sierra Nevadas. He was going to point it out to Armando but he looked lost in desperate thought.

The sun was already behind the mountains by the time Doug set the Cessna back on the runway at Busters. After they taxied to the hangar Doug went inside to make arrangements to leave the plane there overnight. They expected the place to be deserted but the mechanic was still at the radio.

"Surprised to see anyone around here this late. I went ahead and tied down by the hangar. That okay?"

Cal looked up from the radio. "Sure. Only reason I'm still here is to wait till John gets back from Reno. He already radioed at five miles out so he should be in sight right about now." He leaned up from the desk and looked outside. "There he is." He pointed to the landing lights dropping out of the evening sky to the end of the runway.

Doug watched the landing with the natural curiosity of one pilot for another. Nice flare out and he obviously knew the airstrip since he taxied real fast to a spot next to Doug's plane.

"Great. Now I can go home. He went to Reno to replace some avionics in the plane so I guess everything went okay."

John entered the office moments after landing. He put his flight bag down and picked up a clip board.

"Thanks for waiting up, Cal. These aren't more travelers looking for lifts are they?" John grinned at Doug, figuring him for the pilot of the Cessna outside.

"No. We just need to park overnight."

Armando walked in and overheard John's comment. "You asked if we needed a lift. Do you operate an air taxi out of here? I mean . . . do you regularly take riders, like a shuttle?"

"Oh hell no." John laughed. "Just took a couple of

worn out hikers to Reno. It's not a part of the business. We do mostly crop dusting. Some passenger stuff but not much."

"Worn out hikers? You mean like backpackers?"

"Yeah. These guys were the real McCoy too. Had good gear and all. They said they had to get to Reno and didn't want to hike into town. Looked to me like they bit off more than they could chew. Know what I mean?"

A smile crept up Armando's face, but never reached his eyes. "Yeah, I know exactly what you mean, my friend. So where did they say they were going in Reno?"

"They didn't. A cab took them from the airport." John had a flash that he had already said too much. "Well, if you gentlemen will excuse us we'll be closing. I can't afford a lot of overtime here."

"I think we are leaving, too." Armando looked at Doug then back to John. "Thanks for the rent-a-truck and all but we're flying out tonight."

Doug looked out at the near night sky. "Two clicks turn on the lights?"

"Sure does," said John as they left the office. "Nice meeting you." He looked pointedly at Doug when he said it. "Just leave the keys in the truck."

They put their bags back in the plane and taxied away from the hangar. Doug keyed his mike twice and the runway lights came on. After a rolling takeoff Doug and Armando were soon a receding, blinking speck in the night sky.

Armando felt comfort in action. He didn't know if these hikers had his uncle's money, but hearing about the hikers here at this airstrip just happened to be too coincidental to pass up.

He didn't believe in coincidence. When he was twelve, a nun at the school his uncle made him attend to learn English had said a coincidence was but a minor miracle where God chose to remain anonymous. She meant to uplift him spiritually with that lesson. He liked the concept and chose to look upon all coincidence as indicators of facts too subtle for others to accept or use.

Years later, after attending the school, there had been an accountant in his uncle's business whose job it was to keep track of the money his uncle siphoned from the North American aid. He also kept track of the household expenses for the villa in the mountains that served as a hideaway where there were just as many maids as there were rooms.

Each maid was young and beautiful, handpicked from villages in the mountains, and each maid owed her life and allegiance to Uncle Lucho. This fact he drove home by threatening the life of at least one family member of each maid. They would do whatever was asked of them for whoever asked them.

As the plane droned toward Reno Armando remembered the coincidence of the family caught trying to leave the country with more cash than a peasant would see in a year, namely enough to leave the country. It was the family of a girl the accountant always asked for when it was his turn at the hideaway. Armando told his uncle to kill the accountant without further investigation after making sure every bit of memory had been screamed through his tortured lips. His uncle at first did not want to believe a man had served him for so many years and betrayed him, but Armando convinced him and the accountant confessed to this crime and a long history of skimming money.

Armando drifted into sleep with a smile and hoped he would have the opportunity to extract the life story of those hikers who had his uncle's money.

Doug was exhausted. He had too many hours in one day in the cockpit of an airplane. His eyes felt gritty and his stomach hot. It was with great relief that he saw the town of Carson City give way to the scattered lights of the Washoe Valley, then Reno beckoned with the promise of sleep.

He went through the radio channels to get clearance for a landing on the shorter east-west runway. He had to stop and wait at the intersection of the main north-south runway while a Southwest commercial jet took off. He awakened Armando and taxied to the Butler Aviation building. A ground attendant in a bright orange vest directed them to a tie down spot near a larger hangar complex, then walked off without conversation. Not quite as casual and folksy as Buster's Flying Service, thought Doug as he shut off the engine and got the plane tied down.

They walked to the small building where the three hikers had been just hours before. As they approached the building a cab darted from the line of cabs at the main terminal in a move Armando had seen many times before by the cabbies hustling around the airport back home. He smiled. Another coincidence.

"Where to?" asked the cabbie as he reached for their bags.

Armando hesitated for just a moment. "You work this location a lot?"

The cabbie looked askance at Armando. "Yeah, I do," he retorted with the hint of an edge to his voice. "Usually the people who land at the private plane part of the airport are pretty nice. Why do you ask?"

Armando smiled at the way the cab driver set them up for a tip. "Don't get defensive." He took a fifty dollar bill and flashed it to the cab driver. He saw the man perk up and grin. "We had a couple of our friends here earlier in the day, maybe you weren't working then, but they had backpacks and looked tired."

"So."

"So does that ring a bell?"

The cab driver looked pointedly at the fifty. "Sure. I remember them. Good tippers they were."

Armando held out the fifty. "Can you take us to

the same place they went?"

The grin spread to his whole face, eyes and all, and he took the bill from Armando's hand. "Sure thing, Pal. Hop in."

The cab driver started his patented stream of chatter and Armando listened for a couple of minutes. Sounded just like back home only in a different language. Probably was identical to the chatter the last rider got. Armando interrupted him three blocks into his pitch. "Tell me about the backpackers."

"I don't really remember them too good, you know, a guy sees a lot of people during a shift, especially when a shift is twelve hours long to meet the damn bills. Then the government takes half of what you manage to scrape out of the day. Ain't fair. You know what I mean?"

Jesus. This guy must have brothers working the airport back home. Armando sighed and handed the driver another fifty. "You shouldn't take advantage of the tourists, my friend."

The cab driver laughed. "Well, there were three of them. Backpackers. One guy, maybe in his forties, tall, about six-two or so with a rugged face and bright blue eyes. I remember 'cause they were so bright I thought he may be wearing contacts or something but I don't think he was. Then there were two younger guys in their thirties . . . probably. One stocky and sandy haired, the other lean with darker features. All of them looked tired, like your friend there." He nodded toward Doug who was propped up against the door snoring softly. "They each carried a backpack. Not the puny ones you see students and the like toting around but real backpacks like you could move into. You know what I mean?"

"Yeah. Anything else?" Armando was not in the least surprised at the wealth of information the cab driver remembered.

"No, except they tipped real good." He smiled to the

rear view mirror when he said it. "Well, here's the spot."

They pulled up to the hotel entrance of the CircusCircus. Doug shook himself to clear his head and they got out. "I hope to hell a little sleep is on tap for us here, otherwise I'm going to fall down. There'll be no more flying until I get eight hours of continuous and uninterrupted shut eye."

Armando laughed. His spirits were soaring. Each step toward the hikers felt like a step further from the grave. No, it wasn't a feeling . . . it was a fact. Armando knew his uncle too well to believe anything else.

"You'll get taken care of very well, my friend, very well." He put his arm around Doug's shoulder and walked toward the front entrance. "Don't you worry about a thing. Let's get a room and some food, and some rest." They leaned against the front desk. "I'll take good care of you tonight. Very good care of you." Armando hugged Doug to his side and released him to face the counter.

The girl at the counter looked at the two of them and put on her customer-is-always-right smile. "May I help you?"

"My friend and I would like a room for the night. Do you have any vacancies?"

"Certainly." She smiled with effort. It was now the end of her shift and she was getting a little worn with the general public. "We have one with queen beds. Will that be okay?" She gave just a bit of emphasis on the word "queen".

"Yes. Of course." He began to fill out the information card. "Our three friends checked in earlier . . . worn out looking with big backpacks. Do you remember them?"

She smiled. There must be a "queen" convention in town. I thought the gay rodeo was no longer being held here in Reno. "Yeah, they checked in quite a while ago. Do you want me to ring them?"

"No, I think we want to surprise them. What room

are they in?" He handed back the completed form.

"Here, let me check for you." She turned and walked to the other end of the counter. Armando watched her swaying hips with appreciation. What a muffin she would be. She looked great coming back too.

"Wait a minute. The computer says they checked out already. Do you still want a room?"

Doug shot Armando a chilling look. "Yeah. We'll catch up with them later. Maybe something came up." Armando tried to catch the name written on the registration slip the girl carried. He could read the first name but her thumb covered the last. "Maybe Shawn won too much money and had to leave."

The girl laughed. "Sure, it happens all the time around here. You'll probably win so much you'll be gone by morning." She handed him two room keys and a receipt. "Enjoy your stay."

"Thanks."

Once in their room Doug took about a two minute shower to rinse off and was asleep in another five. Armando showered and thought about how to get a better line on the hiker named Shawn.

Food. That's it. They had to be hungry and wouldn't go out if they had the money with them. They would stay in their room and order up from room service.

Armando called room service, ordered dinner and waited.

He felt good knowing he had made some headway toward getting back his uncle's property. If he could recover the money after having it disappear like this then his position in the family would be just about impenetrable. Checking his watch, he realized it was almost time to call Uncle Lucho.

Finally room service arrived. Armando smiled as the Hispanic waiter brought in the food and set up the small table. "How are you, my friend? Enjoy your work?" asked Armando in Spanish.

"Mas Y Menos." the waiter replied. "Mucho

trabajo, nada dinero."

Armando laughed. He wondered if the man had a green card. He read the name tag. "You like money, Juan?"

Juan smiled, but just a little bit. He waited to see what the game was going to be. "What you want? Girl? Smoke?"

"No. Just some information. There were three men who checked in earlier, backpackers, two in their thirties and one older, late forties. They were whites and the older one had real blue eyes."

"I can keep my eyes open for them."

Armando pulled a fifty from his wallet. He was getting low on money in a hurry. "No, these guys already checked out."

"Oh. There were three guys like you describe but they had two women with them. It might not be the same ones."

"Hookers?"

"Not these women, too classy to be working girls. I thought it was a little strange. I took the order in to them when I first got on shift and it was just for the two women. It was kind of funny though because when I got there I had to take out the dishes from when the three guys had eaten earlier. You know . . . like these women had shown up a couple of hours after the guys checked in or something."

Armando handed Juan a twenty for the food and then the fifty. "Tell me about these women."

CHAPTER EIGHT

Shawn drove down I-80 and took the Madison exit. Marlene stirred, looked up and straightened from Shawn's shoulder. "That's the way to get from one place to another, just have someone else drive while you sleep. It's almost like time traveling. Blink, you're in Truckee, blink, you're home."

Rhonda had been asleep in the back seat and woke up with the change of speed and direction. "We're here." She reported out loud.

Her voice woke up Max who was asleep against the passenger door. Shawn pulled into the all night garage where Max had left his jeep. Unlike the Wagoneer, it sported faded out paint, a front tow bar and winch, a canvas half-top with a roll bar and no back windows. He waved to a chorus of goodbyes and went inside the garage to settle up for the parking rent. He felt a lot better about leaving his jeep here rather than on the streets. Nothing pissed him off more than getting in to drive off only to find no response from the gaping hole under the hood where his engine used to be. It had happened once and that was enough.

Shawn and Marlene waved as they watched Nolan and Rhonda drive away. They went inside and never made it to the bedroom. Hell, they never made it to the couch. Shawn put the backpack down in the entryway, reached out and took Marlene's arm as she walked toward the kitchen nook and pulled her to him. He held her for a moment, his left hand caressing the back of her neck and toying with her blond hair, then he began to kiss the smile she couldn't keep from her face. He kissed the hollow of her neck and was rewarded with a hardening of her nipples beneath his fingertips. "I wanted to do this in the car," he said.

"Let me show you what I wanted to do to you back in that hotel room in Reno."

She unbuttoned his shirt while kissing him, her tongue darting between his lips. Then, she began a slow trek down his chest. He moaned and grabbed the railing separating the entryway from the living room. She paused, kissing his navel while undoing his belt. He worked off his shoes, not wanting to stop her from her task of driving him out of his mind. His jeans fell to the floor; Marlene still teasing him with her tongue as Shawn raised up on his toes and cried out.

They proceeded to ransack each other like teenagers in the back seat of a borrowed car; clothes were scattered and thrown in a trail leading from the front door to the living room. The two of them finally ended up with Marlene arched over the back of the reclining lounge chair in a position the manufacturers never envisioned. While surrendering to their third free falling climax, Shawn held her down, her legs wrapped tightly around his straining back as they both collapsed in sweat and laughter. Their heads were almost touching the floor anyway and now they slid helplessly into a giggling heap at the foot of the chair.

"Good thing we didn't do that in the hotel room in Reno."

"We might have shocked even our friends," Marlene replied. "Personally I'm disgusted."

"Me too. Want to call me a doctor now?"

"Okay, you're a doctor." She rolled out of his reach and ran chuckling down the hall. "Now don't bother me, I'm going to take a shower."

He followed her and raised his voice enough to be heard over the shower. "You realize, of course, you can't wash me off. You are actually rubbing me in by trying."

"What?"

"I said is my finger in your ass too much?"

She opened the shower door and looked at him. "What?"

"I said . . . do you figure I'm asking too much?" he said as he got in the shower with her.

Marlene laughed. "I heard what you really said. Now you have to soap my back."

"Fate worse than death." He took the soap and did as she asked. He shampooed her blond hair twice, rubbing the lather into her scalp, then the cream rinse. She purred in appreciation. Then they were at it again, Marlene holding on to the shower wall as they made love again. This time it was slow and relaxed, maybe because of the shower or because they were almost spent. The only haste at all was when the water began to lose its heat but that was more a matter of releasing what they were holding back.

Lying on the bed, finally satiated, Marlene looked at the ceiling. "I feel like I'm floating in a warm pool of happiness. Do you know what I mean?"

"Sure, I do. I'm in it with you." He thought for a moment. "You know what?"

"What."

"I didn't think of the money once while we were making love. I don't think it could buy someone happiness if they weren't already happy."

"I couldn't agree more. So are you going to quit your job and stay home to do me more often?"

"Actually, I'm going to get a pickup, put one of them big tool boxes in the back, get a large dog, have it ride in the back and call myself a contractor like every other unemployed young male in the foothills. What do you think?"

"I'm sure you'll be a big success, dear. Will you have to chew tobacco too?"

"Of course. And you'll have to put on about fifty pounds." They laughed together and all was right. "Do you think Nolan and Rhonda are having this much fun?"

"Doubtful." Marlene remembered Rhonda's decision to leave Nolan. She too wondered if they were having any fun at all.

Nolan drove in silence until they were half way home. He spoke to Rhonda without turning his head from the road. "You've been pretty quiet. Are you worried the money is going to change us?"

"In what way?" Rhonda sighed. This wasn't going to be easy. Here she was, riding along using a bag full of money as a pillow, and she had problems. "Do you feel different at all?"

"Yeah. I do. I really feel this is a great thing for us. Maybe you think I haven't noticed but there has been a lot of unnecessary distance between us." Nolan rubbed his eye with his index finger and inspected the results.

"How do you think the money is going to change that?" asked Rhonda.

"Maybe, with more time together, we can re-fire

the spark, so to speak." They pulled into their sloping driveway.

"Maybe we can pave this damn driveway."

Nolan parked in the garage. He turned on the light, unlocked the door and walked down the hall to the back of the house. "This can't hurt us, that's for sure, and I personally feel tonight will be a new start for us." The sound of his voice retreated with him till she could barely hear the last part from the back bedroom.

Oh brother. Was this his idea of fire? He hadn't even held her since they got home.

She left her handbag on the couch and drifted back to the bedroom, all the time hearing his chatter.

"I really think it has just been after Tawna's dying that we've gotten so out of synch. There should be time now for just the two of us to go somewhere, Mexico or Alaska or someplace, and just be a couple again."

She realized this was probably the height of passion, him gargling in the bathroom, getting ready to mount her. Was she stalling telling him it was over because of the money? She didn't think so. The house was hers. It had been her mother's after her dad died and she got the house three years before Nolan came around.

Nolan entered the bedroom. He stopped and looked at her. "Aren't you going to get ready for bed?"

"Just waiting for you to get done." She kicked off her shoes and went in the bathroom. Jesus. He still hadn't touched her. It was going to be nothing until penetration. Okay. She had better do her part.

She brushed her teeth and washed her face. She thought about growing up in a house where no one hugged or said "I Love You." Maybe it was true . . . you married your father. Even if she didn't want to leave because of some misguided fear of failure she realized this barren landscape was a continuation of the empty house she grew up in.

"Well. What have we here?" Nolan reached over and rubbed her breasts with the palms of his hands.

He pulled her to the bed and kissed her breasts, her stomach, then her neck as he tried to enter her.

"Slow down, I'm still a little dry there."

"Sorry." He began to rub between her legs and she let her mind wander, conjuring up a good fantasy to get aroused. She wondered briefly what he would think if he could read her mind. Come on now . . . be serious.

She imagined someone kissing her deep and patiently. On the mouth, not on the neck as Nolan was doing now. It would be a warm kiss with little nibbles on the lower lip, then a darting tongue, mirroring the hands and fingers caressing the other lips beginning to get wet down below, the promise that tongue and fingers would soon trade places. She was really wet now and Nolan penetrated her. He probably thought his expert technique had done the job. Her fantasy pulled back to look lovingly down at her. She gasped as Max's face came to her mind's eye.

Nolan gasped. For different reasons. He was done.

Max sat at the kitchen table and sorted through two weeks' worth of mail. It didn't take long. It was a task he performed with a trash can at his feet and the pile quickly became a small stack of bills. He had checked his answering machine and had only one from his insurance agent and one from the gym, reminding him of his dues.

He had opened a bottle of wine, a Liebfaumilch that had been around for some nebulous occasion. He poured a glass and lit a cigarette. The cigarette was fresh since he opened a pack to get it. He never felt any craving for nicotine and maybe smoked one every week or so. An oddity, he knew, but he just never wanted more than that. The same with the wine. He knew the rest of the bottle would go out with the trash since a glass was enough. He passed this off as discipline to those who might ask. No one had in quite a while.

Jazz played over the radio on the public broadcasting station. He liked to keep it tuned there since they played everything. Jazz, blue grass, classical, rock, and a mix of other musical treats, and he wanted to get a little of it all. Someone had once accused him of being musically wishy-washy. He thought he just liked a lot of different kinds of music.

He took a ten second inventory of his life. The house was on a six month lease; he had no pets or exotic plants, a full tank of gas in the jeep and a million in cash. So now what?

He remembered the small village down near Acapulco where he had stayed for a year after coming home from Vietnam. His only remaining relative, his mom, had suffered a massive heart attack and died two days before he left Fort Dix, New Jersey. In the opinion of the general public he had wasted his time over there or worse, was nothing more than a murderer of women and children. He felt cold from the inside out. He went south till he felt warm and found a place where no one had an opinion one way or the other about the war.

The village wasn't exactly a movie set. The huts weren't made of grass but rather salvaged wood, corrugated metal and lots of painted cinder block. The people were generally happy and the town kept quite clean. These people were poor but it was no slum.

He had rented a place on the beach from a fisherman and his family for a pittance. It was mostly open air when he raised the wood flap window coverings. There was a wooden deck of mismatched material about three feet wide running completely around the hut.

He settled in and waited for time to do its magic. The sound of the waves had eventually washed away what remorse and bitterness he had in him and he returned to the States. He knew most veterans of the war were scarred in some way but maybe they all should have been required to do what he did before returning to the real world.

He thought now of being back at the hut on the beach only not by himself. He was sick of being alone. What good were sunsets and sunrises on the beach if there was no one to share it with?

Pretty damn melancholy Max. Snap out of it. Just think of a place where you can live peacefully. The South Pacific had innumerable islands where no one asked how you got your money and it went a long way. How about the Caymans? Man, they really didn't care where your money came from. They'd even help you launder it.

Okay. Here I am, on a beach. At least that much is consistent; I want a warm spot with a beach. I'm well off with no big money problems and I am not alone. Someone will be there. I don't have to be alone.

He let his mind stay with it and fill in the blank spot where the other person should be . . . she was loving, fun, dark hair and almond eyes. She looks up at him as they stand on the beach, whichever damn beach it is, and she smiles at him. He sees her face.

Rhonda's face.

Great.

He stubbed out his cigarette, rinsed out the glass and walked to the bedroom carrying the backpack. Maybe things would look different in the morning.

Maybe.

CHAPTER NINE

Shawn looked on appreciatively. It was going to be a great day. Marlene, dressed in a pair of her panties and one of his T-shirts, prepared breakfast of blueberry pancakes, eggs and bacon. He took several sips of his coffee without thinking as he watched the fabric of his cotton T-shirt attempt to conceal her supple form. "This is what I missed most of all on the hike."

"What's that? Seeing me in your T-shirts?" She struck a pose.

"No, hot breakfast."

"Rat." She tossed the dish towel at him and laughed when he made no attempt to dodge it and continued to drink his coffee with the towel draped over his head. "Here, you insensitive slob." She pulled the towel off his head and put their plates on the table.

Marlene drank her coffee and looked at Shawn. "Do you feel any different now?"

"Yeah, I feel like a million bucks. How about you?"

"At least that good." She started in on her eggs.

"This may sound silly but I want to keep working. I don't want to lose my perspective about the whole thing. You know what I mean?"

"Sure. I understand how you feel, just don't get upset if I don't share your perspective." Shawn poured syrup generously over his pancakes. He ate everything on his plate in a pile whereas Marlene finished each item separately.

"Is there anyone you want to give a financial hand to?" he asked between bites.

She started on the pancakes. "Actually no. Not because of greed so much as there just isn't anyone I can think of." She paused for a moment. "I do have a cousin in the mountains of Colorado who could use a leg up. She and her husband don't have much money but they started taking in foster kids when they found out they couldn't have any of their own."

She smiled now thinking of the barely controlled pandemonium that existed there and all the love she felt when she visited two Christmases ago. Each kid received a handmade gift both thoughtful and special. "Yeah, there's a family that could use a little help and could stretch each dollar till you could read through it. How about you? You have anyone you want to blow our fortune on?"

Shawn half snorted. "Sure, I'll just track down every member of my family and split it up amongst them. They shouldn't be hard to find . . . I'll just hang around down by the bank till they come in to visit their money."

He finished up the last of his breakfast and sat back in his chair. "No . . . my family blew me out when I didn't go to college like all the others. I haven't heard from any of them since. I guess we are just going to have to spend it ourselves."

"Tough break." She finished her bacon and began to clear away the dishes. "Figured out where to put it for now?"

"I thought we'd just bury it under the crawl space for

the time being. Maybe under the bedroom. It might just spice up our nights knowing what we're sleeping on. I was going to call Nolan over to help with the hard stuff."

"You mean like the actual digging, right?"

"Right." He walked up behind her and gave her a hug. "This could turn out to be fun." He reached under the T-shirt and found her breasts. "How about a rematch of last night?"

She spun away playfully. "Animal," she scolded. "I'm going to work now. Mostly out of self-defense."

Max took the backpack and his coffee with him to the workshop. He unlocked the heavy metal double doors and switched on the overhead florescent lamps revealing a well-equipped workroom with sanders, a lathe, power saw, portable welding machine and other tools. It was one of the reasons he had taken the place.

He took the five-gallon gas can from the jeep, flushed it with water to remove any lingering fumes and went to work. He fired up the cutting torch and carefully split the can along its base. He then took a rubber bladder container originally designed to hold fuel for an Ultralite one-man helicopter. The bent parts of the helicopter were scattered around the shop following an unsuccessful attempted take off on its maiden and final flight. He carefully split the bladder at one end. Next, he punched small holes every half inch along the split and inserted metal grommets with a hand press.

Using piano wire he stitched the top together and held it under water in a large sink to check for leaks. He couldn't coax any air bubbles out. Satisfied that it was watertight he put as much of the money as would fit, all but two hundred thousand dollars, into the bladder.

He took the base of the can and welded a one inch piece of metal so when the two pieces were put together the base would fit snugly inside the canister. This piece he fitted with a latch clip that could be tripped by pulling up on a strip of metal attached to the inside of the canister, out of sight but reachable with a pair of needle nosed pliers from the top. He cut a piece of gas line and stretched it around the base to seal it then carefully put the bladder inside the two halves of the gas can and fitted it together.

The final test came when he filled the can with water and jostled the can around, even dropping it on the ground. It didn't leak. Satisfied, he emptied the water out and left it to dry while going back to the house for a coffee re-fill and to drive the jeep into the shop.

Next, he improved the gas can lock on the jeep by replacing it with a steel bar that could not be cut since it had a separate bar inside which would turn if someone cut through the outside shell. This was secured to the jeep with an extra strong padlock. He concealed the padlock inside the rear compartment so no one would wonder why such an elaborate lock was used to keep eight bucks worth of gas from being stolen.

By now it was late afternoon and he hadn't eaten all day. He filled the can with gas; it took less than a gallon now, put it back on the jeep, locked it and thought about food.

Max drove across the American River and up Highway 50 toward Placerville. A new Mercedes passed. Too bad the guy couldn't get a car worth as much as his jeep. He pulled into the parking lot at the High Way House just as the sun set and darkness began to claim the foothills. He went inside and was glad to see Marlene working the restaurant.

"What's this? Your hobby?"

Marlene laughed and handed him a menu. "Just don't try to skip out on the check. I've seen your kind of deadbeat before."

Max sat at the table she indicated and handed her back the menu. "Surprise me. I'm starving."

"Okay. What do you want to drink?"

"How about iced tea?" She left and went into the kitchen. He looked around the dining area and saw all couples with only one exception other than himself. A family of five looked to be having a birthday party for grandma.

Marlene came back with his tea and went to join a group of waitresses, busboys and a waiter singing "Happy Birthday to Grandma" over a single piece of cake with a candle in it. When the song was over Marlene waved to him and went to the bar, returning a minute later with Rhonda in tow. "I brought you some company. Do you mind?"

Max tried to act calm. "No problem." He stood up intending to offer her a chair and hesitated, not being sure if he should offer her the one across from him or next to him. Marlene ended the moment by pulling out the chair next to him and dropping a menu. "I'll join you when I get a break."

"Fancy seeing you here." Max immediately wondered why he said that. *Oh great. Why don't you start talking about the weather next?*

"I came by to see Marlene and she told me you were here. Have you eaten yet?"

"No. It's on the way."

"What did you order?"

"I don't know." Real impressive so far Max. Why am I worrying about how I come off here, anyway? She is someone else's wife for Christ's sake. "Marlene is going to surprise me."

"She'll do that alright. I think I'll order for myself." She caught eye contact with Max and felt the same electricity she remembered. Maybe this is someone I can spend time with someday, like, say, the rest of my life. I'm certainly not going to come on to him now . . . he'll think I'm a tramp. Anyway, he probably doesn't know I'm alive when I'm not right in front of him.

Marlene came back with a salad for Max. He

wrinkled his brow. "Don't worry, there's more coming. What are you going to have, Rhonda?"

"Prime rib. With everything."

"As you wish. I just hope you two know how to tip." She left quickly.

Max had control of himself now, at least on the outside. "So what do you think of all this?"

She knew he was talking about the money. "Actually, I'm not impressed. Not that it isn't a lot of . . . you know . . . but I don't think I want to worry over it." She wanted to tell him she was leaving both Nolan and the money. "What about you?"

"After I bought groceries and filled my gas tank there wasn't much left anyway." They both laughed and Max was caught again in the melody of her being. It was pretty cruel of whoever was in charge of this spinning dirt ball to show him someone like Rhonda then keep her from him. Rotten trick.

Marlene brought their dinner and they didn't talk much. He liked that. Nothing worse than being asked something each time you took a bite of food and having them look to you for the answer while you chewed. He remembered doing exactly the same thing to others in the past for sport.

After dinner Marlene sat with them for a minute. "So?"

"So?" asked Rhonda, expectantly. "So what?"

Marlene looked at Max. "Did she tell you?"

"Tell me what?"

Marlene sighed. "The only problem with you Rhonda is you have no nerve." She looked at Max. "She lives in the Gobi Desert of love but is afraid to let anyone know." Marlene looked from Max to Rhonda. "Of course far be it from me to butt in so I'll get back to my work. Bye."

Rhonda sat in embarrassed silence while Max just froze with the water glass half way to his lips. In somewhat of a shock Max put his drink down and cleared his throat. "Why doesn't she just say what she means?"

"Yeah right." Rhonda turned back to Max. "So what's her point?" She fiddled with her water glass for a moment. "She means well but, I'm reluctant to talk about any of this right now. I hope you understand."

Just like that. He thought about the implications of what Marlene had said. Had they been talking about him before? His every impulse was to go slow but a large part of him, the part talking the loudest, wanted to pursue her now, to reach across the table, hold her hand, tell her he had those same feelings. Not now. It would have to be when her situation changed. Like if someday she became single. How's that for wishing someone good fortune?

They filled up the holes in the conversation with small talk till Marlene sat down again.

"I'm off work." She tossed her small apron on the table. "Tough way to make a living. Do you guys mind taking me home?" She looked at both of them. "I called to let Shawn know I'm off early but something must be wrong with the phone." Max reached for his wallet to pay the check. "Too late for you, buddy, I already paid it." She grinned and got up to leave.

Max followed Marlene and Rhonda in his jeep. He felt uncomfortable on the drive over but had the feeling there was more at stake here than his present comfort. When he pulled his jeep up behind Rhonda's red Olds at Marlene's house a chill came over him. He sensed an uneasy tug behind his testicles. It brought back bad memories of danger behind beautiful jungle walls. It urged him to leap from the car and get in front of the girls.

"Hold it just a minute will you?" He held up his

hand to them. Nolan's car was parked behind Shawn's Wagoneer meaning they were both here but no sound came from the house. The garage door stood open. The girls stayed by the Olds while Max carefully entered the garage. He still could hear nothing from inside the house. He saw the phone wires leading along the ceiling, down the door jamb to where they had been cut. Not broken . . . cut.

CHAPTER TEN

Boyle had gotten his assignment early that morning. Three in the morning, actually. Armando had learned the name of one of the hikers and what kind of car he and his friends had left in by spreading a few more fifties into the proper hands. The room service waiter got fifty by getting Shawn's last name from the desk clerk. The valet attendant had his memory return at the sight of a fifty, describing the Wagoneer, its occupants and the fact that it had California plates.

Boyle took what information Armando had and told him to return to the compound in northern California. Armando didn't object. His uncle had already implied during the last phone conversation that just maybe Armando's efforts had been enough to lead them back to the money. There was too much money in the vaults of their northern compound to have Armando absent for long.

Boyle went to his small office in the San Diego suburbs and started his search before sunrise. His office was located in one of the ubiquitous business parks of concrete and glass, lots of concrete . . . little glass, which housed everything from pool builders to microchips companies.

The office next to his was already full of young telemarketers who sold ball point pens, key chains and toner for copying machines over 1-800 lines. The morning shift was already at work hammering east coast contractors before they could escape to their contracting. The telemarketers inundated the contractors with the deals of the year; mostly shoddy products at about three times legitimate prices. What a great country, thought Boyle.

He unlocked his office and turned on his computer. As it warmed up he opened the cup of coffee bought at an all-night market and bit into a glazed donut.

He had begun computer hacking about five years ago as a means to locate and blackmail people. He became so good at it he could have made a legitimate living if he was interested. He wasn't.

First he listed the search parameters. Pretty cut and dried. Shawn Sanders. Drives a Jeep Wagoneer. Lives driving distance from Reno. Almost too easy if the Wagoneer is really his and not the woman's. The DMV hack job was so simple. After he had bought a password from an employee who liked money, he had installed a macro command that did all the things necessary to get into the system.

Since the women had arrived just a few hours after the three hikers checked in, they had to have driven less than three hundred miles or so from Reno. That left anywhere from Modesto, Santa Clara, San Francisco, Ukiah, Redding and everything inside that circle. The DMV search gave him two hundred possibles without the Wagoneer but twenty-five possibles owning Jeep Wagoneers of various years.

He went to work on the twenty five Sanders, Shawn, Sean or S., that had Wagoneers registered. Going by date of birth he eliminated twelve as too old to be hiking the Pacific Crest Trail. Five more were eliminated by race being black. Three had handicapped plates issued to them and were unlikely hikers. The remainder he listed by distance from Reno, three in the bay area, one in Redding and one in Placerville.

After printing out the list of names and addresses he accessed the appropriate phone books and got home numbers for all of them except the one in Redding that was unlisted or had no phone. Two of the listings in the bay area had office phone numbers, one being a doctor, and one selling insurance.

By now it was a quarter to nine. He took a break and ate the second donut, washing it down with the remainder of the coffee that he heated up in the microwave.

He dialed the insurance agent's number first. After the second ring it was answered by a professional voice.

"Sanders' Insurance, how may I help you?"

"Yes. This is Art Bloomer. I called last week and was told Mr. Sanders would be out all week. Is he back in?"

"I don't know why anyone would tell you such a thing. Mr. Sanders has been in every day. Do you want me to connect you?"

He hung up. He got the same results with the doctor. Calling the third candidate in the bay area produced a woman who wanted to know why someone wanted to talk to her husband three weeks after his funeral. Apologizing he hung up.

His next call was to make a flight reservation from San Diego to Sacramento. It left him one hour to get to the airport. He shut down the computer and left the office.

Either the Sanders in Placerville was the one he wanted or he wasn't. If it turned out to be a dud then he would just drive up to Redding but he had a strong feeling about the Sanders in Placerville. It was so obvious. Only two hours, three at the most, from Reno and if he was to pick a possible spot for a hiker to live it would be Placerville. He made the decision to go there directly instead of phoning. He didn't want to spook his prey.

The commuter flight left San Diego Airport and headed north up the Central Valley. He dozed fitfully in spite of his eagerness to close on his *assignment*.

He flew under the alias of Clint Rucker. What a great name. A whole shit pot better than Boyle. Why had his father hung that on him? Sounds like Boil. Like something you would go to the doctor and have lanced. Boyle. Boil.

He remembered when he had really gotten out from under his father's hold. He had just turned thirteen and his birthday party was a miserable attempt on his mother's part to pretend he had a lot of friends. The funny part was that he didn't mind not having friends. What would he do with them anyway? Share his secrets? Fat chance.

He had been loafing down near Crystal Pier in the Mission Beach area of San Diego, when a young fag had approached him. They had gone under the pier away from the view of passersby. He let the fag rub against him and waited till the young man had gone to his knees. As the man loosened the drawstring on Boyle's swim trunks Boyle pulled back. "No," said Boyle. The young man looked confused. "I want to see yours."

The young man smiled. He undid his pants and pulled his swollen member out. Boyle had him spread his legs. "Now close your eyes." As he did so Boyle kicked him hard to the groin. As he fell to the sand Boyle brought his knee down on the back of his neck.

Boyle smiled as he remembered how he had beaten the young man long after he was unconscious. How he had picked up the two by four and beat him till his arms ached and the shape on the sand stopped looking like a man. More like cast off meat. He had sat and looked at his work and knew in that moment he had separated himself from the rest of the world and he liked it. That night he had looked at his father with new eyes. Free eyes. His father pretty much left him alone from then on.

The plane began its final approach to Sacramento Metro Airport; the stewards walking through . . . seat belts and seat backs . . . touch down and taxi to the terminal. Boyle rented a white Dodge because no one could ever remember what kind of car it was if they saw it. He rented it under a fake Clint Rucker credit card. It was now a little after one in the afternoon.

Boyle stopped at an office supply store and picked up a Thomas Brother's map of the area. As he drove up Highway 50 toward Placerville he listened to country and western music on the radio and looked at the baked dry foothills. Man, I wonder what a well-placed match would do here.

He found the house listed for Shawn Sanders in a mix of very expensive and almost shoddy houses. This one fit at the lower end but was neat and well-tended. It was a single story wood house, about five years old, with an attached two car garage located at the front of the house forming a fat L shape. The garage was almost as large as the rest of the house and the door was open.

Boyle parked down the block and took stock. There was a Jeep Wagoneer parked in the garage and no other vehicles in sight. As he contemplated his next move another car drove up. A man in his thirties with dark hair stepped out of the car and rang the bell. He was greeted by a blond man, also in his thirties, with the comfort and ease of old friends. They went inside.

After fifteen minutes or so they both came around from the back of the house and went in the garage. They picked up some type of garden tools that Boyle couldn't quite make out and went back inside the house.

Boyle drove past the house; circled and parked so the garage shielded him from the front windows. Getting out of the car he took the map book, flipped it open, held a pen and drummed it on the map like a meter reader and walked to the garage. The first thing he noticed was the now empty backpack lying against the garage wall. Listening at the back door for a full two minutes he figured they were somewhere in another part of the house. After pulling on a pair of ultra-thin leather gloves he cut the phone wires next to the back door and tried the door knob. It was locked. No big deal there. The locks on the inside doors aren't made to slow anyone down much.

He took a sharp folding knife with the tip altered to the shape of a small fork. He slipped it between the frame and door and forced back the bolt. There were no signs of a dog, like scratch marks on the door or food bowls, so he wasn't concerned about an alarm being raised.

He pushed the door open slowly. The only sound he could hear was muffled conversation from somewhere inside. He walked into the kitchen and stopped. He loved this part. He felt hypersensitive, every nerve ending ready for flight or fight. He spun around at the sound of the refrigerator motor coming on and silently chided himself for being so jumpy.

He pulled his tool kit out. Leather jewelers wrap about eight inches by ten inches with pockets sewn in to keep each highly polished item from rattling against another. From this he selected a bone handled thin curved blade of surgical steel six inches long but sharpened like a razor on both edges. Returning the pouch to the inside pocket of his windbreaker he continued toward the sounds of the two men talking.

Down the hallway he went, the sounds getting louder. He stopped behind the door to what should be the main bedroom. Sure they were inside, he poised to enter. He would try the nonchalant method of walking in like he belonged and using the element of surprise to enable him to cut the first one he came to. No way they would expect that. He almost giggled.

He took two breaths and walked into an empty room.

He looked around in confusion for a moment. He

could still hear the sounds of their conversation only it was slightly muffled. It came from the vent at his feet.

He knelt slowly and listened. They were talking about how what they were doing resembled work and their joking was punctuated by the thunking sound of hand shovels and gasps for breath.

Now he had to think. There was no way he could just stroll into the crawl space under the house like he belonged there. “Hi, just dropping in to look at the bottom of your house.” No . . . wouldn’t work. He decided to set up somewhere and wait for them to come back inside. He walked carefully so as to make no noise. Once he got to the front room he sat down by the sliding doors to the back yard and waited.

They came in so soon it almost caught him unaware. “I guess we should have taken a few beers with us,” Shawn said as he walked in past where Boyle crouched. Shawn turned to look at Nolan and saw them both. His eyes registered danger as Nolan turned toward Boyle.

Boyle had meant to cut the man bad enough to get absolute compliance without killing him. He brought the wicked knife up in a slashing motion to split him from hip to shoulder. Nolan reacted quickly and instinctively, reaching for the blade before it could cut him. The blade being sharpened on both sides, cleanly removed the little and adjoining fingers of Nolan’s left hand. Nolan looked at them in disbelief as they dropped to the floor.

Shawn lunged for the lamp and held it over his head. As he went to attack Boyle, Nolan tried to grab Boyle with his right hand. Boyle ripped the knife back at Nolan, no longer worrying about finesse, cutting his throat cleanly. The move took the blade all the way to the spinal cord as surgical steel sharpened to perfection went through skin, cartilage, blood vessels, muscle and windpipe like a hot knife through butter.

Nolan had the dubious distinction of witnessing his own death in the mirror over the fireplace. He was quite alive as he watched his head nearly separate from his shoulders. His eyes registered the look in his own eyes before his face turned from the mirror and joined the rest of his dying body on the floor just inside the sliding door. He could see into Shawn's backyard between the bottom of the drapes and the carpet as the afternoon breeze lifted them to give him one last glance at this world before going into the next.

The forward slash caught Shawn in a vertical motion across his upraised arms, cutting through the left biceps, laying open his cheek, through the bridge of the nose all the way to the bone, across the other cheek and through the right biceps. As Shawn dropped the lamp from his now useless hands Boyle kicked him hard in the stomach and the cry of pain died in his throat.

Boyle stepped over Nolan's body and shut the sliding door. Shawn had not lost consciousness. He was bleeding profusely from his wounds and would probably die without help. Boyle knelt next to him.

"Do you want to live?"

Shawn could not speak. His eyes showed terror and the beginnings of physical shock. "Too bad about your friend." He sighed like he had been an innocent bystander instead of the perpetrator. "I just want what you took from us. It's not worth what I'll do to you to find out." He reached down between Shawn's legs. He showed the blade with his other hand. "You want to tell me don't you?"

The terror was complete. Shawn could barely talk through his butchered face.

"In the crawl space."

Boyle knew there was no lying left in this man. He walked behind Shawn and pushed him to the floor. Shawn was still conscious but could not move. He felt his life pouring from his arms. Boyle laid the curved blade on the coffee table and took the jeweler's pouch from his jacket. There was no blood on him at all, the sign of a true professional. He selected a wider blade with the handle grooved for a better grip. He knelt and pushed Shawn's feet together so the backs of his legs faced the ceiling.

He held the knife two-handed in a prayer-like position, putting his weight to it, drawing it across Shawn's legs four inches above the knees, cutting through muscle and tendons completely to the femur. Blood gushed from the wounds. Shawn felt the knife going through him as though he had been given some anesthetic. In fact, he had. His body had gone into shock to shield him from what was happening. He lost consciousness before Boyle wiped the blades on Shawn's pants and set them aside for later use.

Boyle rose, reached into his pocket to rearrange his erection, and looked out the sliding glass door. Satisfied no one was witness to his work he picked up Shawn's baseball cap with the Sacramento Kings emblem that had fallen to the floor, then he stepped outside.

The deck extended most of the length of the house. The ground fell sharply to the fence separating this home from an empty wooded lot. He took the steps leading to what passed for a back yard and walked under the deck. Instead of a short crawl space, the rear wall under the deck was easily nine feet tall. One of the wood panels had been removed allowing access under the house. Stepping through the opening Boyle looked up at the flooring, covered in insulation, with a maze of heating ductwork and pipes. At the far corner stood two shovels next to a freshly dug hole about four feet deep and half as wide. It was empty.

Returning upstairs Boyle carefully stepped over Nolan's body. Shawn had regained consciousness and had crawled to the end of the couch dragging his useless legs behind him. He had somehow pulled the phone off the end table and was trying to dial. Boyle smiled, stepped around him and walked to the rear of the house.

He searched the house casually, looking for things that might help him later. In the bedroom he picked up a small picture of the man in the front room who was trying to dial the phone, and an attractive blond woman. In the picture they were wearing sombreros, swimsuits and sandals and smiled into the camera from a beach in Cancun, Mexico. He slipped the photo out of its frame and put it in his back pocket.

He noticed little of interest in the other rooms except proof that the man in the front room lived here with the woman and no one else. He walked back down the hall, past Shawn who now stared numbly at the ceiling with the phone across his nearly motionless chest, and into the kitchen. He picked up an address book lying on the counter near the wall phone.

Then he saw the ice chest on the sink counter. Nice touch. He opened it. It was almost full of money bundled and wrapped in cellophane. Reaching down into the chest he could tell this was not all of the money he was sent to recover. That didn't surprise him. He would see if the one trying to phone eternity could still talk. Not that it mattered much. He would play this one out as three separate jobs.

Next he washed the knives in the sink, tested them with his thumb, satisfied they were not nicked, he went to Shawn's side. "Can you hear me?" Shawn's eyes barely responded. "Good. Now look down here."

He tilted Shawn's head so his chin rested on his chest. "I think you'll find this of some interest. At least in the anatomical sense." He cut away the front of Shawn's shirt and trousers. "Now pay close attention while you can."

Starting the incision at the sternum and continuing down in a wide circle to the groin area Boyle went to work.

CHAPTER ELEVEN

Max considered the options. Something was wrong here. Terribly wrong. He knew it. He should go around the side and enter that way. He opted for the direct approach. He tried the door. It was locked. Moving to the front of the house he told the girls to stay in the car and if anything bad happened or if he didn't come back out in ten minutes they were to call the police. He took Marlene's door key off the ring and handed her back the keys. "What's wrong?" asked Marlene.

"I'm not sure. It might be nothing but I'd rather play it safe. Just stay here and don't go in by yourselves no matter what."

He returned to the garage, picked up a pair of long handled pruning shears, unlocked the back door and pushed it open. Even with what he'd been exposed to in Vietnam his mind wouldn't register what he saw at first. The copper smell of blood, feces and death filled his senses.

He stared for a full minute at the open refrigerator.

There, on the first shelf next to the milk, cheese and leftover chicken lay two nearly identical flaps of muscle and skin which could only be stomach and genitals. He tore his gaze away and saw the two bodies laid out in the living room. Two thoughts passed through his mind. Defenses against madness like the sick humor of doctors or undertakers.

First, it wasn't fair to call it a *living* room anymore.

Secondly, somehow, someone was going to have to identify the bodies and then match them to the pieces in the fridge.

He raced to the trash can in the garage and was violently sick.

After calling the police it was all Max could do to keep both women away from the house. They cried but believed him that what waited inside was something they should not see. By the time the police arrived all three were in a state of numbness. Sheriff's units filled the street with lights flashing. The area was taped off as a crime scene and even the most hardened veterans were visibly shaken.

The coroner arrived and Max was asked if he was sure of the identity of the two bodies. He told the coroner and the uniformed officer assisting him that they were the two bodies of his friends. The bodies were photographed from every angle imaginable. The hands were bagged in case either of them had managed to struggle with their attacker.

Max tried to remain strong. Occasionally either Marlene or Rhonda would come to him and start to cry all over again. Sorrow was one thing Max felt. The other was a feeling that they were caught in the sights of a snipers scope. He felt an itching between the shoulder blades and kept turning to look into the darkness past the revolving emergency lights on the roofs of the ambulances and police cars on the street

The man in a dark blue, well-tailored suit seemed to be in charge of the investigation. Detective Drew was a twenty year veteran and didn't miss much. He followed his gut most of the time. His gut told him this was no thrill kill. After hooking up the phone line he hit the redial button. A voice came on and told him the correct time and temperature. Gee, when they did that on television the murderer usually answered. Oh well, got to go through the motions.

He looked up to see Max, Marlene and Rhonda huddled together like refugees seeking warmth. He let his instincts move him. "Officer..."

"Dantley, sir."

"Yes. I want you to take someone with you and get those three separated. Are the forensic guys through with the back rooms?"

"All but the master bedroom, sir."

"Okay. Let me know when that one is done. Meanwhile get those three apart just long enough for me to get some kind of statement from them."

He walked out to his car and overheard two young patrolmen talking. "What do you think happened? Did you see that shit? Pretty sick stuff."

In an attempt at humor, or maybe to impress his partner, the other officer responded. "I think it was a double suicide." Straight faced.

The other patrolman laughed in spite of himself. Drew stepped between them. They both snapped to attention. Drew fixed them with a withering stare.

"Sorry sir. I guess we're a little nervous," said the older of the two.

Drew walked off without a word. The two patrolmen breathed in relief and exchanged sheepish looks.

He questioned Rhonda in a smaller bedroom off the hall. It could have been called the sewing room or den.

It contained a mismatch of items like dressers, a desk covered with magazines and unanswered mail, a couple of file boxes, Christmas paraphernalia, a guitar and case and other assorted items that went with no particular decor. Rhonda sat on the edge of a twin bed made up for guests. Drew pulled up a folding chair.

"I'm sorry about your loss. I am also sorry to have to ask you these questions but getting the answers right away might help us to catch the one responsible for this. Do you understand?"

"Yes."

"This will take just a minute. Are you sure you're up to it?"

Rhonda sat with knees together clutching a Kleenex. "Yes, I think so."

"Okay. Do you know why your husband was here?"

She took a deep breath. "He was visiting Shawn. They were good friends."

"Did they visit each other on a regular basis? I mean, did they visit every Monday?"

"No. Just whenever."

"It looked like they were doing yard work. Did he say anything about that?"

Rhonda looked up. "No."

"Can you think of anyone who might want to cause your husband harm?"

"No."

"No arguments with co-workers, neighbors?"

"No. Not that I can remember. Not at all."

"How about the other man, Shawn? As far as you knew, did he get along with most people?"

"There was nothing like that. They both were easy going."

After a few more questions about their relationship, he thanked her and left.

In the hallway he motioned to the uniformed officer again. "Is the master bedroom done?"

"Yes sir."

"Put the other woman in there please."

He entered as soon as she was in the bedroom. "Ma'am, I'm very sorry for your loss. But I need to ask a few questions. This won't take long, I assure you. I hope you understand."

Marlene just looked at him through tear-swollen eyes. She appeared to be a very strong woman, belying her diminutive stature.

"Did your husband have any enemies?"

"Shawn was not my husband. We lived together." She looked evenly at him as if waiting for a comment.

"Yes. Well, has he mentioned anything that might reveal someone who would want to cause him harm?"

"No. Shawn got along with everyone." She wiped her eyes with the back of her hand.

He handed her his handkerchief. "How well did he know Nolan?"

"Very well. In fact they just got back from a hike."

She stopped the sentence short, a fact that did not escape him. "What hike?"

Marlene shifted on the bed. Her jaw took on a tighter look. "They just got back from a camping trip."

Drew mentally noted the change in attitude. He continued. "Is there anything missing from the house?"

"Not that I can see." Except an ice chest full of hundreds, she thought.

"Could you walk around with me and look please?"

"Sure." She was glad to get up. She dug her nails into her palms as she looked at the nightstand where the picture of her and Shawn in Cancun used to sit. She said nothing, walking and acting as if she were searching for missing articles.

They went from room to room, all except the living room which was still being gone over inch by inch in search of clues. In the kitchen she hesitated near the wall phone. "No, I don't see anything missing at all."

"Thank you Ma'am. You've been very helpful."

He talked to Max in the garage. "I hope you don't

mind. I have just a couple of questions."

"Sure, no problem. Anything to help."

"How well did you know the deceased?"

"Pretty well."

"Did you see them regularly?"

"Often."

Not much in the way of information for someone who wanted to help. Okay, if that was how it was to be played. "Did they have any enemies that you know of?"

"No."

"They just went camping together. Did anything happen that they might have mentioned?"

"No, not to me."

Dantley knocked on the door and put his head inside. "Sir?"

"Excuse me please." He said to Max and followed the officer out to the driveway.

"Just thought you might want to know. They weren't doing yard work sir. It looks like they were burying something in the crawl space."

Under the house, a couple of flashlights and a lantern lit up the site. An area was taped off where the hole had been dug earlier. Detective Drew noted the two shovels. Was the hole finished? If not, how big was it going to be? There was nothing else below the house except the two shovels so what were they going to put in the hole? Why did they go back inside? Did they know the murderer? "Take some casts of the footprints. I want to know if there was anyone else down here besides the victims."

"Yes sir."

He returned to the garage. Max hadn't moved. Either he was an ex-soldier or ex-con. They seemed to be the ones who could wait forever and still look like it was their idea. "Did you see either of the victims today?"

Max hesitated. "No. I spent today at home until about five-thirty or so then went to eat. I ate where Marlene works. Rhonda was there. Marlene wanted a ride home cause she got off early and the phone here didn't work. Rhonda gave her a ride and I followed them. I wanted to visit with Shawn and Nolan. We got here I saw the phone lines were cut so I went in first. That's my dinner over there if you want to check." Max indicated the trash can where he had lost his dinner after seeing what was in the refrigerator. He looked the detective in the eye. "I can't help but notice that you're not writing this down on paper. Unless you're wired for sound I'm just going to have to repeat myself in a formal statement so do you mind telling me why you're doing this?"

Drew looked back without blinking. "What were they burying under the house?"

Max blinked. He continued to lock on the detective's eyes. "I don't have the slightest idea." *And neither do you*, he thought.

Drew sighed. "I'm going to ask you not to leave town for a while. I hope you understand. You're right about the formal statement. I need you to come in tomorrow to the station. Can you do that? Say about ten?"

"Sure. Now if there's nothing else I'd like to go."

Drew waved his hand at the door. Max walked out on the front lawn to where Marlene and Rhonda sat on the hood of Rhonda's car talking in low voices. They looked at Max as he approached.

Marlene smoked and hugged herself. "There's some stuff missing from the house."

Rhonda touched Max's arm. "It's not just stuff. Tell him Marlene."

"There was a picture of me and Shawn in Mexico. It was in the bedroom on the nightstand and it's not there now. Also our address book is gone."

Rhonda looked at Max. "How did this happen so fast?" She shuddered. "Just last night we went and got you guys in Reno. Now they're at our door. Nothing is worth this."

"I know. I know." Max looked from Marlene to

Rhonda. "I can't believe this went down like it did. There are two scenarios that make any sense." He pointed to the house indicating what had happened to his two friends.

"This could be a random act of violence and whoever did it found the money. Now they have your picture and address book." He paused and looked to the sky. "Of course it could also be the ones the money belonged to and they have your picture and address book. If it is, then I just don't see how they managed to find us so fast."

"And?" Rhonda asked.

"And, either way, someone real bad has your picture and our names."

They stood in silence. Marlene broke into a sob. "I can't believe this has happened. It's like we're being robbed of our time to grieve. It's not fair."

Max took her by the arms and looked in her eyes. "Fair or not, we're stuck with it. If we don't use our heads here we might not survive. There'll be time later for grieving and maybe even revenge. Right now we need to stick together. Agreed?"

Marlene had no problem with that line of reasoning and Rhonda couldn't see it any other way. None of them wanted to be alone tonight

The detective approached them from the house. He motioned to Max. "Can I speak with you a moment?"

He and Max walked to the front of the garage. Drew glanced at the two women and back to Max. "I'm going to give you a little information . . . of course you know there's no way you could have heard it from me. Got it?"

Max nodded. "Got it."

"There was something about this killing that stuck in my mind as far as how it was done. So clean. Well . . . relatively speaking. Anyway, the MO matches the work of a killer, man or woman we aren't sure, who strikes about once a year. Because of the slashing and all we first thought he or she was a psycho. We still think so but we also think whoever it is, is a professional. That means it was done for a reason . . . probably financial." Drew lit a cigarette. "Do you know what that means?"

Max tried to look as blank as possible.

Drew continued. "Look. I'm not sure what went down here but you three might be in a lot of trouble if this is the same person we think it is. I guess what I'm saying is to watch your ass."

Max searched Drew's eyes and trusted what he saw. "Thanks. I'll take what you say to heart. I will."

Drew extended a hand. At first Max started to shake it. Then he saw the card. "Call me if you get talkative. Okay?"

"Sure." Max read the card and put it in his pocket and walked back to the car.

Rhonda and Marlene seemed to be pretty well composed, all things considered. It was time to get down to business. Here they were at probably the most tragic moment in these two women's lives, and they had to attend to the ugly business of survival. Max knew from experience how necessity and convenience don't come at the same time.

"Okay, girls, it's time to make plans. Are you up to it or do you just want to give up?"

They both looked to him with even gaze and determination. Marlene spoke first. "Let's do it."

"Let's get somewhere with lots of people around so we're safe but can still talk. We need to decide what to do right now."

As Max returned to his jeep the itching between the shoulder blades was so intense he almost dove into the front seat. Whoever killed Shawn and Nolan was out there. He felt sure he was being watched. Whoever that person was knew who they were but they had no clue about who might come to kill them. That meant they could trust no one for now. Max wasn't sure how, but he intended to even up the odds a bit.

Boyle watched them leave through high powered night glasses. He smiled and left the hiding place on the ridge and went to his car to follow.

CHAPTER TWELVE

Max drove to Bob's Big Boy in Placerville. Since it was right off Highway 50 it had customers almost all the time. They took a booth by the window but not near the phones or restrooms. They wanted privacy yet the safety of a public place. All three ordered coffee. Rhonda looked to Marlene. "I know we're going to feel a lot worse about this later on but right now I feel numb. How about you?"

"Yeah. Same thing here." She looked at Max. "Just how bad is this mess we're in?"

"This is as bad as it gets. I wish we had never found the money and if I'd have known it would lead to this I would have left it there. Right now there's nothing we can do about it."

"Could we give back the other two shares?" Rhonda asked. "Would that help?"

"No. I don't think it would get us out of the woods with these guys." He rubbed his chin thoughtfully. "The opposite just might be true. Keeping the money just might help us survive."

"Then what?" Marlene asked. "What good does it do us to just survive? I don't want to be on the run for the rest of my life."

"Well I'd much rather be on the run than caught. Do you know what I mean?" Rhonda replied.

Max looked to them both. "Actually, I'd rather get even."

"How?"

"Every day we stay out of their reach is a bad day for them. If that was all we could accomplish it would be something at least." He drank from his cup and looked around the restaurant. "For all we know the person who killed Shawn and Nolan is in this restaurant right now. We should act as if that's the case."

"Or the people who did it," said Marlene.

"No, I think it is just one person because of the way it was done." He shuddered at the memory. "I find it hard to imagine someone who did that to Shawn and Nolan actually hooking up with a partner."

They sat in silence, each sipping coffee and coming to the same conclusion. Max spoke first. "Look, in order for us to get help from the police we're going to have to tell them about the money. If we do that then we have to give up the money to the authorities and even that might not do the trick. We might still come up short on the protection deal."

"You don't think they'll protect us," asked Marlene.

"Oh, they'll want to. They'll do their best but eventually they'll get bored. They can't and won't keep us under guard forever. Six months, a year from now, we will be in the same boat as now. Someone will still be really pissed off because they don't have their money and it will be our fault. We will be without protection except our own wits. But there will be one very big difference."

Rhonda and Marlene waited for the rest of the statement. "What big difference?"

"We won't have the money."

"So what do you want to do?" asked Rhonda.

"I intend to run. It has to be easier to hide out if you have plenty of cash at your disposal. At least this way we can hide out in style. I have a place to go for awhile."

Marlene sat down her cup. "I have one too. I have someone whose name wasn't in the book." Marlene said. "It's someone who moved to a remote place in . . ."

Max held up his hand. "I don't think you should say anymore." Rhonda looked at him quizzically. "I don't want to know something I might reveal under the wrong circumstances."

Rhonda reached over and put her hand on Marlene's arm. "I can let you have half of the money I have."

Max looked at her. "I don't think we can take the risk of going to get it. There might be a good chance it's no longer there."

"We were sitting on it driving over here." She smiled. "It's under the front seat. We were going to hide it later."

Max considered this new development. "Now we have another problem. Your car is real hot. The police and the killer probably know about it. If we're going to make a run for it we need to get something else to drive." He drank the rest of his coffee. "I'm going to make a phone call. Don't get up for anything. Okay?"

"Okay." Both said in unison.

Max went to the bank of phones near the restrooms. Putting his back to the wall he dialed a number as he watched for anyone who might pay extra attention to his movements. He could see no one who appeared to be alone. There was a group of young wanna-be gangsters in a corner booth, a few couples and families, and at the counter were two men; one older gentleman talking to a younger man maybe late twenties or early thirties.

The phone was answered on the fifth ring. "Hello?"

"Hi. Jim?"

"Yes?"

"This is Max."

"Max. Great to hear your voice." Jim replied with genuine pleasure. "We don't see each other enough. What's up?"

"You know how you're always trying to get me to trade in that old jeep of mine?"

"What happened? Did it blow up or something?"

"Very funny. Do you want to sell a car or not?"

Jim laughed. "Since you only get a new one after the wheels have fallen off the old one I'd have to be dense to pass up this chance. Why don't you come in tomorrow morning and I'll take care of you."

Max smiled. "Look, this may sound odd but I need to do this tonight. I know it's late so don't tell me what time it is. Here's what I want you to do . . ." He laid out his plan.

Max returned to the booth. No one paid him any attention but that didn't mean much. The gangsters had left in a noisy mob, the waitress not looking pleased at the tip they left, and the older man at the counter was telling the younger man something about fishing. He caught snatches of their conversation on the way past. ". . . you need to put the hook through their backs, they live longer and wriggle more . . ."

"Have you two given any thought as to running versus giving up?"

Rhonda now had a more determined look in her eyes. "I personally have been ripped off by drug dealers worse than anyone here, first Tawna then Nolan, so if just staying alive and keeping their money fucks with them . . . I'm all for it." She smiled. "In fact, I'd rather burn it than let them have it back."

Marlene sat up straighter. "Anything I can do to foul up their lives is fine with me too."

"Great. We have to stay here another thirty minutes

so we may as well try to eat something. Then we're getting out of here and starting our run." He looked at Rhonda. "Do you have someplace to hide or . . ."

Rhonda was not about to let this man out of her sight. She might not have long to live, the way things were shaping up, and there was no way he was getting away. Besides, she really didn't have a place to run.

"I kind of hoped I'd stick with you for awhile."

Max felt happier than he had a right to, considering the circumstances. He smiled at her. "Let's order something."

When they had finished eating what they could, Max went to pay the check while the girls went to the restrooms. The restaurant crowd had thinned out, only two couples and the same father-son fishermen at the counter. He could hear the older man spinning some fish tale. " . . . Yes siree, it was raining like a cow pissing on a flat rock but I weren't about to leave. We musta' ate for a month on the fish I pulled from that hole . . ."

Oh brother, welcome to the foothills. When the girls came back they walked quickly to the parking lot. Max waited till the Olds was pointed out to the street then he whipped around it and sped down the main street toward the north end of town. Rhonda followed right on his heels. They didn't see the younger man at the counter throw a couple of bills down and race to the parking lot next door.

The older man kept right on talking.

Max drove to an unlit but large used car lot. At the curb there stood a fake bear that mechanically waved to passing motorists during the day but now slumped silent like a huge puppet at rest. Behind the bear was a tall pole about three feet around with an old VW bus welded to the top. On the side of the bus was painted *THE BUCK'S USED CARS*.

Normally there would have been cars parked to block the entrance at night but one had been moved to allow them to enter. They drove to the rear of the lot to a Quonset hut about fifty feet long with *SERVICE* painted on the door that closed behind them. They sat in darkness, engines off, listening to the popping sounds of cooling metal. A light came on revealing several bays for working on cars.

In the first two service bays sat cars with their hoods removed. They appeared to be in the middle stages of tear down or rebuild, it was hard to tell which. From behind two newer white Chevy Blazers walked a smiling man nearly bobbing with enthusiasm. "Can I help you?"

"Just looking." Max replied. They laughed together with the ease of two men who had done so many times before. After hugging each other Max brought him over to Rhonda and Marlene. "I want you to meet Jim. He's one of the reasons I'm still alive. Jim, this is Marlene and Rhonda."

"How'do, ladies. Don't let him fool you none. It was him what saved my life." He fairly beamed at them. "Glad to help." He stopped smiling. "I'm real sorry you folks have trouble but if I can help I sure will."

The girls smiled in spite of the circumstances.

"Let me show you these two buggies I picked out. I hope they suit you." He walked to the two Blazers just like it was broad daylight and he was selling a car to a couple of tire kickers. "Almost new. Got them from a mining company that just went under. That's why they're identical. Lots of power, all the goodies and four-wheel drive." Rhonda actually kicked a tire. "Now normally these would sell somewhere in the neighborhood of twenty thousand but the current administration had that neighborhood torn down. You can have them for a song." He looked at Max. "So start singing."

Max laughed. "What about the plates?"

"The mining company sure ain't going to argue if you use them. They're good for another five months. I'll hold the titles as inventory till then." They started to walk back to Max's Jeep. "As far as the DMV is concerned, both of these rigs will still be on my lot."

"You don't know how much I appreciate this, Jim." Max put his hand on Jim's shoulder. "You are probably saving our lives here."

"Well, it won't make us even. I've enjoyed a lot of years I maybe wouldn't have had if you hadn't been in that chopper that day so don't sweat it." He tapped out a cigarette and lit it. "Is there anything else I should know about this trouble?"

Max took the gas can off the back of the Jeep. "I don't know what you should be careful of. I don't think you will be sucked into this but cover your ass." Max emptied the gas out and undid the latch. "Treat it as though you're in danger. This person is a butcher." He laid out the bladder of money on the cement floor and started transferring it to a canvas tool bag. "I'll call your business number late at night and leave a message from time to time. If anything goes wrong on this end, or if there's something I should know about, just mention *Blazer* in your message and I'll call at exactly midnight at your house first chance I get."

Max counted out forty thousand dollars, hesitated, and put down another ten thousand. Jim didn't insult him by telling him it was too much but put it in an inside pouch of his windbreaker.

"I'll be careful." Jim pointed to the end of the hut. "I have a paint booth down there. Your Jeep will be yellow and that Olds might be camouflaged green by morning. Just sign these forms for me." He took a couple of mileage statements and owner transfer slips from a file cabinet against the wall. They walked over to the Olds where Rhonda had emptied out the car and taken the money from under the seat. "Here, miss." Jim handed her the forms to sign.

As she signed the form she indicated the two small bags of money on the hood. "I split my part with Marlene. Do you want me to chip in on this?"

Max did some quick math. "No. That's fine the way it is. We better get a move on." He looked at Jim. "Do you have any coffee here?"

"I can make some up while we move these cars around. I'll let you take my thermos."

They parked the Jeep and the Olds against the wall and brought the Blazers up to the front door. As the coffee was making, Jim rummaged through the ancient metal desk finally pulling out a Rand McNally road atlas. "Do you need this?"

Max shook his head. "I know where I'm headed."

"I could use a map." Marlene took it and put it on the front seat.

Jim motioned for Max to follow him to a small tool shed. "Do you want to take this?" He held out a 38 caliber snub-nosed revolver and a box of shells. "It might come in handy."

"Do you have anything else? You refused to even touch one after coming back from Vietnam."

"No. This is the only one I have."

"Jim, I don't want to take this. In fact, I want you to carry this damn thing with you till this is over." He looked Jim in the eye. "It will be over. I don't intend to stay on the run for the rest of my life. I've got a few connections and I like revenge better than hiding."

Max looked over at the two women talking in low voices. They seemed to be saying goodbye. Both of them had tears on their faces. "Somehow I'm going to find out who killed my friends and then I'm going to rid the earth of that trash. There's no other way. Right now though I want these girls to be somewhere safe." They walked back to the two Blazers. "Thanks, Jim. Take care of yourself."

They shook hands. Max and Rhonda got in the Blazer closest to the front door, Marlene started up the one behind it. "Let's hit it," said Max.

Jim hit the button that rolled the doors up and Max pulled out over the curb. Highway 50 was only one block away. Marlene pulled up behind him at the light. There was no other traffic. When the light turned green Rhonda waved to Marlene. Max turned right up Highway 50 and Marlene turned left. They hoped it wasn't goodbye forever.

Behind them Boyle sat crouched down in the front seat of the Dodge. He had to make a decision quick. They were obviously running or they wouldn't have switched vehicles. Maybe whoever was at the car lot would know where they were headed but if not, he'd lose them by trying to get the information from him. Anyway, he could always come back. He already had the money from the girl riding alone in the one Blazer. He also had her address book so she was findable. He waited till the other Blazer was onto the highway before he started up. He might even find out where the one woman was going from the other two. He pulled out and followed Max and Rhonda, staying well back, sure the driver would be watching for a tail. He considered working on the man and woman at the same time and grew excited. God, how he loved this job.

CHAPTER THIRTEEN

Marlene drove down Highway 50, then Highway 49, retracing the route she and Rhonda had taken yesterday to Reno. Jesus, had it only been yesterday? How things had changed. Her whole life had been scattered to the winds. In one day she had gone from being broke to being rich, to being broke, and back at least to being well off financially. She had gone from being comfortable to running in terror. Just yesterday she had worried about when to get her car's oil changed and whether or not to go to aerobics class. Seemed trivial now. The man she loved so much had been taken from her. Tears began to flow again and she wiped them to clear her vision.

She drank from the thermos of coffee and listened to obscure western music stations as she drove on through the late night, through Reno without stopping, past towns called Trinity, Lovelock, Imlay, and finally Winnemucca. Who named them?

She pulled in at a truck stop in Winnemucca to fill

up the tank. She could hardly keep her eyes open but didn't want to stop yet to sleep. The attendant inside wiped the counter furiously while rapidly chewing gum and bouncing to the music playing too loud on a boom box behind him. Ghetto blaster, Shawn used to call them. This much energy at three thirty in the morning could not be just youthful enthusiasm.

Marlene paid for the gas and when he gave her the change she touched his hand and smiled. There were packs of NoDoz for sale on the counter. She picked one up and looked at him. "Do these really work?"

"Sort of. How long do you want to stay up?"

"Do you have anything better?"

He looked at her for a moment. "Sure." He took out a ChapStick, popped off the bottom and shook several small white pills into his hand. "Take a couple of these with coffee. But don't think about going to sleep for awhile." He handed her a half dozen of the pills.

"Thanks." She took them with coffee, refilled the thermos and drove onto I-80. Within minutes she was wide awake and feeling pretty damn euphoric for someone running for her life. She had taken speed when she was younger to cram for exams in school or on long weekends. She knew the price of this false euphoria would be a terrible emotional crash later on.

She drove east with the singing of the tires and Hank Williams on the radio. More towns came and went . . . Valmay, Beowawe, Deeth and Pequop . . . all small and some no more than a gas station and a smattering of houses off the freeway. She hoped to be in the mountains of Colorado before she slept again.

Her cousin's number was not in the address book taken from the house. It was on the letter she had in her purse. Written just a week ago, her cousin, Alice described her newest foster kid. She wondered how they would feel about a hundred and twelve pound addition. She could certainly cover the room and board. She had called her as soon as the letter came to congratulate her but hadn't entered the number in the address book. Good thing. It gave her a place to run to now.

The sun began to lighten the sky with changing shades of pink and orange splashed across a layer of thin clouds. She entered Utah at a town called Wendover. She pulled in to fill up, looking at the casinos crowding the state line and wondered how Rhonda and Max were doing and if she would see them again.

Max and Rhonda drove up Highway 50, Rhonda silent in the seat next to him as Max tried to see if the lights he had noticed were following them. It was hard to tell since once you were on this road most people followed it to Lake Tahoe some sixty plus miles away. He pulled off the highway at the town of Camino to let the cars behind him pass. Then he got back on the highway and alternated between driving fast to just under the speed limit to see if any cars stayed with him. He could not be sure.

He didn't press Rhonda for conversation as they entered the town of South Lake Tahoe. He pulled into a motel parking lot and watched for several minutes to see if they were followed. Satisfied, he drove down to Tahoe Keys just blocks away.

Tahoe Keys is a resort, marina and a complex of homes that sits on tributaries leading out onto Lake Tahoe. It is man-made and each canal behind the homes is about as wide as the street in front with occasional lights for boats to find their way down the waterways to the entrance of Lake Tahoe.

He drove slowly, reading the addresses until he pulled in the side yard of a house at the end of a cul-de-sac.

From the outside the house could have been in any nicer tract anywhere in California. There were no curbs or sidewalks giving it a casual air. The house was ten or fifteen years old with an attached garage. Where Max had parked, between the garage and a wood fence, was a concrete slab for a motor home. They sat for a few minutes. "Come on. We should be safe here."

Max turned off the dome light before opening the door; they didn't have much to carry. Max carried his bag of money and coffee thermos. Traveling light, as they say. He walked around to the rear of the house where a deck extended from the back doors in descending levels to a combination dock and boathouse. Small pine trees grew up through the decking in circular spots cut out for them. Built-in benches were scattered at intervals and large pots of ferns and flowers completed the landscaping. He stopped at the largest pine tree, looked for and found the hummingbird feeder and took the key from a concealed flap underneath. He turned and smiled to Rhonda. "Your room is ready, ma'am."

Rhonda carried a canvas sport bag of money and her purse. She was tired and aching, both emotionally and physically. Her eyes felt as if they were filled with sand and she wanted to take a shower. They stood in the shadows of the recessed rear entry and Max unlocked the door. Rhonda looked at him in the dim light. "Are we breaking and entering?"

"No." Max walked in and checked the drapes to be sure they were all closed before hitting the light switch. "This place belongs to a friend of mine. He's a geologist. Right now he's in a Winnebago in Death Valley checking to see how old the rocks are. The Government is anxious to know."

He looked in a couple of cabinets in the kitchen. "Looks like we have the makings for a breakfast here. At least we won't have to go shop before we eat." There was no kitchen table but rather a small breakfast nook in the corner with windows facing onto the lake, probably a great view in the daytime. Two bar stools and a counter divided the kitchen from the living area.

Rhonda sat on the sofa facing the fireplace. "So

what's the plan?"

"I thought we'd get some rest first, then try and figure something out in the morning. We should be safe here."

"Should be?" She ran her fingers through her hair and yawned. "That's comforting to know."

Max was checking the windows and doors as he talked. "I know a few ways to make us more secure." He walked to the back of the house carrying their bags.

Rhonda got up with effort and followed. She could hardly keep her eyes open. "All I want right now is a long shower and sleep." She walked into a huge master bedroom. A row of French doors looked out onto an enclosed area with a grape arbor and hanging plants surrounding a covered hot tub. Vintage California, she thought. Max checked these doors also.

"Why don't you go ahead and take a shower while I go check the perimeter." He caught the look she gave him. "I mean I'll check around outside just to be on the safe side." He was starting to revert to being a soldier again. That was probably a good idea.

She walked into the bath area, it was too big to call a room. The central feature was a large shower with two built in seats and two showerheads surrounded by glass brick. Next to that was an antique bath tub of enormous dimensions, with claw and ball feet. "This guy doesn't live like any geologist I ever met." She shut the door and began to undress.

"He's not like anyone I've ever met either." Max replied. He waited till she shut the door to leave. An image of Rhonda nude and wet came to mind. He shook it off. Now was not the time. The way things were going in his life *the time* might never come.

Rhonda opted for a shower and indulged herself by turning on both taps. Once completely clean, shampooed, rinsed and scrubbed, she sat on the built in seat and cried. She let the water wash over her as if it would clean her mind of what had happened. She felt her being on the run, Nolan's murder and Tawna's death, no . . . murder might be the right word to describe Tawna's death, were all connected to the type of person who now pursued them. Drug money. That's what Max had said it was. Drug money. She cried till the water became as cold as she felt inside.

Max found electrical tape, fishing line, pliers, and paper clips in a drawer under the phone. This must be the junk drawer. Every house had one. He also found a ring of keys marked *Boat*. These he put in his pocket. To this he added a box of *Crispy Chex* cereal and several empty cola cans from a container marked *Recycle*. With these in hand he walked around the outside of the house, checking for places an entry might take place.

At logical entry points he strung fishing line at random heights and taped several cans to this making sure to conceal the cans. He went down to the boathouse, unlocked it and went inside. There was a narrow walkway he took around to the other side of the small shed. The waves made slapping noises as he pulled back the canvas cover to reveal a twenty-foot Bayliner with a small cabin area under the enclosed bow. The decal on the side said *Cuddy Cabin*. What's a cuddy?

He stepped into the boat and tried the main power switch. Nothing happened. He lifted the engine cover. The battery cables had been disconnected, probably to save power. He slipped them back on, tightened them with the pliers and tried the switch again. The battery gages showed three-quarters power. Good. The fuel tanks registered full and he expected nothing less from his friend. Jack was a meticulous guy. If the batteries had been dead there was no doubt a charger around here somewhere.

Max strung fishing line at the front door, then

attached two cans with paper clips and tape, so the slightest pressure would send them clanging to the floor. He returned to the rear of the house. He walked along and looked in the windows. He could not see in except for a small slit at the bedroom window. He looked in and checked to be sure which one it was so he could tape it over.

What he saw was Rhonda toweling off with her back to the window. She arched her back to reach between her shoulder blades and Max thought she looked like a sculpture. Only prettier. He watched a moment longer, sighed and went to the back door.

He spread the breakfast cereal around on the back deck and under the windows. He was glad to note they blended in perfectly. He stepped on one to register the sound in his mind. He went inside.

Rhonda gave a start when Max walked in. "I guess I'm still a little jumpy." She had found a flannel shirt about five sizes too big in the closet and looked like she was wearing her big brother's clothes. "Are we all safe now?"

"Safe as a babe in mother's arms." Max went to the window and pulled the curtain tighter. He checked to see if he could still see out. Rhonda looked at him and wondered how he knew which curtain to adjust. "We should be able to get some sleep now. Tomorrow we'll take a little boat ride over to Emerald Bay. Have you ever been there?"

"I've never been on the lake at all."

"You'll love it." He went into the shower, closed the door and raised his voice to talk. "It's a large bay that used to be owned by some Scandinavians who built a house right out of a story book, like Vikings should live there. An island in the middle of the bay has a tea house that looks more like a miniature castle." He turned on the water started to soap down when the water turned cold. It could be a good thing, he thought. With her in there he needed a cold shower. He finished quickly.

He walked out with a towel around his waist. Rhonda was under the covers, dwarfed by the huge bed. Taking a pair of boxer shorts from a drawer, a bit too large with red ants stenciled on them, he put them on and went to the closet.

"They call it Emerald Bay 'cause that's what the water looks like. A huge emerald. A real tourist attraction." He pulled down a couple of blankets from the top shelf. "Twice a day, maybe, they bring in boat loads of tourists, big paddle wheelers that look like they should be cruising the Mississippi River. You'll love it. Want to go?"

No answer, except a gentle snore. Not really a snore, too high pitched. Kind of like a sleep-giggle. He smiled. Well, no temptation tonight.

He spread the blankets on the floor at the foot of the bed and lay down. He was so tired he could have slept on a rock. Tomorrow he would have to see about getting a gun. There wouldn't be one in this house. His friend Jack vowed to never touch one again as long as he lived. When Jack said something he usually meant it. Somehow he had to find out who it was that had done in Shawn and Nolan. A few people came to mind that might be able to help but he would have to be careful.

The police would wonder why they had gone into hiding. If he were a cop he would have his suspicions about a man who ran off with the wife of a murder victim the same night the murder took place. That meant they would have to hide from the police too.

There was an outside chance the detective named Drew would be some help. When the opportunity presented itself he would find out. They were safe for the time being. He let sleep take him.

When he awoke his heart was pounding. He listened

to the darkness, trying to locate himself. Oh yes. On the floor, Rhonda asleep in the bed. Lake Tahoe. He listened and wondered what had awakened him. Maybe it was only the house creaking in the night.

No, he heard it again. A crunching. Now it's stopped. Max rolled to the window. Pulling aside the curtain he had peeked through last night, he caught a glimpse of a shadow moving to the side of the house and through the bushes; without making a sound. This shadow was a man. A gun would settle this now. He wished for something to shoot him with. He had the crazy thought of using Jack's camera.

Crawling to the bed, he held his hand over Rhonda's mouth. She awoke with a stifled scream. Max motioned her to silence. "Get dressed. Quickly." He whispered. She was done before he was.

Damn. If he were alone he would try to take this person out. He wasn't worried about a fight but was more worried about what would happen to Rhonda if he lost a fight with this madman and left her alone with him. He couldn't risk it. They had to run.

Max motioned for Rhonda to stay where she was. Then he crawled to a window facing the front of the house. Before pulling the drape back he waited, listening, mouth open to help hear. No sound. He pulled the drape back slowly. He had a good view of the front yard and the tailgate of the Blazer. A shadow moved near the fence by the Blazer. Now he saw the shadow move along the fence toward the street. A white car was parked in the shadow of a neighbor's pine tree. Max could not remember a car being there when he pulled in. He listened intently. There, a soft click as the door of the car was opened. No interior light came on. How many people set their dome lights so they don't come on? This was trouble. It was time to go.

CHAPTER FOURTEEN

He returned to the bedroom and Rhonda. "We've got to go. There's a man outside, but he's in the front." Rhonda started to shake violently. Whoever had butchered Shawn and Nolan was here! Max gathered up the bags with the money and then grabbed her by the arm. "Look, I know this is hard for you but we've got to keep our heads. He's in front and is probably just watching the Blazer for now. We have the advantage because he doesn't know we know he's here. Follow me." He stayed in a low crouch and moved down the hall to the kitchen.

"He's expecting us to leave the way we came so let's give him a surprise. There's a boathouse at the end of the dock. Do you see it?"

Rhonda peered through the parted rear curtains. "Yes, I see it."

"Okay. I've set several noise making booby traps. There are cans set to clang together if we hit a piece of fishing line just outside the back door. We just have to step high over that second board. See it?" Rhonda nodded. "Then at the boathouse there's another one." He gave her what he hoped was an encouraging look. "When we get to the boathouse we'll take the boat and go from there."

"Go where from there?"

"I'm not sure. I just know we have to leave here. Are you ready?"

"Ready."

"Follow me."

Max opened the back door and they carefully stepped over the trip line and made their way down the decking. At the door to the boathouse they stopped. Rhonda listened for noises while Max disarmed the makeshift alarm. They entered the boathouse. There were two plastic translucent panels that let in some of the pale moonlight. It took a moment for their eyes to adjust. Max pulled the canvas back quietly and put it aside. He took the two bags of money and stowed them under the bow. Maybe the bags were "cuddy." He wished there were some quiet way to open the door leading to the water but he knew it was going to be loud. It was a standard roll up garage door with a Sears motor. The remote was taped to the dash of the boat. He took out an oar and sat it on the deck between the seats in case he had to push off. Then he untied the lines to the dock, hit the starter button and the remote control to open the door.

The motor came to life with a healthy roar. He started backing up as the door slid upward. The boat moved back with agonizing slowness, the flat stern of the boat pushing a wide wake. Max was reminded of dreams where the earth turns to Jell-O and you can't move fast enough to escape whatever is chasing you. The boat cleared the dock and Rhonda gasped to see a surprised figure standing near the back door of the house.

The figure ran across the back yard to the edge of the canal. Max spun the wheel and pushed the throttle forward. The boat leapt in a tight circle throwing Rhonda, who had been standing next to Max, hard into the rear seat.

Boyle jumped a fence, ran out onto the dock of the house next door, and launched himself in the air toward the boat. His timing was nearly perfect. His hand found Rhonda's collar and gripped tight. She was almost torn from the boat but managed to grab a tie down and hold on. She tried to scream but the collar of her jacket cut off her air. Concentrating on getting to the middle of the canal as fast as possible, Max didn't see Rhonda's predicament. Boyle tried to pull himself into the boat. Rhonda managed a shout. Max looked back as Boyle pulled himself up on the rear of Rhonda's seat and reached for his pocket. Max knew he couldn't let him bring out whatever he went to his pocket to get. Max picked up the oar and swung it in an arch, striking Boyle on the shoulder and throwing him over the side.

When Max had let go of the wheel the boat continued in its tight circle. Coming around again Max thought he heard the bow strike something. He hoped it was a deathblow. He took the wheel, cut power back and circled around near the dock. Lights had come on up and down the waterway.

A man shouted to them from a nearby house. "Hey. What's going on out there?"

"Sorry," hollered Max; looking to see if their attacker had resurfaced. "The damned throttle stuck." The man went back inside. Max idled in a slow circle. "Maybe we did him in."

Rhonda held on to him and looked at the water. Suddenly she squeezed his arm and pointed to the shore. "Look there."

Boyle was climbing up the bank, blood streaming from above his eye. He staggered and swayed, looking at the boat in the middle of the waterway. Suddenly he turned and sprinted around the side of the house.

"Where's he going?" asked Rhonda.

Max considered the question for a moment. "He's going to his car. Let's get out of here." He gave the motor more throttle and went down the canal toward the channel that would take them out onto the Lake. It was maddeningly slow going. Signs along the narrow waterway said "No Wake" but he figured the penalty for speeding couldn't be as bad as what their pursuer had in mind for them.

It took several turns to get to the marina area. They had gone maybe four city blocks before they finally had a straight run at the channel to the lake. As they neared the mouth of the channel a hole appeared in the windshield. Max ducked and looked over his shoulder toward the parking lot behind the marina.

Boyle knelt in the classic rifleman's position for another shot. The rifle he held was an ugly item with a large scope and silencer mounted on the barrel.

Max pushed the throttle to the limit. The right side window exploded at the point where it met the front windshield. "Get down." He pushed Rhonda toward the bow and she crouched low. Max heard two more bullets strike somewhere on the side of the hull. They sped around the rocky point of the breakwater as a bullet ricocheted off the rocks. He swerved to miss an incoming fishing boat; the surprised passengers yelling and one giving him a single finger salute. "Sorry." He shouted back as he headed for open water.

The Bayliner planed through the water at about fifty miles an hour, top speed; not too bad considering this lake was over a mile high. The Chevy V-8 whined slightly as they sped north across the Lake. Max looked at Rhonda huddled in the entry way under the bow. "Are you okay?"

"Sure. This is how I always like to wake up." She pulled herself up to stand next to him. It was early morning and to their left there were still stars over the mountains. To their right the sky was lighter shades of purple and blue but the sunrise that had just welcomed

Marlene to Utah had not yet made an appearance here. The water was smooth as glass, something a person could see only at this time of morning here.

"Do you have some plan or are we just getting an early start on that visit to Emerald Bay to avoid the rush?"

"Well, I think our best bet is to go straight north across the lake to Incline Village or Crystal Bay. There's no way that guy can drive around the lake in the time we can get there with this boat. Then we can try to get a car, or even a taxi, and put some quick distance between us and him."

"How'd he find us?" Rhonda rubbed her neck where she had been choked by her collar.

Max touched her neck softly and looked at the raising welt there. "We'll get something on that quick." He picked up a towel from the gunnel, and held it in the spray alongside the boat and handed it to her. "Here."

She massaged her neck with the wet towel.

"I guess he is better than I gave him credit for. I just didn't think anyone could have followed us without my noticing him." He squinted at the shore. "I was wrong." He tried to see the cars along the shore road. "I won't underestimate him again."

Zephyr cove was over their right shoulder when Rhonda walked to the rear of the boat. Her feet sloshed in ankle deep water. "I think we got a little problem here."

Max turned and saw the rising water. "Shit." He turned on the switch to start the bilge pump. He watched the water level. It continued to rise. "Can you swim?"

"Like a fish," she replied. "How about you?"

"Like a rock." He looked embarrassed. "I grew up in the desert. What can I say?" He angled the boat toward the shore. Ahead was a huge rock outcropping rising from the tree-covered shoreline. A tunnel had been carved through it for the road around the lake. "There's Cave Rock." He pointed. "Let's try for that."

They almost made it. The boat began to wallow. The rising water flooded the engine compartment and they lost power. Rhonda stood up to her waist in water, both bags of money strapped to seat cushions. Rhonda had located life vests, helped Max put his on and got hers tightened just as the boat went under. "Don't panic," she said.

Max nodded, then did exactly that as the suction of the sinking boat pulled him under, trying to get him to follow the boat to the bottom some eighty feet below. He sucked in water involuntarily and choked. Before he could suck in more water Rhonda had a grip on his vest and yanked him to the surface. He came up choking and thrashing. She kept hold of him till he started breathing normally again. Somewhat normal. "Here, hold on to this strap and try to paddle." She gave him one of the handles for the seat cushion and they started for shore.

It was slow, Rhonda towing two seat cushions with the bags of money on them and Max's two hundred plus, water logged pounds, but they reached the rocky shore line in a matter of minutes. They were both blue since the water in this lake was not much above freezing even in the summer. They shivered on the shore, catching their breath.

Max was sure hypothermia was setting in fast as a breeze began to blow across the lake. No one had witnessed their fiasco. The shoreline was deserted. He could hear a car passing on the road nearby, then another. That galvanized him into action. He stood up to see where they were.

Fifty yards away was the Cave Rock boat dock. It was a small boat launch with room for only two boats at a time. It was in an area sheltered by a short breaker made of large, angular rocks about the size of small cars. There were two pickup trucks parked in the lot with empty boat trailers attached. No one manned the small ranger's booth at this hour.

"Come on," he said, chattering. They stumbled over the large rocks to the sandy portion of the parking area.

They ducked down at the sound of a passing car. Max tried the doors of the first truck, an older Chevy. Locked. The second truck was a newer Ford Pickup and was also locked. He was going to break the window of the older truck, figuring it would be easier to hot wire and less likely to have a locking steering wheel. A car drove by on the road and he ducked down by the front tire. When he held on to the top of the tire he brushed his hand across the set of keys stashed there by the fisherman. He looked up at the sky. "Thanks."

He unlocked the door just to make sure it was the right set of keys. Then he unhitched the boat trailer and motioned to Rhonda. She sprinted to the passenger's side, dragging the two bags of money and shivering mightily. He started the truck and turned on the heater as she jumped into the seat beside him

Soaked to the skin and an unhealthy shade of blue she turned to him and attempted a smile. "You can't swim for shit Max but you're sure a great car thief. Did you hot wire this thing?"

"Too hard." He said, shivering. "I just made another key with my chattering teeth." They laughed and pulled onto the road going north.

The heater began to work but not nearly fast enough. They both shivered violently as they drove. They got some relief by taking off their shoes and jackets. By the time they were half way down the mountain they had warmed up enough for normal conversation. Rhonda had her head bent over the heater vent drying off her hair. "So?"

"So?"

"So what do we do next?"

Max rubbed his chin, a mannerism she was used to by now. "Actually. I was thinking that this is a good thing."

"You bet."

"No. Really. That detective told me this was one person, probably too hard to find a partner when you work like that, and . . . since that person just tried to kill us . . . Marlene should be okay."

As they drove down from Lake Tahoe, the road hugging the edge of the mountain in many places, they could see into the valley toward the towns of Minden and Gardnerville, a scene idyllic on any other occasion. It unfolded like a carpet purchased in Europe and spread out here between the mountains and the desert.

"Something else too. That man would have tried to follow us. He either tried to follow us in a boat, in which case we lost him, or in a car. If he followed in a car he had a fifty percent chance of picking the right direction so he may have gone to the wrong side of the lake." They were nearing the junction to Nevada Highway 395. "I think we lost him for now. I also think I'm sick of not being able to shoot back. I'd like to go on the offensive. Whoever it is behind this would never expect it. How about you?"

Rhonda rearranged the bags of money so that the heater would help to dry them out. The money itself hadn't gotten wet except for a little at the edges. "I personally would like to get that man in the sights of a gun. No, better yet, chained to a front bumper. What do you have in mind?"

He slowed a bit at the highway junction then turned left and headed toward Carson City. "Let's go get something to fight back with."

CHAPTER FIFTEEN

They drove to Carson City and took the exit for Highway 50 heading east. The terrain and scenery went from scattered trees and grass to desert and sage brush. The pickup they drove blended in with every other pickup taking someone in the *trades* to work. Carpenters, drywallers, roofers and all the other construction workers lucky enough to be employed this fine morning were on their way to work. About half of them gave a casual wave with the driving hand and Max would wave back. He wondered if commuters in big cities would wave . . . with all the fingers extended.

Once in Silver Springs, some thirty-five miles east of Carson City, Max turned south again on Highway 395 and drove through town. Maybe town wasn't the right way to describe Silver Springs. Towns were churches, businesses and houses grouped together in a valley or on the plains somewhere. This was a collection of mobile homes and single story, mostly square, houses with one thing in common. Sand. Some homes were a city block from their nearest neighbor. The ones that had been there the longest were differentiated from the newer arrivals by mature trees bent to the east by the evening winds.

Once they entered the suburbs of Silver Springs, meaning there were almost no houses visible at all, Max slowed at each street leading off the highway. At one street he stopped, started to turn, then changed his mind and continued down the highway.

"Do you know what you're looking for?" Rhonda asked.

"I've got a friend that lives here but I go through this every time. All these streets look identical to me."

"That's because they are."

"Here we go." He turned east again on a graveled road that turned to dirt and finally became just a track as it looped around man-made Lake Lahonton. Even at its best this lake was shallow, but after several years of drought the water's edge was quite a hike from its old shoreline where cottonwood trees grew between water and desert. Some five miles further they passed through a sandy draw and entered a box canyon.

The canyon walls were only about twenty to thirty feet high. Yet it served to keep the house in the back of the canyon, and the canyon itself, hidden from view. Few people knew this place existed unless invited out. "Nice place your friend has. Do you think he's home?"

Max stopped the truck on a rise several hundred yards from the house. "Oh. He's always home." He opened the door and stepped out onto the road. "Get out for a minute. He has to see who we are first or he might shoot us." Rhonda did so with a sideways look at Max who grinned back at her. "He's such a paranoid. You've just got to love him."

There was no movement from the house for several minutes. Max honked the horn and waited. Finally the front door opened and a man in denims carrying a rifle waved to them. They drove into the yard, past a couple of older Ford pickups and a Land Cruiser all with the Vietnam service ribbon painted on the back bumper. The man leaned the rifle against the railing and came around to the driver's side.

"Max!"

Max got out and hugged the smaller man, lifting him off his feet. Then he held him at arm's length and looked him over like a mother would a returning son. "Well Danny, You don't look like you missed many meals. Are you doing okay?"

Danny grinned. "I can't complain. It's better now that I don't go to see those damn VA docs anymore." They started to walk to the front door. "Are you going to stay for awhile?"

"Just a short stretch. I need some help."

They were almost on the porch when Rhonda cleared her throat loudly behind them. They turned to see her still in the seat looking at them. "Oh." Max walked back to the truck and opened the door for her. "This is Rhonda, Rhonda, this is Danny. He and I were in Vietnam together . . . about a century ago."

"Hi."

"Hi," Rhonda answered. "Nice place you got. I wish we were here last night."

Max smiled at that. "Yeah, so do I. If I'd have thought it was as bad as it was . . ."

Danny looked at them both; standing there still damp, looking like one would after being awakened from a sound sleep and thrown into the icy waters of Lake Tahoe.

"Hey, maybe you both should come inside. I just brewed a fresh pot of coffee and I'm sure we can scrounge up something to wear. Don't get too many females by here but I've got something that will fit the bill. Come on in."

They followed Danny up steps and into a surprisingly well done living area with Indian throw rugs, woven wall hangings, a huge polished redwood burl supporting a thick slab of smoked glass fronting a comfortable looking loose cushion sofa. A large fireplace dominated one wall. Max put the two bags down next to it. A red tiled hall led to a kitchen that was made for someone who liked to cook . . . not microwave. The thing that seemed most conspicuous by its absence was any reference to the war in Vietnam. No memorabilia. No photos. Nothing.

Danny walked with one stiff leg and at first Rhonda thought it was a limp. When they sat down at the kitchen table he shifted his weight and collapsed the knee to sit down.

Max nodded toward Danny's leg. "That thing looks like it's working pretty good."

"Yep. It is. I finally gave up on those VA docs. They tried long enough though to get one that felt right. I got this one from a guy in Philadelphia. Cost more than a real one." He and Max laughed together. Danny looked at Rhonda and saw her discomfort. Not so much at the leg as not knowing if she should laugh with them. "I misplaced my leg in Vietnam." Danny said to her. "The VA said I lost it but I don't want anyone to think I was being inattentive. I know just about where it is." He grinned and she finally laughed. He liked the sound and his grin turned to a smile.

"There's a bedroom straight down the hall with a shower, please make yourself at home. Come to think of it, there's some freshly laundered clothes on the bed, see if something will fit" He handed her a cup of coffee. "Want anything with that?"

"No. Black is fine. Thanks." She took the coffee, sipped at it, smiled and walked down the hall.

After she left Danny turned to Max. "That looks to me to be a special lady. Is she? Maybe I'm thinking this because you've never brought anyone here before?"

"Yeah. But my timing really stinks."

"So fill me in."

He brought Danny up to date. By the time he had finished, so was their third cup of coffee. "These people play real strict, Danny."

"So what can I do to help?"

Rhonda walked in and stood combing her wet hair, studying them both. Max looked at her directly and answered Danny's question. "I think we are through being on the defensive."

She nodded at Max and sat down next to him at the table. She wore a pair of Danny's khaki shorts and a denim shirt.

Danny looked at her appreciatively. "Those clothes never looked that good on me." He stood and began walking down the hall. "I guess it's time we checked out the den. Come on, kids."

He led them into a large room with long windows maybe a foot high against the ceiling on two walls. The effect was that of a World War II pill box or machine gun roost. Along all four walls were probably two hundred guns, some encased individually and others racked. Under each one were drawers built in that held ammunition, scopes or special equipment for that model such as silencers or adapters for infrared scopes.

"Remember these?" Danny handed Max an M-16.

"Yeah, sure do. Made by Mattel . . . they're swell." It did, in fact, resemble a toy. Light weight and black plastic, it felt more like a toy than what it was, a highly efficient weapon for spraying lead at a target very quickly. It held a clip of sixteen shells and could fire semi-automatic or in a short burst. "This would have come in handy last night but I think we want something we can conceal. We'd like to surprise them if we can."

Rhonda was looking at an ugly, short Calico model M-961A 9mm submachine gun. It was so short that she could conceal it if she had to but could fire between 600 and 700 rounds a minute if it had a large enough magazine. This one had a 50 round magazine.

"I know how to fire a weapon, I was an Army brat till my parents divorced, but I never thought I'd want to use one of these as bad as I do right now." She held the 9mm Calico in her left hand and stroked the barrel with the fingertips of her right. "This thing legal?"

"Most people are afraid to ask. There might be a felony or two in this room. You don't plan to register it do you?"

"No, I just want to use it once."

Max walked over and picked up an Automag III that looked like a large .45 Cal. automatic. "Does this use 9mm?"

"Actually, that uses 30 carbine. Makes a hell of a hole in whatever you manage to hit with it." He pulled out a box of shells. "Hollow points with a drop of mercury inside. They go in small . . . then explode."

"Nice. Any other toys you think we might need?"

"Here's a real argument stopper." Danny took a Mossberg 5500 autoloader shotgun from the wall rack. "You just keep pulling the trigger and it fires more 12 gauge shotgun rounds than you'll ever need. It can certainly clear a room for you. Do you want to try them out?"

Rhonda looked at the smaller handguns. "Yes. I'm real rusty. Can I try that snub nosed 357 Magnum there too?" She pointed at a Colt King Cobra 5 shot revolver with a 2" barrel.

Max looked at her with renewed respect. He wondered what other surprises she had in store for him. He hoped he would get to find out.

They went out the back door and past a garden where large watermelons and cantaloupes grew from the sand in neat rows. Danny stopped in a depression between two large sage bushes. Years of blowing sand had collected around the bases. By growing to stay alive they had created an interconnected elaborate root system easily five feet high from which the sage brush grew, sprouting small yellow flowers that danced lightly in the morning breeze. Here Danny had built an unpainted plywood table on two-by-four supports with a slanted roof of corrugated metal to keep the sun off.

There were different targets arrayed along the wall of the canyon from fifty feet to two hundred yards away. "You'll notice that some of the figures are good guys like the coffee cans with happy faces in those two old cars. And some are bad, like those fifty-gallon drums with target circles on them and the two sets of metal lockers with stick figures painted on the doors. Use some discretion, please."

They tried out the different weapons, enough to get comfortable with them but a long way from the Olympics. Satisfied, they returned to the house where they broke each one down for a good cleaning.

That done Danny asked the obvious. "So what's your first move?"

"Well, I think we need to go back to the only place they could have picked up our trail."

"You mean Reno?" Rhonda asked.

"No. They had to pick us up in Lone Pine. If we start quickly just maybe we can find out a little something about our pursuers." He yawned. "Can you get us some wheels?" He asked Danny. "We also need to leave that thing we drove up in for a few days."

"I got places here to park that truck till you're ready for it. In the meantime you can take that blue Ford out front."

"Then we need to settle up." Max went and retrieved the money. After paying for the weapons, and something for the truck, Max took out fifty-thousand to take with them. Then he pointed at the two bags of money. "I hate to ask, but could you hold this for us? We're better off not trying to keep track of it. Seems like we're always leaving places in a panic."

"Sure. But I want you to check in with me every so often. Can you do that?"

"Good question. Can we do that?" Max made a sweeping gesture with his hand. "There's no phone here. I just always assumed I had to come here in person. You mean to tell me I could have called you instead of bothering to visit?"

Danny grinned. "Great. Now that you know, I'll never see you again. Actually, you call the number for the volunteer fire department and ask for Will. He has a radio and buzzes me that way." He wrote the number on a business card someone had left him and handed it to Max. "I expect to hear from you at least once a week till this is over. Monday is best."

"I hope this is over by Monday. Right now we could use some food and a little rest."

Rhonda nodded at this and wondered if they were reading each other's minds. It seemed that they were in constant synch. They moved together. Where she had never been able to communicate with a man before she now did so without a sound. She wanted more of this. What would happen when this was over? Does he feel the same or am I reading more into the situation than exists? Stop it, she thought. Let's just keep to the job at hand and grow up.

After a late breakfast, they slept for an hour and awoke somewhat refreshed. While they had slept Danny gassed up the truck for them and stashed the shotgun and the Calico submachine gun under the seat. The 357 Rhonda had selected and the Automag that Max picked out would be carried or at least in hands reach.

There was no question that Danny would help Max. Danny was a quiet, private person with few friends. If he took count of those he would be glad to see showing up at the door, including relatives, it came to three. Now four with the arrival of Rhonda. She gave him a good feeling and hoped Max could work it out with her. Personally, though, he was happy for Max's opportunity and shared a vicarious pleasure in his chance for a relationship. Danny just preferred to live alone. Maybe if someone came along who liked living here in the desert it would be different. But the possibilities were limited on meeting that person since even the mailman didn't stop by. He chuckled at the thought of an attractive Avon lady coming by. Oh well. He liked his own company and it was a good thing too.

Danny showed them the opening above the fireplace. "Here's where your money is in case I drop dead while you're off on your adventure. Are you sure you want to start on this today?"

"We have only one advantage that I can see. Doing the unexpected. If we leave now we can get to the airstrip in Lone Pine before they go home for the day. They think we're going to hide. It's like the hunter who tracks the tiger in the jungle and realizes the tiger has doubled back and is now behind him." Max looked at Rhonda. "I want them to feel uneasy for awhile. Plus the fact that as long as we have their money it's a moral victory."

Rhonda had her Levi's and cotton shirt back. "If we don't get back you can keep my share or burn it. Just don't let them get their hands on it."

"Oh, you'll be back. I have good feelings for both of you. I'll be here. If you need help at all just get the message to me."

They walked to the old blue Ford pickup and Max climbed in the driver's side. He adjusted the mirror, being several inches taller than Danny, and looked for the starter. "This thing runs okay, right?"

"You could take it to New York right now. Also, if you come here at night in this thing just honk." He pressed the button and the air horn kicked in with a loud ear-piercing roar that made Rhonda and Max jump. Danny laughed. "I'll know it's you." He patted Max's arm.

"What?" Max pretended he had lost his hearing, which wasn't far off the mark.

Rhonda waved goodbye as they drove up the winding,

dusty track and over the rise. Looking back after they had traveled only a few hundred yards Rhonda could see no sign of the house or even a clue that there was a reason for the road at all. She turned and looked out the windshield. What day was this? Tuesday? Had her life changed this much in just a few days? Losing Tawna put her life into low gear. Tawna had been "experimenting" with drugs . . . so damn stupid. Such a waste. It was as though her life moved in slow motion until Sunday and then entered some kind of hyperspace. Were there people who lived at this pace normally? No way. Life had taken on a dreamlike atmosphere. A video game. Could she reset the game? She missed Tawna.

Once on the main highway they traveled down to Yerington where Max pulled in at a quick stop market. Armed with several dollars worth of quarters, he used the pay phone for two calls. The first call was to Jim at the car lot to give him a description of the man at the Lake Tahoe house and to let him know they were okay. Jim said no one had asked for them or came around looking suspicious. Hell. He hadn't had a customer since they left.

The next call was to the home number written on Drew's business card. Max figured there would be no tracer on his home phone. It was also unlikely that he would be put on hold. He wasn't expecting anyone to be home and figured he would just leave a message on the reorder. By surprise, Drew answered on the third ring. "Drew here."

"I've only got a minute. Please listen carefully. This is Max. You told me not to leave town. I did."

"Where are you?"

"No. I can't say. I do have a description of the one who might have killed my friends. Interested?"

"Why don't you get to a police station and make a statement?"

"He's about six feet tall, medium build with thinning dark brown hair."

"Max. We can't help you if we don't know where you are."

"He looks like a yuppie. Very mousey. He also has a bruise and probably a cut over his right eye."

"Where are the ladies? They seem to be missing too."

"They are both safe. This guy tried to kill us last night at the Tahoe Keys. Know where that is?"

"Hey. I'm stubborn, not stupid."

"Got anything that might help?"

"You might tell me why this guy is chasing you. He doesn't do it for sport but he seems to enjoy his work."

"Can't do that. You could check the house at the Keys, he may have left a print or something." Max gave him the address of Jack's house at Lake Tahoe. He looked through the dusty panel of the phone booth at Rhonda sitting in the truck looking at the map, drinking a Diet Pepsi and eating potato chips. He liked her more all the time. "Look, I'll check back in with you. We're not coming to the surface till this thing is ended. Anything you get that might help would be appreciated."

"Tell me where you are."

"'Bye." He hung up.

They drove on in silence, making their own way through the emotions thrust upon them in the last few days. Max wished for a moment that they were on a vacation trip that would not end. He felt good with her sitting next to him but knew there were too many obstacles to overcome. How long before the bad memories faded and a new life could begin? Why would she want him to be a part of it? Wouldn't he forever remind her of the tragedy that had paraded through her life like a slow moving tornado?

He shook off such morbid thoughts and concentrated on the task at hand. If there was to be any life for them he must find a way to bring this to an end. Instinct dictated action. Quick and unexpected. It had served him well in the past. No reason to change now.

Anyway, what was he to do, wait till this freak found him? No thanks.

They drove down through Smith Valley, finally reaching the floor of the eastern slope of the Sierra Nevadas. These majestic mountains remained constant companions out the right window as they continued down Highway 395 reaching Bishop California some two hundred miles and four hours later. They stopped to fill up and stretch.

McDonald's supplied the afternoon meal; burgers, fries and Cokes devoured without much thought as they sped on, eager to make Lone Pine before nightfall.

CHAPTER SIXTEEN

When they pulled into the gravel parking area at the air strip Rhonda read the sign on the building and looked to Max. "How do you expect to hear the truth from these guys?"

It took a moment for that to sink in. "Well, Buster sold out to John . . . he never lies."

They walked past the pickup with the BOB1 plates. "I knew it," said Max.

"What's that?"

"Nothing. Let's see who's here." They walked through the hangar door, past the Piper Lance that appeared to be finished, and into the office. Cal was seated at the desk, working on some unidentifiable electronic apparatus. "That's not the part you sent to Reno is it?"

Cal looked up, rather startled, thinking he was all alone. "Oh, Bill. Right?" He set aside the avionics part and stood up, extending his hand. Max shook it and Cal indicated the avionics gear on the desk. "Yeah, the same part went out again so I'm trying to see if I can break it here and save the trip to Reno to have a professional do it." He looked at Rhonda.

Max put his hand on Rhonda's arm. "Cal, this is Donna, Donna, Cal."

"Hi Cal." She felt a sense of surrealism that Max was Bill and she was Donna and the guy with Bob on his coveralls was Cal. On top of it all, they were about to act as if her husband and Shawn weren't brutally murdered yesterday; and they weren't both the hunted and the hunter. No problem. "Nice to meet you."

He shook her hand and said to Max. "This is kind of unexpected. I didn't think you'd ever come back this way, especially so soon. Did you forget something?"

Max couldn't help but like him. "No, just needed to ask you a couple of questions. Is that okay?"

"Sure. Do you want some coffee? There's none like it anywhere."

"I'll vouch for that." Max saw that the pot was full having just finished its cycle. It was almost quitting time and a fresh pot just got made. Maybe Cal had a little overtime in mind.

Rhonda started to sit down on the green sofa. "Don't sit there," Cal said. She gave him an odd look

"Trust him on that," Max said. He turned back to Cal. "So, we need to know if anyone has been asking about us."

"Sure has been." Cal handed Rhonda one of the nicer cups. "There's cream and sugar over there on that counter." He pointed where packets of instant creamer and sugar sat in a cup with a broken handle.

"Thanks."

"There was a plane that came in as you were taking off to Reno with your buddies." Rhonda flinched at that. "Had two guys in it. They didn't ask for you specifically but John mentioned taking you up to Reno while talking to the pilot of the other plane. He seemed pretty nice and I think he was hired by the other one."

Max drank his coffee and searched Cal's eyes. "So tell me about the other guy."

"Bad news. The pilot was okay enough. In fact John was talking to him when the other one came back from the rest room and put a chill on things. That one smiled a lot, but not with his eyes. You know what I mean?"

Max nodded. "So what did they do?"

"That's what was so strange about it all. They rented my truck and had already tied down for the night." Max looked confused. "I mean that they tied down their plane like they were going to stay for a while till they heard about you. Then they took off for Reno." Cal looked at them both. "Are you two in trouble? Or is it none of my business?"

Max put down his coffee and walked back and forth across the small space between couch and desk. "Look. If we tell you what kind of trouble we're in it might not be information you want to have. Let's just say that anyone who might ask about us, unless they happen to be the law, are very bad and very dangerous. I doubt if they would come here, they picked up our trail here. No reason to start over, but if they do . . . then the less you know, the better. Okay?"

"Okay by me," said Cal. "How can I help?"

"How about telling us what you can about them."

Cal leaned forward. "Well, the pilot flew a Cessna 210 with a home airport of Bieber. That comes off the log here." He pointed to a sheet used to keep track of tie downs and other services. "The other man seemed to be snaky. He was Hispanic. I didn't like him from the beginning. I think he hired the pilot and plane."

"Did he leave his name?" Max looked at the log. There was a place for the time, the services needed, the plane numbers and the pilot's name. Cal looked at the same sheet.

"Doug Peters." Cal took the log. "I know it's correct because the numbers on the plane matched the log."

Max and Rhonda shared the same sense of

frightening acceleration and excited fear. Max recognized it from the moment before battle when a fire fight started or when a person came swooping down in a Huey to a hot LZ, or landing zone, and they knew the shit was flying.

Rhonda felt a sense of exhilaration that now they had become the hunters instead of the hunted. Maybe she was masking her grief over Nolan and Shawn with anger. Maybe. So what? "Bill. Let's get moving."

Max took Cal by the hand as if to shake in a traditional fashion, and then put his left hand over the other and gripped firmly. Cal looked at his eyes and was struck by how flinty blue they were . . . how they held strength deep under the surface, like a current, strong and cold at the bottom of a still pool. "Thank you."

Cal was always more comfortable in shallow social surroundings. He was not an intimate person. "Hey. Okay." He retreated as Max released his grip. "Do me a favor and let me know how you come out on this. Will ya?"

Rhonda answered. "Cal, you'll be one of the first to know." She smiled at him and he could not help but smile back. He felt like a part of an adventure and he didn't have a clue as to what it was.

They got up to leave. Cal copied down the registration numbers of the Cessna and gave the slip of paper to Max.

Night was fast approaching as they drove into Lone Pine. They were too pumped up to sleep so they began the trip to Bieber. "What's the map say?" Max asked.

"Pretty complex," Rhonda replied. "We stay on this road for about three hundred miles, turn off on a little state highway in Susanville and that takes us to Bieber."

"Sounds tough to me. Maybe by the time we get to Susanville we'll be ready for rest."

"All I know right now is I'm happy to be on their trail for a change." She watched the lights of the oncoming cars turn to stars before passing and leaving imprints on her vision. She tried the trick of closing one eye as the cars passed and opening it again after it passed. No loss of vision. How come she remembered that, of all the things her dad told her? She remembered how he had said that during the war, the big one, WWII, he always pronounced it double-u double-u eye eye, when he was at sea on a destroyer the lights in the cabins at night were red. The eyes don't recognize red light as light so the pupils don't contract. That way when a person walked out of a room lit with red light onto the deck at night the eyes were already adjusted. She always wondered if her friends who wore red lensed glasses during the day when they were so popular didn't fry their little rods and cones and go blind sooner.

She wondered why she was even thinking about this.

She hoped Marlene was okay.

Right now she wished they had a way to get in touch with her. How would they let her know it was over? It would probably be in the news. Sure. Kind of getting ahead of yourself, aren't you?

They had been driving for a couple of hours and were getting close to Mammoth Lakes. Few words had been spoken since Lone Pine. She thought perhaps Max was trying to let her work through what was happening. It was time to start talking. They had been silent for so long she didn't know how to start.

Bugs were thick and hit the windshield like slow sick rain. Suddenly a huge insect splattered against the windshield on Max's side. He flinched.

"Yes," Rhonda said dryly. "That was a gerbil with wings, there's lots of those down here." Max turned on the wipers, making a slick smear across the windshield. "Hungry?" she asked.

Max kept looking through the windshield. "Yeah. Maybe lemon meringue pie and coffee."

"How about yogurt?" That brought a chuckle. "Custard?"

They broke into easy laughter. Max gave up on the wipers. "We need gas anyway. Let's stop here in Mammoth."

They gassed up at an Arco station then went into a restaurant that boasted home cooking. Anyway, it had lots of cars in the parking lot. A sign read "Please wait to be seated." They did. Several plaques were visible from where they had to wait . . . *The Kiwanis Meet here, each Tues. 3:30 . . . Toastmasters International* . . . etc.

"What time is it?"

Max looked at his watch. "Almost seven."

"I feel safest when we're moving." The waitress whose turn it was to be hostess approached them.

"How many?"

They looked at each other. "Two." They said in unison. As they followed her to a table Max leaned toward Rhonda. "I thought she had us stumped for a moment."

They ordered coffee and water, read the menu and decided on toast and salad. "I'm not as hungry as I thought," Rhonda said as they drank their coffee.

"How far are you willing to take this?"

Lots of answers to that one, she thought. "Meaning?"

"Well, we are now in hot pursuit of a killer who needs us dead or at least the money we have. Either way we die. He's probably been hired by a group of criminals, drug smugglers or the like, who have no sense of humor."

"So what's your point?"

"So the point is that we need to take out more than one person to end this. Do you really want to take part in this?"

"Look. Let's get something straight here." She caught and held his gaze. "There's no way I would ever know when it was finished unless I stick this out to the end. I'm not as tough as I'm trying to pretend I am. I'm scared." Her look got darker. "Anyway, these scummers stand for everything I hate. Druggers took my daughter and my husband from me. I'm not happy. If I can hurt them somehow then I've done my part."

"I just want to let you know what this is about. If I hadn't acted so sure that we should keep this money Shawn and Nolan . . . ."

"Yes. That's 20/20 hind sight and we all have it. I know I want to have that asshole in the sights of one of those high caliber toys Danny gave us." She took hold of Max's free hand. "This will always affect my life but if I want to have one and spend the money Nolan and Shawn and maybe a few other people died for, then this is something we can't avoid. This is the real war on drugs, isn't it?"

"You put it well. I want you with me. I'm afraid for you to be in danger and my feelings are getting in the way here." Now he felt flustered.

"Quit worrying about how odd this feels and follow your heart. Okay?"

Max nodded and finished the last of the toast. "Let's get going then."

They paid the check and went back to the truck. The night had turned chilly and a breeze was blowing through the trees. Max unlocked her side and she held his arm. He stopped and met her eyes. "Max. There's a life after this and I, for one, can't wait to get started on it."

Max paused for a moment, tried to think rationally, and then put his arms around her. She did not resist. She buried her head against his strong chest, where she could feel his heartbeat. They said nothing. Clinging to each other while a family of five went past to their Dodge Caravan parked next to them. The parents studiously ignored the couple while the three kids tittered amongst themselves. They held on to each other for several minutes after the family had driven off. Rhonda's eyes were wet, her arms aching to hold this man forever.

Max broke the silence. "I guess we just raised the stakes in the game, didn't we." They pulled apart like two Velcro fasteners. He wanted this woman. He wanted to pick out Christmas gifts and birthday presents. When was her birthday? How old was she? Where was she from? He felt great. There existed a whole life in this wonderful person and he had yet to learn of it. He wanted to wait and savor it. He also knew they had to put it off until after this was over. At least he knew now that it was possible she had the same feelings as he. What a relief.

"Let's get going while we still have the advantage of surprise." Rhonda got in the truck, wiping her eyes, while Max went around to the other door. "Hell. It's so crazy to attack the jerks that it just might work. I would be willing to bet that they are not used to being on the receiving end."

Rhonda smiled at him as he started the truck. "You're right. They have to be thinking that we're in hiding." They drove back onto the highway heading north.

The moon had come up now and the mountains to their left glistened with the snow at the higher elevations, a stark contrast to the black background of the forest. Max drove till they got to Gardnerville and they changed places.

Max was relieved that Rhonda felt some of the same feelings for him as he did for her. They talked in an easy, comfortable manner about of the basics of their lives; schools, where they grew up, their parents. They skirted the more painful issues by unspoken agreement. It was still too early and too raw. They said nothing as the lights of Reno came and went. Soon after that, Max dozed off.

Rhonda kept driving, listening to AM radio, an oldie station from Denver loud and clear then dissipating into static, some cracker-jack top notch farm reporting from Idaho that continued strong and showed up every time she searched for a new station, then there was a potpourri of religious broadcasting from several northern California stations.

She listened to Max snoring softly and felt a connection she hadn't had with anyone for a long time. For an instant she considered what it would be like if they ran off and hid somewhere. She bet if they moved to Boise they could disappear. She had read somewhere that each year thousands of people drop out of the mainstream. They just disappear for all intents and purposes. They were passing through the town of Doyle. Small. Discreet. Who would ever look for them here? No one, right?

That's right. But the fact that no one was looking for them would not make them comfortable. How would they know? They would forever act as though someone were just about to get them. Kill them. Butcher them. Would they live that kind of life? No.

Tears came unbidden. Christ. How long would this go on? Point was . . . if they were really going to live a life, one that had children and family and old age in it, they had to face this task and get it over with.

She had always taken it for granted that her life would be comfortable. That was before Tawna had been taken. Then all this had happened. Mediocrity now seemed completely worthwhile. Nirvana. Xanadu. Home. She had wondered in the past how people stayed happy just doing the mundane tasks of life. Now it seemed like a fairy tale scene to fix Max breakfast, and the kids maybe? Or Tawna to share it with? How about an evening in front of the fireplace? Or on a porch? Norman Rockwell images came to mind in rapid sequences. How cornball could she be?

Suddenly she was a great fan of cornball. She was going to risk her life in the next few days and it would not be to grab the gold ring.

It would be for cornball mediocrity.

CHAPTER SEVENTEEN

Boyle threw the rifle in the trunk of the rented Dodge and drove away from the Marina. He wanted to bang his fists against the steering wheel in frustration but resisted the urge. That shit was for amateurs. He felt his poor shooting had been pretty amateurish but he hadn't been able to get his breathing under control for the shot. Oh well. There'd be another chance.

A quick glance in the rear view mirror told him he needed a place to regroup. He held a rag against the cut on his head. The bleeding had nearly stopped. A deserted parking area permitted him to change out of his sopping wet clothes. Damn the water was cold in this lake. With the heater turned on high to drive the chill from his bones he figured his next move. The man and woman in the boat were gone; so the logical choice was the other girl. She shouldn't be all that hard to find. Rest and recovery first, then back to work.

Warmed up by now, he put on a baseball cap to cover the cut on his head, pulled into a convenience store and bought bandages and antiseptic. He drove back to the Motel Six near the marina and checked in under the name Roy Houston. He liked that name. Sounded strong.

In the bathroom of his room Boyle rinsed off the cut to his head and inspected it in the mirror. Not too bad, he thought. Getting smacked by the hull of the boat had actually saved him from being mangled by the propeller. Calmer now he took a hot shower, lay down on top of the bed covers and went to sleep almost immediately.

The knock on the door from housekeeping came just before noon. He was lying down quietly, as if asleep, till the door opened and he heard the gasp. "Excuse me," said the flustered maid.

Boyle got up, dressed, packed what little he had and went to the car. Less than an hour later he checked into an identical room in Reno. He wedged a chair under the doorknob, took the money recovered from the house in Placerville and laid it on the bed. He counted four separate banded stacks at random to check for accuracy. Then he counted the number of banded stacks and set aside his twenty five percent. His part he put in a mailer bought at an office supply store earlier and addressed it to his office in San Diego. The rest of the money went back into the paper grocery bag.

That done, he began the search for the woman. From his wallet he took out the folded picture lifted from the nightstand of the house in Placerville. He looked at his quarry as she smiled from the photo. "Where did you go?" he asked with a quizzical smile. "Where are you now?"

He opened the address book and thumbed through the first few pages. Her name and the name of her now ex-lover was listed on the information page. He looked back at the photo. "So, Marlene Peterson, let's see who you know." He started with her work number. They picked up on the second ring.

"Highway House." High pitched but a male voice.

"Yes, I wanted to know if Marlene Peterson is working today."

"Uh . . . can you hold on a minute?" Now he was listening to pop Muzak; Some Beatles number played by an orchestra.

"Hello. Were you asking about Marlene?" a woman's voice inquired.

"I was yes, is she working tonight?"

"No, we don't think so. She didn't call in but we don't expect her to come in. Are you a friend of the family?"

"Yes, I know about what happened to her boyfriend. There's no answer at the house and I just thought she might have called you and left word where she could be reached." He paused for effect. "Do you have any idea how I could get in touch with her? We're just worried sick over her and how she must feel."

The woman on the other end of the line made a clucking noise. "So are we. You might hear from her first."

Boyle sighed heavily. "Well, if she calls try to find out where she is would you? I'll try back later and I promise if I hear from her I'll ask her to contact you too, Okay?"

"Yes, we'd appreciate it. Thank you."

He hung up. He called several phone numbers, posing as a friend of Marlene's, with no success. There were only one or two phone numbers on each page and only a few with addresses.

He checked the *P's* for family members and found a few numbers with the 303 area code in Colorado. A phone call to Marlene's parents in Denver revealed a lot about the lack of close family ties . . . No, they hadn't heard from her in months. Her moving out there like she did . . . and living with that guy . . . Boyle didn't feel she would be hiding out with Mom and Dad.

There were no listings for brothers or sisters. Either there weren't any or they didn't rate an entry in the book. There were numbers for an aunt and uncle in Durango, Colorado but when he called all he got was an answering machine. He made a note to call back. A phone number for an "Alice and Randy" caught his attention because there were several names listed beneath the phone number with birthdates. It looked odd in a way he couldn't put his finger on at first. Then it hit him. He figured the names were for children but the names were "Nathan, Roberto, Ashad, Carrie and Pat." They didn't match, and some birthdates were less than nine months apart. Too close even for Irish twins. It sounded more like a United Nations group than a family. He tried the number but it turned out to be disconnected anyway.

He picked up the photo and looked at Marlene's smiling face. "I guess you're not going to make this easy are you?" He put the picture in his shirt pocket and stood up. "I'll just have to do this the hard way."

He took out five thousand dollars from the grocery bag of money and stuffed it in his pants pocket, took the bag and the envelope containing his own share and left the room. He dropped off his envelope at the Post Office and drove to a computer store where he bought a notebook with enough power to run a small government. Nothing on par with his usual equipment, but then he was in the field.

Back in his motel room he hooked up the equipment and dialed a phone number in the Pacific Bell building in San Diego that he had first called almost a year ago.

He had acquired the number to make finding people easier. First he had spent almost a month locating a suitable candidate for his computer piracy. Lyle Wilson won that dubious honor. He was a steady employee destined for long term employment with almost no bad habits. Boyle's new step daughter, Kelly would call him a nerd. Lyle worked with computers in the credit and billing section of Pacific Bell.

Boyle waited until Lyle went to work one morning,

went up to his front door, knocked to be sure no one was there, slipped the lock and went in. Lyle's office was neat and organized as expected. Boyle located his computer, and after checking for a modem line, began opening the case. He connected Lyle's drive to a ribbon cable draping from a machine he called his leech. Within a matter of minutes the leech had copied Lyle's drive to memory. Then he reconnected the computer, closed the case and left.

Back at his own office Boyle connected the leech to his system and powered up. With only a few adjustments and two utilities he'd downloaded from the net he had Lyle's computer on his desk . . . virtually. Now, Boyle had the scripts Lyle used to access his computer at work. Like most programmers Lyle used his computer to work from home. And, like most programmers, he had automated all of the logon process, since programmers placed efficiency above security. Now, Boyle had the same connectivity to Lyle's office system. Boyle waited until lunchtime, used his own line to call Lyle's office and made another leech copy of that system's drive, which was configured to connect to Lyle's house. While Lyle wouldn't be concerned with security his administrators were. Each month they made everyone choose a new password for the network. If Boyle could not connect to Lyle's office he would simply connect to his house to copy the new connection configuration. As long as Lyle had a job at Pac Bell, so did Boyle.

Now Boyle could browse through any billing or credit records for anyone serviced by Pacific Bell in California, which was virtually everyone. He couldn't change or alter any records but he could look.

Boyle had accessed smaller phone companies, hacking his way in by phone link, but since Pacific Bell used a large main frame computer he had to resort to someone else's identity. It had been worth the effort.

He dialed and got a busy signal at Lyle's office, meaning the computer was being used. He tried several more times at fifteen minute intervals with the same result. He paced and visualized his prey getting farther and farther away while he sat doing nothing. He had to get Lyle away from his desk. Finally he called Lyle's main office number.

"Pacific Bell, billing."

"I need to speak with Mr. Lyle Wilson, is he in? I'll hold."

"Just a minute."

If it weren't for the music Boyle would have thought he was disconnected. It was a full three minutes later when a voice came on the line. "Lyle here."

"Mr. Wilson? This is Frank Arson at the air freight terminal for Pacific Air. We have a package that arrived for you."

"Yes?"

"You are Mr. Lyle Wilson right? Okay. The reason I'm calling is because we have a problem. We have a package here addressed to you that was damaged in shipment. Some of the contents appear to be broken. We could hardly make out your name and number."

"Who is it from? Is it to me personally or the office?"

"We can't tell who it's from; we can't read the return address. It is addressed to you personally with your work phone number for verification. We would ship it to your house but the box is broken open and we need you to come look at it and fill out some paperwork for the insurance. It looks like the contents are pretty badly damaged."

"What's in it?"

"Oh, it looks like computer equipment of some kind. I couldn't tell you what kind since I'm really not too familiar with these things. Anyway, we're open only till four this afternoon. Can you get out here today?"

"Can I come out tomorrow during lunch?"

"Actually, we're moving our counter to the main terminal over the next couple of days. We wanted to be sure and contact you today because we're tearing everything out of this place to move. We don't want to lose anything in the process. I'm really sorry for the inconvenience. If you can come now, I'll wait here for you and try to get you taken care of right away."

There was an audible sigh at the other end of the line. "Oh all right. How do I find you?"

"Just go like you're driving to the main terminal but take the turn off that says *Car Rental Return* and take that road all the way to the chain link fence. You'll see our office; it's a modular with a large brown and white sign that says *Pacific Air Freight*. You can't miss it. How soon can you be here?"

"I'll leave in about ten minutes."

"Great. Goodbye."

Boyle waited several minutes before calling Lyle's office computer. He worked fast and pulled up Marlene's phone bills for the past four months. He performed a *screen capture* as quickly as they came up. He was out of the system in a matter of minutes.

Next he entered the numbers from the address book and sorted them numerically. He did the same with the numbers called on the phone bill. Comparing the two lists he could see how many times each one was called. Some numbers showed up on the billing that weren't in the address book. He dialed them and got a succession of take-out food places, road weather, time, a couple of service companies like cleaners, a camera shop, etc. The billing showed only one call from the house after he had "visited" and that was just a few hours later. He dialed it and got the correct time and temperature in Placerville. Funny that. It was also the last number called before he had done his *work*.

Going back through the address book he checked off those numbers in Colorado he had already verified.

She hadn't called her Parents or her Aunt and Uncle in the last four months. There was one call to the disconnected listing for "Alice and Randy" in Colorado from three months ago. The only other Colorado number on the billing that remained was one called two weeks ago. It didn't match any number in the address book. "Hello, what have we here?" Boyle said out loud.

He dialed the number. The phone was picked up before the first ring was finished. A small voice answered in a frantic chorus of . . . "Hi. Hi. Hi."

"Is Alice there?"

Boyle yanked the receiver away from his ear as the child screamed . . . "Alice."

"Ashad, don't yell into the phone like that. Now put that phone down. No. Not there . . ." The connection was broken as *Ashad* hung up on him.

Boyle smiled, stood and stretched. The noose was tightening. He took out the photo of Marlene and her "late" boyfriend. "You've been very naughty, Marlene. I hope you realize that this kind of behavior cannot go unpunished. It won't be long." He ran the tip of his index finger along the outline of her bikini clad likeness in the photo. "You won't be able to get away as fast as your boyfriend did, he went much too fast to be any fun. You will go slow, I'll make sure of that."

He licked the tiny beads of sweat that appeared on his upper lip. He took his finger off the photo and touched himself where he began to swell in anticipation. This part of the chase was always so sweet. Kind of like foreplay.

He shook his head to clear it and dialed Colorado information. They gladly told him the town where *Alice's* phone number was and verified the address for him.

It was now nearly eight at night. Boyle considered his next course of action. He packed in minutes, went out for pizza and drove east on Highway I-80. In less than a half hour he pulled off at the *Mustang Ranch* exit, followed the road past the first building, which he considered a tourist trap, and pulled up to his favorite building.

There were no horses or cattle here, although there was a bit of leather and maybe a saddle or two. It was the largest legal brothel in the United States. This was the third of three buildings. As he went in the *Hostess* called for the girls. Seven prostitutes in an assortment of see-through nighties paraded in, stood for him to look at and said their names.

Boyle took the photo of Marlene and Shawn from his pocket, looked from it to the girls standing before him and pointed to a diminutive blond who looked close enough physically for his use. She went by the name of Shari. They went down a hallway to a small room she called her apartment. Once inside she asked how he preferred it.

"I'll make it real easy for you. Shari's not your name so if you don't mind I'd like you to go by Marlene till I'm done. Okay?"

"Sure, it's your money. What else? Oral? Dress-up? Straight? I got a few ideas of my own."

"How about some light spanking while you beg to do me orally? Can you handle that?"

"Sure. You can even tie me up if you like. Only no real rough stuff." She reached across a vanity and took down several velveteen ropes, knelt before him and held them out for him in supplication. She looked up at him with pleading eyes and he felt himself grow. "Please. Please," she intoned, in a barely audible voice.

He took the ropes from her outstretched hands. "You can do better than that, can't you Marlene?"

Two hours later and several hundred dollars lighter he walked out feeling like a new man, and the new man wanted to go to work. He felt better than he had in months. He drove out to Highway I-80 and headed toward his next task. God he loved this kind of work.

CHAPTER EIGHTEEN

Marlene checked the map. This has to be the turnoff. She turned up the drive past a little shelter that looked like a gingerbread house, just tall enough for kids to stand in out of the weather. That must be for the children to wait for the school bus. It was recently built out of plywood and painted to look Hansel and Gretel'ish. Visions of Hobbits sprang to mind. The track led up the side of a hill with the Rocky Mountains towering behind it. The slope was grassy, rather than wooded, with a stand of spruce bordering the road.

Driving up the hill she went over in her mind what to say. The euphoric effects of the speed had worn off and been replaced by feelings of impending doom and emotional fragility. Impending doom. Shit. This is not impending doom at all. *This is doom.* The one man in her life she visualized growing old with had been brutally taken from her. When Tawna had died and people asked Rhonda what happened she used to break down trying to explain the whole thing . . . how she had ditched school . . . hung around with those kids . . . using drugs like they couldn't kill her . . . till finally she had condensed the story to a short sentence. "She was killed in a car accident."

Marlene drove up the slope, the house visible now, just as she pictured it except with more space around it. They couldn't possibly own all this land. There just aren't that many people who wanted to build this far out. What a playground for the foster kids.

She stopped on a rise with an unobstructed view of the deep, long valley spread out below her. She shut off the engine, put the windows down, and looked at the view. With the mountains towering to the east behind the house the line from the sunrise moved like a tinted cut out, starting at the top of the hills on the west and marching toward her across the valley floor.

Okay, someone asks me "How did Shawn die?" and I'll just say . . . "Oh, he was dissected by a madman" . . . and, oddly, she almost laughed at that. Shawn would probably get a kick out of that answer.

Once, when they were watching the nightly news, there had been a part when an anchorman had asked a young wife how she felt about her husband's death. They had kept the cameras on the young woman's face until they got the desired response, the response that brought ratings to the news cast, the woman cried into the camera. Seconds later they were selling deodorant.

"Do me a favor," said Shawn, "and attack the cameraman if you're ever in that position."

"What about you?" Marlene asked around a mouthful of popcorn. "What if I die first? What will you do if they ask you?"

"Oh, that's easy." Shawn stood up and acted like he was the nightly newsman, holding a half full longneck bottle of beer as if it were a microphone. "You sir," he said into the beer bottle. He made a whistling noise by blowing across the top and tapped it a few times. "Is this thing working? I've got some news to do here." He looked behind him as if at some invisible crew of technicians.

Marlene laughed and rolled back on the couch, lifting her feet up and throwing pieces of popcorn at him as he continued.

"Sir. You haven't been told yet, we drove here at about a hundred miles an hour to beat the cops that were going to tell you first. Your wife was just killed when an improperly attached cement truck cylinder fell over as she was passing it on the highway. We're here, as responsible television, to show you these pictures we took of the horrible scene . . ." he held out the palm of his hand like he was showing her a photograph, " . . . you can see part of her body right there, see?" Shawn smiled into the make believe camera. "Well, sir, how do you feel?"

Marlene howled and hissed. "Boo."

Shawn stepped to the side and took the position like he was being interviewed. "Well America . . ." He turned around, bent over, dropped his sweat pants and mooned the five o'clock news.

"Bravo." Marlene clapped, threw popcorn and whistled. She remembered they had made love on the floor afterwards, the TV still running, Shawn on top in a traditional position, and Marlene started giggling.

"What's so funny?" Shawn asked, arching back to look at her face.

"Earlier you mooned America and now you're doing the same thing to Johnny Carson's monologue."

"Yeah," said Shawn. "It's a good thing TV doesn't work both ways. We're not the only people who do this to the Tonight Show."

Marlene smiled, and had hoped she would never lose the memories.

"Hi."

The sound jerked her back to the present. It came from the freshly scrubbed face of a five-year-old boy standing on a boulder near the passenger side window.

She wiped away the tears streaking her face with the back of her hand and said, "Hi to you too."

"You lost, or are you coming to visit?"

God, kids are great. Right to the point. She could have kissed him. "Coming to visit. Wanna ride?"

"Yeah, but I can't 'cause I don't know you." The boy looked from Marlene to the house "But I'll race you."

"Okay."

As soon as she said the word he took off, running around the Blazer and over the boulders, he was twenty yards ahead of her in a flash. She made a display of gunning the engine and spun the tires before driving up the last hundred feet to the house.

There, on the back step of the house, wide enough to be called a porch anywhere else, stood her cousin Alice, wiping her hands on her apron. She squinted to see who was at the end of the road, coming to visit here. Several children stood with her, different shapes, sizes and hair colors.

Marlene pulled to a stop and felt the weight of loneliness and pursuit fall from her shoulders. She felt safe and calm for the first time in days.

CHAPTER NINETEEN

The multi-colored neon sign said *Melody Arms Motor Lodge*. It was a U-shaped single story building of early fifties architecture. A gravel drive led to a covered entrance in front of the first bungalow. The sign over the door said *Office*. Rhonda pulled in and stopped the engine. The popping sound of the motor cooling vied with the buzzing of the vacancy sign. It was on the verge of burning out. A blue bug light hung from the rafters of the overhang and sporadically electrocuted moths and flying insects with a zapping sound. It contributed a faint ozone smell to the pine, earth and cooling asphalt odors in the air. Flowers and shrubs grew from truck tires painted white and cut at the tops in a pointed fashion to show that they were intentional and not discarded tires with plants growing out of them.

Each small unit had a one-car garage next to it with the garage attached to the next unit. Room, garage, room, garage, etc.. Max figured it was a terribly inefficient use of space. The garage units could have been changed to rooms by now.

They checked in. At first Max wondered how they would register. Mr. and Mrs.? It never came up in the conversation. He rang the bell and listened to the sounds of David Letterman emanating from a television. A door opened, David Letterman got louder for a moment, and the strong smell of spicy food cooking followed the manager to the counter. "May I help you?"

He wasn't what Max expected. It was the turban that threw him off. He was expecting some kind of retired logger. This man was from India. Oh well. He was no Native American Indian either. "Yes. A room for the night."

"How many peoples?"

"Two."

"Queen Bed?"

"Twins."

"No twins. Only queen bed. Is okay?"

"Sure." He filled out the card with a fake name . . . fake everything. The only thing not fake was the number of people.

"Twenty-nine fifty with tax."

Max paid in cash.

"That's number twelve. Right at the end of this row."

"Thanks."

Max drove to number twelve and noticed the beginnings of construction to turn the garage attached to each side into new units. They went in and Rhonda went straight to the shower. Max fidgeted while Rhonda showered. He wasn't sure where to sit, stand, or lay. Sleep on the floor again? Give this thing more time? When she came out wearing an under shirt and towel he took the easy road.

"I'm going to get cleaned up." He went in the shower and let her answer the question of sleeping arrangements.

When he came out Rhonda was lying on one side of the bed and the covers were turned down on the other side. He sat for a moment. He usually slept in the nude but wore his underwear now. He lay back and contemplated the situation. He wanted to at least hold her. The one foot distance between them felt like a deep, bottomless chasm separating their two bodies. What should he say? How about talking about how uncomfortable he was about talking? Even that sounded confusing to him. He decided just to start talking.

"Tomorrow when we get up we can buy us some clothes. These we're wearing have about had it."

Rhonda looked over at him. "We probably should have done that today."

"Well, if we buy stuff up here we will blend in better with the locals. It's impossible not to stand out in these little towns 'cause no one knows you. You have to be a tourist or a transplant of some kind.

After a minute or two of silence Max yawned and continued. "I want you to know a little about me. I don't make a lot of friends easily. I like treating the ones I have as special. Maybe I just don't want to have a life filled with acquaintances who find out you've passed away from other acquaintances." He rubbed his chin. "I remember my uncle said an acquaintance is someone you know well enough to borrow money from but not well enough to loan any to." He wondered if he was getting off track. "Anyway, I also don't have a lot of women in my life. Wait a minute. I don't have any in my life. I just don't pick out women to spend my life with at random. I don't want to marry or live with an acquaintance." He took a deep breath and plunged forward. "So . . . I was shocked at the effect you have had on me. I feel good about you. No. I feel I would like to loan you money. 'Course you don't need any but I mean you don't fall into the acquaintance category at all."

He hoped he didn't drown in this morass of words.

"What I'm trying to say is you are special to me. Even Danny noticed it. Sure, the timing is bad but the same uncle said that opportunity and convenience never come to town on the same bus. He also said the money runs out before the good deals do. That doesn't have anything to do with this but the part about opportunity and convenience does. There probably could not be a worse time to meet the person you should spend what time is left with. We might not have much time left at all. But even if I had met you under perfect conditions and not in the midst of this terrible situation I would feel the same."

Max swallowed hard and went for it all. "I want you to know that I think . . . no, I know, I love you and want to spend my life with you. I want to be responsible for every laugh line you ever get from now on. Do you understand what I'm trying to say here?"

"Rhonda?"

He rolled on his side to look at her. She slept soundly. He continued to gaze at her. She slept with her hands clasped alongside her face. Angelic was the word that came to mind. He sighed, reached over her and switched off the lamp on her side. He smiled and lay back down to go to sleep. Then he said to the darkened room. "Well, that went pretty good I think."

In the morning they were up early and ate breakfast at a good coffee shop that had a bustling crowd to vouch for the quality of the food. Rhonda asked for and got the location of a second hand clothing store from the cheery waitress. "Why a second hand store?" Max asked.

"Wearing these same clothes for days might make us stand out but so would two people showing up with all new outfits."

He hadn't thought of that at all. They were waiting at the door of the used clothing store when it opened up. They bought enough clothes to last a week or so, flannel and cotton shirts, Levi's, sweaters and jackets. They got everything except shoes and underwear. These they picked up at a K-Mart style store, along with a suitcase.

Back on the road they took Highway 139 north through some great scenery, past Eagle Lake sitting like a blue-green jewel in a mounting of fir and pine. They passed a sign that indicated McDonald's had a camp here. "What's that? Does McDonald's have a boot camp now?"

"Nope," said Rhonda. "I read somewhere that it's a camp for underprivileged kids or something like that. Pretty good idea huh?"

"It's in a pretty enough spot. Quite a change for a ghetto kid, I'll bet."

They missed the turn off to Bieber and went an extra few miles to a town called Adin. It cost them about twelve miles but it gave them a chance to scout around the area. The clothes and the truck helped a lot to blend in with the locals. After coffee from a convenience store they located a real estate office manned by a woman. Max wondered if it was politically correct to say manned by a woman? How about womanned by a woman? How about this woman? She filled the rather large swivel chair to overflowing; behind a desk littered with listing forms, a notary pad, pictures of houses and relatives, and a coffee mug with *Avon Calling* on the side in gold leaf. She sat reading a newspaper and eating the last few bites of a bear claw pastry. She looked up as they entered. "May I help you?"

"Yes," Rhonda said. "We're thinking of moving up here and want to get an idea of the prices and what's available and all that. Can you help us?" Rhonda flashed a please-like-me smile, and the realtor looked as though she would enfold Rhonda in her huge arms and take her home.

She rose from the chair that seemed to sigh with relief and opened a hinged railing to let them into the area where the two desks sat. "Well, come on in. Let me see what I can do." They sat down in front of her desk. "So what kind of house do you have now?"

"We don't. So we don't have to sell one to buy here." Rhonda squeezed Max's leg to let him know that she would field the questions. "We want to move here in about three or four months. Are we looking too early?"

"Heavens, no. That's barely enough time to get a feel for what's here. How many in the family?"

"Only two, right now, but we plan on more."

"Okay. I have a couple of listings that I need to check on today and I have the time now . . . how about riding along and seeing the countryside here?"

"Great. We don't have any idea what to expect. Maybe you could kind of fill us in on the local history a little?"

The realtor beamed from ear to ear. "Honey, you have got the right person. I've lived here all my life, except for a brief stint at college. Let me get my keys and you can ride with me."

"We don't have much time. Will we be very long?"

"No. We could see every house that's for sale within fifteen miles in a couple of hours. At least we could see the ones that are listed. Everything's for sale, right? It all depends on how much you want to spend." They followed her out and noticed that she didn't lock the door behind her. Definitely not like the city. "Oh, my name's Berta." She opened her door and backed into the front seat. Rhonda made a mental note to start eating less.

"I'm Jean and this is Bob." They got in, Rhonda in the front seat and Max in the back after he made space by rearranging a pile of newspapers, listing forms, Tupperware and a box of Avon products. This lady had to know everyone in town. They drove down the main highway toward Bieber for just a few miles and turned off to the north on a narrow but well maintained road.

"This first house I have to stop at is pretty new, only five or six years old, three bedroom two bath, has a barn and garage combination and acreage, almost six with two in irrigation. They just put it on the market for eighty one thousand."

As the house came into view Rhonda thought she could list the same house for maybe two hundred and eighty thousand back in Placerville. Too bad they weren't really shopping 'cause it was nice. This felt like playing house. Max feigned interest in the barn as Rhonda began to lead the conversation to more informative surroundings. "We have gang and racial problems back home, that's kind of why we're moving. Anything like that here?"

Berta laughed. "No, not around here. I guess everybody would have to wear different colored jackets to get a good gang fight going although they did have a drive by yelling at the high school." She laughed at her own joke and Rhonda joined in. "I'm afraid this is mostly lily white up here." She walked back to the car. "Let's head over to the other house. It's about a hundred years old and so's the owner. It's like time traveling to look at."

Rhonda laughed with her. "But you do have people other than whites here don't you? I mean I heard there was a Hispanic area near here."

"Only two families up here that are Hispanic. I got a nice couple in town that buy their Avon from me and I sold a house to a gentleman up the road last year. That's it."

Max walked up behind them. "That's probably the

guy I met before, honey." He looked at Berta. "Is his name Gutierrez in Bieber?"

"He lives near Bieber, but his name isn't Gutierrez. I think it's Armon something-or-other. He doesn't come around much. He's a loner." Max and Rhonda exchanged glances.

Further conversation yielded no more information except the location of the airport. It was an hour and a half later when they returned to the realtor's office. Nothing was missing and the door was still unlocked. Rhonda thought about the alarm combination and elaborate series of dead bolts and locks protecting the front door of the real estate office she had first started at in Sacramento. There would be maybe a trash can and papers left had they tried leaving that office unlocked and unattended. An elderly man wearing bib overalls and chewing tobacco sat inside reading a newspaper. Berta gave them her card and excused herself. Max wondered if the old man was her lunch date. Maybe he was her lunch.

When they pulled out on the main road Max took a cigarette from a pack he had found in the glove box. "I didn't know you smoked." Rhonda also didn't think it was a big deal. She hoped he wouldn't think she was smoker-phobic.

"I also eat crackers in bed."

Rhonda smiled. "I eat cigarettes in bed. So don't try to scare me off." He relaxed visibly.

"So what's next?" she asked.

"I thought we'd try to locate the pilot first. He'll be the easiest to find. Then we can attempt to unearth the one who hired him."

"What about the other one, the one back at Lake Tahoe."

"I don't think the one that attacked us and killed Shawn and Nolan was the pilot. Chances are he's nowhere near here. If we can get to the one that hired the pilot I would guess we would be able to track down Mr. Wonderful."

"How do you want to play this? I mean, do you

want to get the police in on this?"

He turned to Rhonda. "Look. This is personal now. This is not about turning these guys in to the cops so they can spend the next five years or so in and out of court finding out if they are guilty of a crime that only offers free room and board for life in this state. There is no way to get swift justice around here . . . just ask Charles Manson . . . and they can decide to skip the country and kiss off the bail money. That is not going to happen. These assholes killed two of my friends and they can ruin our life as long as they are allowed to continue to breathe. I'd like to wipe these guys. If you want to sit this out then let me know now. Okay?"

Rhonda returned his level gaze. "I was just wondering if you wanted us to let the cops know where to pick up the remains of these useless turds once we're done with them."

"This is a hell of a way to start a relationship."

"I don't know about that. I was just thinking that you sure know how to show a girl a good time."

"What a guy, huh?"

She smiled and watched him do the same. "Yeah. What a guy."

It was only ten minutes to the airport. It was only ten minutes to everything around here. It wasn't much of an airport. Actually it made Buster's Flying Service look like TWA. Here there was no building that looked like an office at all. There was one building serving as a hangar that could hold three or four planes and an area next to it where another two or three planes could tie down. The hangar door was shut. Two young boys were flying a kite near the end of the runway. They looked to be school age. Maybe it was lunch time. Must not be a lot of air traffic here.

The Cessna 210 they were looking for sat tied down in the grassy area between the rear of the hangar and the edge of the trees.

Rhonda and Max walked to the plane and looked

through the side window. There was no dust inside or on the wings either. This wasn't true of the other planes on the field. The one parked next to this one had a *For Sale* sign in the window. They walked past the two boys flying their kite and Max stopped to watch for a moment. "That's quite a kite you've got there."

"Thanks, mister."

"Say. Do you boys know where the owner of that plane is?" He pointed at the Cessna.

The older of the two boys looked at Max with a sidelong glance. "Do you know his name?"

"Yeah, it's Doug. Has he been around today?"

"He's probably through that door at the other end of the hangar." He jerked his thumb over his shoulder. It wouldn't have surprised Max if he had ended the sentence with the word "Scram."

"Thanks."

They walked to the end of the hanger and found the door they had overlooked before as it was painted the same industrial grey as the rest of the building. It was unlocked. Max lead the way in to a large building that sure felt deserted.

Rhonda followed carefully, the hair on the back of her neck raised. Overhead were several large florescent lights. Unlit. The only light other than what seeped in through various breaks in the construction was coming from an office raised above the floor of the hangar against the roof and accessible by a narrow flight of wooden steps. The shafts of light through the dusty air looked surrealistic. Like a stage set for a rock video or maybe an old Humphrey Bogart movie.

Max made his way carefully to the bottom of the steps. Here he stopped and motioned for Rhonda to wait. He kept his hand on the Automag in his waistband and began a sideways crab-walk up the steps.

Rhonda looked around the hangar, her back to the area under the steps. She glanced up as Max reached the top of the landing and a hand reached out and took her by the shoulder.

CHAPTER TWENTY

She stood frozen and looked at the hand. Every detail etched in her mind. Large. Dirty, broken or chewed fingernails, hairy, with the misshapen knuckles of a street fighter. Finally she reacted. She screamed. A genuine "B" movie scream. Things happened all at once. She jumped forward, expecting the hand to try to hold her. She fell headlong into a rolling tool chest that did indeed roll . . . three feet to the edge of a grease trap where it fell over with a tremendous crash.

Max half ran and half fell down the steps to stop at the bottom, gun drawn and about to fire into the darkness beneath the steps. The man, whose hand so frightened Rhonda turned to flee under the steps. He crashed into a stack of corrugated metal sheets, like those the hangar was made of, causing them to slide like a huge deck of cards to the floor. The accompanying sound was deafening. The metal sheets half buried the dazed man, and triggered an avalanche of six-foot-long florescent tubes from a shelf above them. These broke with individual explosions, each one releasing a cloud of vapor like thick fog. The man scrambled and struggled to his feet.

Suddenly the scene was frozen like a vision in a lightning storm as the rows of overhead lights came on. At the top landing a man, hand poised on a light switch, surveyed the scene below. "What the hell . . . who are you and what's going on here?"

A fair enough question. One Max would have asked himself had this man not beaten him to it. Since no one else had a gun in his hand Max slid the Automag back into his waistband before anyone could notice.

Rhonda stood up shakily and pointed to the man under the steps trying to regain his footing. "I guess he frightened me. I mean he didn't say anything, he just came up and put his hand on my shoulder and I panicked."

The man on the landing began to come down the steps. "I wouldn't think he'd be real talkative since he's a mute." The man walked over to where the mute stood, frightened and shaken. "Are you okay? Can you calm down?" After he got a nod in return, he turned to look at Max and Rhonda. "What are you doing here?"

"We're trying to find a Doug Peters. We heard he was for hire sometimes, him and his plane." Max tried to look sheepish.

"Well, you found him. Come on up to the office while I try to calm old Tom here down." Doug guided Tom up the steps by his elbow.

Behind him came Rhonda and Max. "We're sorry about scaring him. But he sure scared me. You know what I mean?" *And do you know that I'm going to have to change pants after this is over*, she thought?

They entered a well-lit office with two metal desks facing each other and covered with different paperwork, cups, airplane magazines touting the upcoming air races in Reno, receipts, an ashtray filled to overflowing, family pictures in box frames, a pen holder made out of an old altimeter, and a ceramic Snoopy on his doghouse going down in flames while shaking his fist at what must be the Bloody Red Baron.

If the desks looked cluttered then they appeared Spartan compared to the walls. Pictures in and out of frames covered every inch. Smiling people emerging from the cockpit of small airplanes after their first solo, group photos, signed photos of famous and near famous; a business license to run an air taxi and training service; a diagram with the directions on how to get to the front door in case of a fire; two different calendars from local businesses showed the last two months, etc. There was at least a week's reading material here.

"Sorry about the mess, it's the maid's day off." Doug didn't bother to clear a spot for them but sat Tom down in the chair behind one desk and continued to talk in soothing tones to him. "You're just fine now aren't you?" Tom nodded sheepishly and did appear to quit shaking a little. The phrase . . . shaking like a dog shitting peach pits . . . came to Max's mind. He elected to keep the thought to himself.

"We're sorry to have caused any problems. We just wanted to know if you were for hire."

"Sure. Where did you hear of me?"

Max and Rhonda traded quick glances. Rhonda looked down and Max followed her gaze. She was looking at a black leather folder with the word "log" on the front. Max nodded and turned to Doug. "Some real estate lady; mentioned you had a Cessna 210 and took charters or passengers sometimes."

Doug straightened up and looked Max in the eye. "You mean Berta?"

"Yeah, that was her name."

"Well, I don't think so, partner. She and I don't see eye to eye, so if she recommended you there must be a problem with you." He looked from Rhonda to Max and saw what there was to see; two people attempting deception. He was keenly aware of how it looked to deceive. He did it all the time. "I don't think we can do business friend."

Rhonda turned to the door without saying a word. Max followed suit and walked to the door. "Suit yourself, Pal. Sorry we busted up your day." They pulled the door shut and moved quickly down the steps. Rhonda was practically running by the time they got to the outside door.

She flashed the black leather logbook at Max and smiled. "I got us a bonus too." She held up a leather wallet with the *Day-Timer's* logo embossed on the cover.

"So?"

"So? Don't you know what this is?"

He looked at her blankly. "How about if I lie and say yes. Will you still tell me what it is?"

They were five feet from the far end of the hangar when Doug began shouting behind them. "Hey. Stop you two."

They looked back to see Doug running to catch them. They sprinted around the corner, jumped in the truck. Max spun the tires as much as possible to raise up a huge cloud of dust as he fish-tailed out of the parking area and lurched onto the main road, barely missing one of the few logging trucks on the road as it flew by going the other direction. The logging rig had to swerve off the road and raised more dust, laying on the horn as the driver fought the truck back to solid pavement.

The road curved to the right less than a quarter mile later. When he looked in the mirror, they were free. "I don't think he saw what we drove." Max had the truck going about eighty. "Hell. He probably doesn't know which direction we went."

"How about maybe slowing down? We might not stand out so much that way."

"Just another minute. There's a turn right up here . . . there."

He yanked the wheel and took the turn almost on two wheels. He slowed down to a more normal speed. "This is the road we missed coming up the main highway. It comes out five or six miles south of Adin and we can come into town that way. Old Doug there might be calling his friends right now to be looking out for someone driving back to town."

"You're so damn smart." Rhonda smiled

"So . . . what is that thing you stole back there?"

She held up the wallet sized organizer. "It's a Day-Timer. I used one in real estate religiously. Everything I did, when, where, with who, addresses, times, the works. It all goes in these things."

"Wish I had yours."

Rhonda canted her head and looked at him. "I'll give you mine. I want you to know who I am." Max broke off the eye contact and looked back at the road. "Let's see if Doug here is as meticulous as I was." She began looking through the daily planner. "Well, it won't withstand a good IRS audit but it's enough for us. Listen to this . . ."

Max held up his hand for silence. "Wait. Listen."

"What."

"There it is." He pointed out the side window to the left where the Doug's Cessna was just completing a pass over the main road to Bieber. It began to turn toward them, no doubt finished with the other road. Max saw no other cars on the road. "Hold on." He shouted as he jammed hard on the brakes, spinning the steering wheel first to the left to make the rear of the truck to slide and then to the right, as he down shifted. The engine revved up and he released the clutch as the truck completed its spin to wind up facing the direction they had just come from, only now in the opposite lane. He slowed down to below the speed limit. "Get down on the floor."

She crouched down and hid her face. Max grabbed his sunglasses off of the dash board and put on a baseball cap Danny had left above the visor. The Cessna swooped overhead and made a tight turn. Max gave a slight, local inspired wave as it passed. The plane headed off to search the road leading to Redding on the other side of the airstrip. Max turned right at the main road and headed into the big city of Adin.

"Can I come up yet?"

"Let's wait just a minute. That was real close. I don't think he will connect a truck headed toward the airstrip with only one person in it with the one he was chasing. Come on out . . . but stay low and watch for that plane."

She squirmed back to a sitting position. "There's just no end to the lengths you'll go to in order to show me a good time is there?"

"Nope."

"What do you call that little move? I mean it seemed to be planned rather than hoped for."

"That's called a bootlegger's roll. Moonshine runners used to do that to lose the feds. Are you impressed?"

"You bet." They slowed down as they entered the edge of town. Rhonda leafed through the Day-Timer.

"Find anything yet?" Max asked as he drove toward the Denny's style restaurant he had seen earlier.

"Yep. He's got a notation here for Sunday. It says he spent the whole day with someone named Armando. Six a.m. takeoff. Then nothing till the next day. It says he came back late that same night or early the next morning."

"What does the Log say?"

"Wait a minute. It says he flew to Lone Pine, Reno and back here." She thumbed back to the address part of the Day-Timer. "Here we go . . . Armando. No last name. Phone number 932-3699. 13122 Sugar Pine Road. Bieber, Ca."

"Let's get some lunch and a road map." He pulled into the restaurant. They ate a quick meal, bought a local map at the register and went to see where their target lived. They both liked the sound of that. Target.

Now they'd get a chance to sneak up on someone else for a change. Max stopped at a sporting goods store and bought a sophisticated pair of binoculars.

Back on the highway it took only twenty minutes to find the road leading to Armando's place. To take the road to his house wouldn't do anything except announce that they were snooping. There was no other reason to go down that road except to see his house. He had no desire to make whoever was in the house nervous or suspicious.

"Shit."

"How about some other vantage point?" Rhonda said. "I mean like maybe over there?" She pointed to a tree-lined ridge about a mile away that bordered the clear-cut area behind Armando's compound.

"Good idea." Max drove down the main road and tried three side roads that turned into logging tracks and petered out to nothing before finding one that got them close enough for him to look down on the compound. When he could not go any further without running the risk of getting stuck he turned the truck around and stopped. He took the Calico submachine gun out and set it on the seat. He put his jacket over it and checked his Automag.

"Okay. Here's how we play this." He lifted the hood on the truck. "You stay here and watch my back while I go and scope out what we're up against. If someone comes, just say the motor stalled out." He didn't think anyone would be coming down this road unless they were lost or looking for them. "If it's trouble, honk twice. I'm sure I'll hear it."

"With this horn, Danny will probably hear it back in Silver Springs."

Max smiled, grabbed the binoculars and headed

off though the woods. After going about two hundred yards he veered right to a vantage point at the edge of the clear cut. There were about forty acres where everything that grew was cut to the ground. It looked like the scene of an atomic explosion. He stood under a tree easily seventy feet high and looked out over a field of stumps where nothing grew over four feet high. It was eerie. He could see where new trees had been planted and wondered how long it would take for the area he looked at to grow into a forest. Since he didn't know, he decided to withhold any opinion one way or the other. Also, he had work to do.

Work . . . like, how he was going to get close enough to really look at the compound. Through the binoculars he could make out two small out buildings about six feet by six feet, maybe well houses or storage sheds. A barn blocked him from seeing the back of the house so he edged to his right until the back door was visible. A porch ran along the rear of the house. The back door opened and a young girl in a summer slip style dress walked out to toss water from a pan. Then she sat on the edge of the wood porch, lit a cigarette and slouched there, smoking.

He panned the area and saw the first of the dogs tied to a tree some fifty feet from the house. He let the binoculars hang around his neck and began to pick his way across the clear cut. He crouched low and walked crab-like, slowly from stump to stump until he was within twenty yards of the woods behind Armando's compound.

Here the stumps had been removed to make the landing strip. He raised his binoculars again and panned across the property. He counted ten dogs, all Rotweillers, chained at different intervals. He could see a pathway between the pattern of dogs that would allow him to get to the house by using the power pole at the end of the airstrip and the corner of the barn as a point to point reference. He made a mental note to bring some steaks.

He spent the next several minutes marking the location of the buildings, paths, dogs and where the windows and doors were on the back of a business card he found in his wallet.

As he put away the pencil and card, a black Bronco drove up to the house. The driver and the girl exchanged a few words; Max could not understand from this distance. The young girl stubbed out her cigarette and went inside. As the Bronco drove into the barn the tires chirped before the engine stopped. He heard the Bronco door slam and a tall, thin but muscular looking, man walked from the barn. He wore a black baseball cap, Levi's and a tan flannel shirt. The man stopped before he got to the porch, hesitated and turned around. Max crouched lower. The man scanned the woods as if looking for someone. Maybe he sensed Max's nearness. Max noticed that the man's shirt was buttoned at the top.

This had to be Armando and he appeared uncomfortable. Yeah. Be uncomfortable for a while. Armando turned and went in the house, the sound of the screen door's closing coming seconds after Max watched it happen like a cheap movie with the sound track a bit behind the video portion.

Max wasted no more time. The shadows were lengthening as he picked his way back to the tree line. He could smell the sun baked ground, like some huge compost pile, and mosquitoes appeared with the cooling evening, trying to embalm him before he could get back to the truck.

Rhonda paced in front of the truck, swatting at the mosquitoes and grumbling. Her face lit up as Max appeared from the tree line. She shut the hood and walked around to the passenger's side door. "How'd it go?"

Max got in and started the truck, swatting at his neck as he did so. "Went fine. I learned something important."

"What." Rhonda fanned at the flying scavengers to get them outside the truck as they picked up speed.

"We need insect repellent and we need it fast."

Max drove to the main highway and headed back to the town of Adin. They had plans to make.

CHAPTER TWENTY-ONE

Max pulled in to the sporting goods store where he had picked up the binoculars earlier. They bought two spray cans of Cutter's insect repellent, two flashlights, batteries, and a roll of electrical tape. Then at the grocery store they bought a box of Tide, two storm lanterns, a garden hose and ten pounds of steak.

"I don't really think I can eat that much. I'm trying to stay away from red meat," said Rhonda as they loaded the purchases in the back of the truck.

"Actually, I thought we'd eat at the same place we had lunch. We need to get a home base though."

"How about there?" She indicated a collection of cabins and trailer spaces, mostly vacant, with signs painted in peeling green and white on several propped up sheets of four by eight plywood, indicating that the traveler had, indeed, arrived at the home of Shasta Gateway Park, complete with free maps, souvenirs, swimming pool and showers, overnighters welcomed, clean, reasonable, most major credit cards accepted.

From the looks of the near vintage cars and trucks of the clientele they would probably take food stamps.

"It's perfect." Max drove up the gravel drive to the combination office, souvenir shop, shower and Laundromat. "You know what?" He didn't wait for the response. "For a couple of millionaires we sure stay in some classy places. Don't you think so?"

After the quick formality of registering they took cabin number eight at the back of the park. It was perfect. They parked the truck out of sight behind the cabin, unloaded their supplies and walked the short distance to the restaurant. This time they ate like it meant something; cheeseburgers, fries, pie, all in large quantities.

Rhonda remarked after they were ready to leave. "So what do you think you'll eat after you grow up?"

"You mean after this is over and we can actually take our time and choose a place to eat? You mean like dining out?"

"Yeah. I guess that's what I mean."

He rubbed his chin, looking very thoughtful. "I think I'll cook for you. How's that?"

"I can't wait." Smiling, she ignored the honking of a truck full of rowdy teenage boys. Max grinned as though they were complimenting him for being with this woman.

Back at the room, Rhonda surveyed the purchases and decided not to ask what they were all for. She did feel that perhaps this man she was with had gone through a lot to be what he was now.

Max cut a four-foot length from the garden hose and siphoned off enough gas to fill a sauce pan taken from the kitchenette. He poured some of the Tide in the pan and set it aside. Rhonda watched with interest. Maybe she would need to know this stuff later in life. Max looked up at her. "Homemade Napalm."

"I knew you were a good cook. Though I shudder to think of your childhood."

"Plain Southern Baptist. I learned this stuff later

on at the taxpayers' expense." He cleared off the small table and sat down. "Now, if you have that Day-Timer thing I'll outline what I think is a plan and we can refine it between us."

Rhonda took the Day-Timer and the logbook stolen from Doug's office and put them on the table. Looking through them gave up no more information except that Doug Peters was a hard worker and a terrible record keeper.

Max liked that. Taking out the business card he tried to show Rhonda the general layout. "Okay, these here are large trees." He pointed to the X's he had drawn. "The under-growth has all been cut back to allow the Rottweilers room to maneuver. Or maybe they trampled it down themselves."

"Rottweilers?"

"Yeah. Big dogs. They look like Dobermans on steroids. Anyway, this guy's got them tied up to these trees at irregular intervals but I traced what I think is a path through them." He ran his finger across the card. "Plus, I'll have steak to keep them occupied for a time. These here are outbuildings of some kind." He pointed at some O's on the card. "This is the main house and this here . . ." He pointed at a squiggle that looked a lot to Rhonda like all the other squiggles. "That's an old barn. But there's one thing strange about it. It looks like it's about to fall down but I heard his tires squeal a bit when he stopped. That means there's a cement floor in that old derelict. So there's more than meets the eye I'll bet."

"What's that?" Rhonda indicated a series of squiggles on the edge of the card.

"That? Oh that's a phone number."

"Uh, maybe you could copy this onto another sheet here and I'll understand it, too." She tore out a blank page from the logbook where he made a much more detailed drawing. It even had symbols that didn't all look alike.

After finishing the drawing he went outside to one of the barbecue pits and collected a cup of black ashes. Going back inside, he sat with Rhonda. "Here's what I have in mind. In a couple of hours we're going to do some midnight shopping at the co-op store between here and Armando's place. I'm sure they carry prel, actually it's Prilled Ammonium Nitrate but everybody calls it prel."

"Sure, I know exactly what that is." Rhonda rolled her eyes at him.

"It's fertilizer. The stuff they use around here isn't the best for what I have in mind but it'll work if I add a secret ingredient. It will definitely add a little punch to an otherwise mild explosion."

"Explosion, I like the sound of that." Rhonda smiled.

"I recognize a pun when I hear one. I think we should leave them a real message. We'll go back where we parked earlier. You stay with the truck again while I go in and try to neutralize whoever is there. If Armando is the man behind Mr. Wonderful, and we take him out . . . well, there would be no reason for him to keep after us because he wouldn't get paid."

"Do you believe that?"

"I don't know. There is one thing for certain, they won't be expecting this so I'm pretty sure I can pull it off. Also, after what they've done so far I think it's a good bet that either we kill them or they kill us. What's your vote?"

"Easy. Let's kill them."

He looked at his watch. "This may sound like it'll be hard to do but we need to try to get a couple of hours sleep."

"Sure," Rhonda said with a tinge of sarcasm, "I can hardly keep my eyes open. I'm so damned relaxed."

"Well, I can, so try to be quiet for that long, okay?"

"You won't even know I'm here." She ran her index finger across her lips like it was a zipper.

Max took off his boots and lay down. He was asleep almost immediately. It was a trick he'd learned in the jungle . . . how to sleep when the chance came. He once slept six hours standing up, leaning against a tree. When another soldier shook him awake Max immediately took a step forward and fell face first to the ground getting a black eye and some good natured ribbing for the next couple of weeks.

Rhonda sat on the edge of the bed and smoked one of Max's cigarettes. "Since we may die in the next day or two I guess I can take a chance that this isn't the cigarette that will kill me." She spoke to Max's sleeping form. "I hope you're sleeping more soundly than I was last night. I heard all that stuff you said."

She put out the cigarette, the first one in six months and it almost got her high. "I feel the same way about you. Except I'm not in any hurry to get laugh lines. It is cute that you want me to have them. Maybe if we live through this we can find our place to be together." Rhonda moved to the other side of the bed and stretched out. "Going through this has made me appreciate mediocrity and I just want you to know that it is my fervent hope to be mediocre with you as long as time will allow."

She put her hands behind her head and sighed. "Maybe after tomorrow I'll tell you this while you're awake." She tried to relax. "I wish Tawna had lived long enough to meet you, I think she would have liked you a lot." She knew she'd never sleep. She closed her eyes.

It was twelve midnight when Max shook Rhonda awake. "It's show time," Max said. He held out a cup of instant so thick and so strong it was like espresso. Max had laced with four spoons of sugar for a kicker.

"Here, this will put an edge on your senses."

While Rhonda drank her coffee and got ready to leave, Max poured the jellied gasoline into the two storm lanterns. He scraped the black ashes into the empty cigarette pack and put that in his shirt pocket. After testing the flashlights he taped over the lenses with electrical tape till only a slit showed. "Ready?"

"Let's go."

Like everything else, the co-op building was ten minutes away. It was one story white cinderblock; located about thirty feet off the main highway. Around the back was a six foot high chain link fence with "Beware of Dog" signs all over the place. The back of the building was not well lit. Max drove through the parking lot to where it exited to a service drive and parked.

"You're not going to have me sit here again are you?"

"Not a chance, girl. There's real work to do here and I need you to help. This will be fun." He took one of the steaks from the bag and cut it in half.

They waited till no traffic sounds could be heard and sprinted for the rear of the building where the chain link fence met the back wall. There were several pallets stacked up allowing them a relatively easy route over the top. When they reached the fence Max started to whistle. He called to the dog . . . "Here doggie. Here doggie." Then another whistle like he wanted the dog to come. He got an answering growl from a German Shepherd, his tail wagging at the same time. Max held out a piece of steak. "Here you go, boy." The dog sniffed at the steak then began to wolf it down. Max climbed the fence and Rhonda followed.

"The problem with these dogs is they see too many

people in a day and never get steak."

As he figured, the back door lock held little resistance. He almost asked Rhonda to pick it for him. Once inside he made his way down the aisle to the fertilizer racks. The *prel* was in fifty-pound sacks. It looked like round pellets of Styrofoam except for the sharp smell. Max found a flat cart and they loaded six sacks onto it and wheeled it out to the fence. It took another fifteen minutes to transfer it, bag by bag, to the truck. The dog gratefully took the second piece of meat and wagged his tail as they left.

As they drove back toward Armando's, Rhonda turned to Max. "Well, that was fun but how come we didn't just go in and buy the stuff during the day?"

"For one thing, they would start to look for us after we use it. This way they'll just wonder how it happened. And secondly, I didn't think about it till after the place was closed." He shrugged.

They pulled down the side road and parked where they had earlier. Max waited in the darkness till the sounds of the woods had returned. He began putting black ash on his face. "Okay, we'll do it just as before. Two honks mean trouble. You can also use the flashlight if you don't want to make any noise. Shield your flashlight with your hand like this." He demonstrated for her. "Flash once means okay, flash twice means trouble. If you don't get an answering flash from me then use the horn. Okay?"

"Got it. Once for okay, two for trouble. What about you signaling me when you're done?"

"I'll trip the porch light twice when it's okay to come in. Then you can drive to the gate and I'll let you in. If I don't give you some kind of signal inside an hour, or if I'm not back, then get out of here and call Captain Drew."

Rhonda looked at him in the darkness, his eyes almost the only thing that showed with his face blackened. Then the moon came out from behind the clouds, illuminating the cab of the truck. Rhonda moved to Max and kissed him full on the mouth, her tongue darting past his lips. He did not resist. She broke off the kiss and looked hard at him. "You better come back."

"I will." He moved off into the woods and Rhonda settled down to wait. She could see the lights of Armando's through the trees but couldn't make out where specific buildings were. She could hear an owl, probably near the clearing watching for field mice out in the open ground. She could also hear rustling in the undergrowth but decided not to try to figure out what it was.

Max made his way across the clearing, almost invisible with his face and hands darkened. His main concern was to stay quiet. He did not want to arouse the dogs and, since the wind was in his face, he hoped to have them eating steak and ignoring him before they knew he was there. At the edge of the woods he knelt and allowed his eyes to adjust to the darkness of the woods. He could make out the cleared area where the first dog should be. Christ. He could almost hear them snoring. He took a piece of steak and tossed it to the first dog. He never even barked before starting to chew on it. Max moved on.

Armando lay awake, hands behind his head and staring at the ceiling in the darkness. A shaft of light from the moon cut across his chest and the back of Jessica's head as she slept curled up facing away from him. He listened to the sounds of the night. Thinking. Uncle Lucho seemed to believe they would get back the rest of the money.

One million had been recovered, less twenty five percent for the man named Boyle. Armando was angry that Uncle Lucho paid the gringo so much but he admitted that he'd been prompt. What Boyle had recovered would soon be back in the vault. He hadn't delivered yet but Uncle Lucho said it would be here shortly.

He would not know how badly his own standing in the family had been eroded until this was over. That was how Uncle Lucho did things. If he was to be replaced then the first Armando would know of it would be as his successor cut his throat.

Max made his way around the barn and tossed another piece of steak to the dog tied there. If he was correct he could now make his way to the house without interference. He checked the Automag and put it back in his waistband. He took out his buck knife and held it in his right hand, blade tucked in against the forearm. He made his way carefully between the trees and headed toward the back porch.

A red light on the security panel above the dresser began flashing in the dark. Armando rolled from under the covers, pulled on his pants and shoes as he checked to see which one it was. The back entry. Close to the porch. Deer? No, the dogs would have barked. He moved to the window. The moonlight filtered through the trees. He could make out a shape, dark as the shadows, moving from the tree cover out into the open. Where were the dogs? Armando grabbed his pistol and the remote signal to release the dogs. Maybe they were taken out already. How?

Max stopped at the base of the last tree before the

back porch. Turning slowly he checked the corners of the house for movement. Stepping free of the shadow under the tree he moved like slow silk to the wall next to the porch. Putting his back to the wall he knelt to go under a window then rose up to see inside. It was too dark to make out any detail except what appeared to be a sink and counter. He had figured this end of the house to be the kitchen with the bedrooms at the opposite end. He wanted to enter the house here and make his way to the bedrooms and move with the element of surprise. His only concern was the girl. She must be a civilian. He crept along the wall to the back porch.

Armando moved down the hallway to the kitchen. Next to the back door was a Louisville Slugger baseball bat. He checked the remote control and pressed a small button once. Immediately each dog received a shock and stood straining at their leash as trained. Then Armando stood next to the back door and pressed the button to release the dogs. He heard the primal growl of one of the dogs as it sensed a target. Armando smiled as he held the bat in both hands like a major leaguer. He waited for the intruder.

CHAPTER TWENTY-TWO

Max heard the low growl. The sound seemed to come from two directions at the same time. He looked over his shoulder at a hundred pounds plus of motion, seemingly all head and jaws, racing from the shadows toward him. Since Max was crouched low it caused the dog, when it leaped at him, to actually come down on him. Max brought up his right arm in a slashing motion, cutting through the bone, muscle, and tendon of its front legs which had no effect at all on the dogs singleness of purpose. It meant to rip him into bite sized chunks as quickly as possible. Max felt the dog's teeth on his shoulder as the powerful jaws clamped down, very nearly breaking the bones, burying the teeth into flesh. Max shifted the knife to his left hand, brought the blade up under the dog's jaw and cut across the throat of the dog, severing the wind pipe. The dog's grip lessened but did not release. Max thrust the blade into the back of the dog's throat and ripped the blade back and forth in a sawing motion until the spinal cord split and the dog fell limp.

Max fought to stay conscious, kneeling, clutching his shoulder, grimacing in pain and staring at the sightless eyes of the dying dog. Jesus. Where had that dog come from? Max heard the next growl. Could he be hallucinating the dead dog back to life? The next dog hit him from behind so hard that it knocked Max over and hurled several feet past him. Max jumped to his feet. Moving on pure survival instincts he headed for the back door. He could never outrun the dog in the woods or in the open. He needed to escape now and the house seemed the only haven.

Max clawed his way to the back porch. The dog grabbed on to Max's upper thigh, biting through his Levi's and into the meaty part of the leg below the famous Levi emblem. Max ran to the back door, the dog digging in with his legs, shaking his powerful head back and forth, Max dragging the dog with him as he shrieked in pain and yanked the back door open.

Armando hit the button to stop the dog's attack as Max opened the back door. Wow. Here it comes, boys. A fucking grand-slam-game-winning-bottom-of-the-ninth home run. Armando stepped into the pitch. Wham. Right across the jaw. A pleasing crunching sound as the bat met the side of Max's face. The gringo's head stopped but he had so much forward momentum trying to outrun the dogs that his feet flew by, still wind-milling, almost horizontal as the body hit the floor and stayed there.

Armando turned on the kitchen lights. "All right baby." Armando stroked the bat and looked at Max's still form. "All fucking right." Jessica came in and stood silently by the kitchen door. Armando prodded the body with his foot. No response. He noticed blood coming from Max's ear. He felt for a pulse. Tough guy. Still alive. Good. Now he could find out the how and why of the attack.

Armando listened for the dogs. This one came alone or the dogs would be raising hell to get any partners he might have had. Armando ignored Jessica and sat the intruder in one of the kitchen chairs. He took a coil of clothes line from a drawer and cut it into short lengths. As he started to tie Max to the chair Max groaned in pain and his eyes fluttered. Armando stopped tying him and stepped back to look at him. "Come on, my friend, let's see you wake up." As Max opened his eyes Armando reached over, grabbed Max's jaw and twisted it where it was broken. As the broken bone grated against the nerves of his jaw, Max cried out again, stiffened like a baby with colic, arched his back and fell from the chair to the floor, unconscious again.

Armando laughed. "Oh, baby, are you tough."

Jessica covered her mouth, tears in her eyes, and ran to the bathroom, her bladder giving way and urine running unnoticed down her legs. She huddled against the door in a fetal position with her fist in her mouth, rocking silently.

He yanked Max back into the chair and finished tying him. The chair was stout, all dark wood with ornate wooden knobs at the end of the arms and the top of the back, a Mediterranean style captain's chair. Armando wound the clothes line tight around Max's wrists and ankles. He ran two strands across his chest, midsection and thighs. Armando looked with pride at the wounds inflicted by the dogs. Max's shoulder bled slowly through the shirt. Armando ripped the material to expose mangled muscle and pencil-sized holes where the canine teeth had penetrated. The wound at the rear of Max's thigh bled much faster.

"Too bad for you, my friend. Perhaps you will die of blood loss from that unless someone takes you to a hospital real soon." Armando opened the refrigerator and took out a long necked bottle of Dos Equis beer. He opened it, tipped it to his lips and drank enough to make his Adam's apple bob several times. He finished half the bottle at once, stopped, shook the bottle several times and sprayed Max's face with the remainder.

Max came to, shouting in anger and fear; he fought to stay conscious as the pain from his jaw filled every cell in his body. Waves of nausea; his vision fading almost to black; he was swimming back to a world consumed with confusion, pain . . . the shoulder, now the leg, his face wet, foaming, thoughts of a village in South America intruded for some reason, and he forced open his eyes.

"Hello, my friend. Welcome to my house." Armando grinned at him as though he were a friend who stopped by for a cup of coffee and a little chat.

"Su casa es mi casa." Max mumbled. Talk was difficult; not being able to move his jaw without paying a steep price. Max decided not to try to monopolize the conversation. He went through a mental check list of his injuries. Moving his shoulder slightly he didn't figure any bones were broken. He felt a lot of blood. Nothing compared to his ass. He must be sitting on raw meat. His boot squished when he tensed his right leg. He must have bled quite a bit but it had stopped. His jaw was definitely broken. "Where am I?"

"In trouble. At death's door." Armando looked into Max's striking blue eyes. "I've been hoping that we'd catch up with you. Didn't expect you to deliver yourself like a fucking pizza. I don't even care why you're here." Armando got another beer from the refrigerator. "Want one?" He held it out to Max. "Suit yourself. This is the last one anyway." He sat on the edge of the table, left leg on the floor, right leg swinging back and forth. "So. You have something of mine. Where is it?"

Max knew telling him would not save him. He needed time. How long had he been unconscious? "Where's what?"

Armando swung his right leg up to Max's hip and prodded. Max took a sharp breath. "I have little patience. You have caused me enough grief. Now tell me where it is."

"What?" Max spoke through the pain. Armando brought up his foot. Max focused on the sole of a Nike Air Jordan, the famous basketball player depicted in midair, getting ready for the slam dunk.

"We'll talk again soon." Armando pushed with his toes against the broken jaw and as Max began to cry out he pulled his foot back and kicked Max full in the face sending him flying over backwards, his head bouncing off the kitchen floor. Max lost the battle for consciousness.

Armando stood at the counter. Taking the cordless phone he dialed Uncle Lucho. Because of the late hour it rang in Lucho's quarters. "Yes?"

"I have the thorn from our side."

"Where?"

"Resting in my kitchen."

Uncle Lucho considered the options. "All of them?"

"No. Just the man. He works alone. His mistake."

"Alive?"

"Si."

After a pause so long that Armando thought perhaps they had been disconnected Uncle Lucho spoke again. "Wait. Our American friend will be there soon. Let him earn his pay."

Armando felt total rage welling up inside. He knew better than to say anything against his uncle. He waited for him to say how long it would be. All he heard was a dial tone.

Armando stared at the phone in frustration. Fuck! Here he had gotten the one who could tell where the rest of the money was. He should not have called. He should have gotten the gringo to talk first. He threw the phone at a tall china hutch with glass doors which shattered.

Jessica shook her head at the sound of the glass breaking. She looked around the bathroom as if seeing it for the first time. It was odd viewing it from this angle. She looked past the rim of the toilet seat; up at the underside of the sink, at mismatched plastic, steel and copper pipe fittings normally unseen. The old green paint she had tried to cover over with white last winter showed through where she had missed with the brush. She could see individual strokes where the end of each swipe had not quite covered the old green color. She remembered sweating; the heater on high like Armando always liked it. Her bending over and reaching under the sink with the heavy brush and blowing with exaggerated puffs at the strands of hair that had kept falling out of the bandanna and into her face. What an improvement the white had been over the dark green.

Now a large fish in bright colors, distorted by being bunched up instead of spread out, swam crookedly on the see-through shower curtain and watched her from one bright blue, too-large eye in comic fashion. She got to her knees, went to the side of the tub and pulled the curtain till the fish swam straight again.

Rhonda couldn't stand the wait. It had been only twenty-five minutes but it seemed like forever. She tapped her watch and listened to make sure it was working. Jesus she hated this. She had heard noises, dogs growling, a banging sound, unidentified short shouts. What did it mean? Had he finished the job? She strained to see the back porch light come on. She trusted that Max knew what he was doing.

Armando knelt beside Max. He needed him to wake up. He needed him to talk before Boyle got there. If he found out the location of the money he would save the family Boyle's fee, and regain face.

Not only that but it would make him happy to be able to dispose of the gringo. He had caused way too much trouble to live any longer than absolutely necessary.

The beer had worked its way through Armando. He stood over Max and unzipped his fly. He straddled Max's unconscious form. He wasn't sure if this would wake him. Who cared? It would be fun to tell him about it later. He relieved himself, the stream splashing down on Max's chest and face.

Max woke up coughing and gagging, unable to avoid what was happening. He looked up in utter disbelief and disgust. Armando appeared ten feet tall, standing with his feet on either side of his head he looked like the . . . Jolly Green Giant. "What the fuck?" He didn't care that his jaw screamed at him for talking. "Oh God damn. What are you doing?"

Jessica had turned off the light in the bathroom and managed to step into the hallway unnoticed. She stared down the hall at the sight; without comprehension at first. Armando stood over the American who lay on his back tied in the chair. What was Armando doing? Then, as she understood what was happening she retreated down the hall to the bedroom, sat down at the vanity and stared at her reflection there in the mirror. Banded by shafts of moonlight through the curtains she looked more like a captured animal than a young girl.

Armando laughed, put himself away and pulled Max's chair back to an upright position. "Grossed you out a bit, didn't I?" He sat back on the table as before and looked at his prisoner. He wrinkled his nose in disgust. "God, but you stink."

Max couldn't have agreed more. He could smell blood, sweat, beer and piss. He gagged and added bile to the combination. This had to rank right up there as one of his all time worst days. It didn't look like it was going to get any better.

Armando made what he considered to be an executive decision. He would torture this man for a while. He had plenty of experience in getting the peasants to loosen their tongues back home. True, this one seemed made of stronger stock. "What's your name?"

"Aunt Jemima."

Armando stood up, put his right foot in the chair between Max's legs and leaned down. His face only inches away. "Listen to me, asshole. You tell me what I want to know and all this trouble . . ." Armando pressed down on Max's genitals with his toes, ". . . will stop." Max felt his testicles being crushed, he could hear a sickening snapping and popping sound. He spit blood into Armando's eyes. Armando jumped back and kicked Max viciously, knocking the chair back to the floor.

Armando took a towel, wet it in the sink and wiped his face. He looked down at Max and kicked him to see if he was conscious. He got a groan and smiled. "You're pretty tough. Let's see how you feel about being dinner."

Max turned his head till he could see between the legs of the table and chairs across the tile floor. Different fluids pooled around the chair. He watched as Armando went to the back door and flipped the porch light switch. Nothing happened. "Shit, the bulb is burnt out again." He tried twice more then took a flashlight from a drawer and went outside.

Max felt his bonds. They were loosened by his being thrown to the floor. He made a mental note never to use clothesline to tie people up. There were lots of better products on the market. He clenched his fists and worked at the bonds till he could almost pull his hands free. So close. Looking into the darkness of the hall he saw a young girl watching him from a door at the end of the hall. As their eyes met she pulled the door shut.

He could hear scratching and scuffling on the porch. The back door burst open and he watched terrified and helpless as the Rottweiler charged at him. The dog lunged and took Max by the left leg and began to shake him around like a rag doll. Max cried out. Then just as suddenly as the attack started, it stopped. The dog sat panting, froth running at the corners of its mouth. Armando walked to Max and yanked the chair upright again.

Armando snapped on a heavy leash to the thick choke chain around the dog's neck. The dog licked the foam from its mouth but did not take its eyes off Max. Max believed he had never seen eyes more primal than those. He did indeed feel like the main course.

"Well, my friend. This is how it is." Armando sat back on the edge of the table as before. "I am going to ask you questions and you are going to give me the right answers. If you hesitate or lie to me, I will let the dog have you. Do you understand?"

"Yes." Max made the decision there to play down any strength he had left. He let his head hang limp, looking up in complete surrender at Armando.

"What's your name?"

"Max."

"Good. Is there anyone with you?"

"No."

"How did you get here tonight?"

"I drove." Max acted as though he were about to lose consciousness. He overplayed the hand.

"Where's the money?"

"I buried it in the desert."

Armando hit the button on the remote control and the dog leaped on Max's chest biting into the front shoulder that had been injured before. "No." Max screamed.

The chair went over again. Armando stopped the dog's attack and tipped the chair back up on its feet. Max could feel the bonds on his chest slip free. The dog had practically freed him. His hands were so loose that he had to lift them slightly to make the rope appear tight.

Armando grinned at Max. "Okay, now you tell me. Where is the money?" He put down the remote control and picked up Max's gun. Looking at it and at Max. Then he aimed it at Max's kneecap and flipped off the safety.

"It's in a storage place in Reno. It's one of those that has a security guard, and is more like individual vaults than storage spaces. I have it under a different name and you need a number code to get at it."

"Go on."

"The name is Gordon Pierce."

"And the number?"

Max sighed. Two-six-seven-two-two."

Armando smiled. "Good." He picked up the remote but kept the gun aimed at Max's knee. "Say goodbye asshole."

The dog rose up on its haunches to attack. A gunshot rang out. Max thought Armando had shot him. The dog yelped and slumped to the floor. Both men looked at the dying dog, blood pumping from where its face had been, then turned to see Jessica standing in the kitchen doorway, smoking gun in hand.

Max reacted first. Freeing his hands he grabbed the gun and Armando's other arm and fell forward, taking them both to the floor. The chair came with them. Armando tried to roll over to protect his back from Jessica. Max got his finger into the trigger guard, twisted the gun into

Armando's chest, and pulled the trigger. Armando rolled back and stood up. Max fired four more times into his chest. Armando jerked back each time till he reached the counter where he fell back. Looking at the ceiling momentarily, he flopped back, face first, into the mess that surrounded the dead dog.

CHAPTER TWENTY-THREE

Rhonda strained to hear what was happening. It had been over an hour now and she had to make a decision. Then she heard the shots. She grabbed the Calico submachine gun and started for the back of the property. She knew what Max had said; to leave and make phone calls. You bet. Right now she thought the man she loved was either dead or in trouble. She stumbled and fell at the edge of the clear-cut area. When she stood up she could see the back of the house clearly.

Max untied the ropes holding him to the chair, took the flashlight Armando had used, and went to the back porch. He pointed it toward where Rhonda was parked and flashed it twice. He waited a moment and did it again. Finally he heard what sounded like a semi truck horn answering him back. He went back to the kitchen and slumped to the floor.

Jessica walked to the sink and drew water. Dipping a towel in it she took it to Max; knelt at his side and began to clean his face. Max opened his eyes. "Can you help me?"

Jessica nodded.

"I need you to unlock the front gate. There's a girl coming in a blue Ford pickup. Can you let her in?"

"Sure." She went into the hallway and returned wearing a jacket many sizes too big for her and carrying a ring of keys. She picked up the remote control for the dogs and pressed the button for them to return to their stations.

Rhonda pulled up and was surprised by the apparition holding the gate open. Jessica looked like a character out of a Dickens's novel. The night's events had left her quite pale. Rhonda pulled past and waited for the girl to relock the gate and get in the truck. As soon as she sat down Rhonda asked. "Is he okay?"

"He's alive but he's not what I would call okay."

"Oh God!" Rhonda raced to the house and slid to a stop at the back door. Running inside she stopped short and took in the scene. It looked like a meatpacking house. She ran to Max and cradled his head in her lap. "Max?"

He opened his eyes. "What."

She was crying and laughing at the same time. "You stink. What's that smell?"

"You don't want to know." He pulled himself to a sitting position. They looked at Jessica standing by the table. She looked like she was in some state of shock. "This girl saved my life."

"What's your name?" Rhonda asked.

"Jessica."

"Well Jessica. Thank you. Do you have any bandages?"

"Yeah, in the bathroom."

"Could you help me get Max in there?"

"Sure."

One on each side they supported Max and got him into the bathroom. Setting him on the edge of the bathtub they cut away his clothes and cleaned his wounds. His jaw had swollen considerably. Jessica brought ice packs from the kitchen to help reduce the swelling. Rhonda cleaned out the dog bites with peroxide and bandaged them. Jessica went and got some of Armando's clothes for Max.

"Who are you?" Jessica asked them. Max looked better; now dressed and no longer smelling like an outdoor toilet at a construction site in July. They sat in the living room, Max and Rhonda on the sofa and Jessica dwarfed in a recliner with her feet tucked under her.

"You related to the man in the kitchen?" Max nodded his head in the direction of the hallway.

Jessica laughed. "No, not hardly."

Rhonda leaned over and touched her arm. "We aren't here to hurt you."

Jessica looked from Max to Rhonda, hesitated, and began to talk. "My family lives on the property that borders this one. I haven't been there for a while." As Jessica told her story she went from a hardened woman to a young girl. She talked for about twenty minutes while Max and Rhonda sat and listened. When she finished Max asked what she wanted to do.

"Well I sure as hell don't want to go home. I want to go to school and be a nurse." Jessica laughed, rich and free. "Don't you think that's stupid?"

Rhonda answered. "Jessica, no dream is stupid. You can do whatever you want. Right now I think we should make a move to get out of here. Can you walk okay?"

Max straightened his leg. "Sure. I feel like we've been here too long already. This place is hotter than Hell." Max looked to Jessica. "Does Armando have many visitors?"

"No. Hardly ever. He runs this place by himself.

Look. Can I go with you?"

Max and Rhonda answered in unison. "Sure." They laughed.

"Well, then, I think you should see this." Jessica led them out through the side door; avoiding the kitchen area, past the porch and into the barn. She switched on a low voltage light allowing just enough light to make out the shape of the Bronco they had seen earlier. The floor was new concrete as Max had thought. "Over here." She moved to a corner of what would be a tack room if there were any horses, and knelt down by a stack of crates and tools piled up. She pulled a concealed lever and the pile slid out from the wall revealing a flight of steps. They followed her down the steps for ten feet or so and stopped on a landing. Jessica flipped on the lights.

They were in small room, a sort of entryway, with two doors. They tried the one to the right and entered a large room. Two desks faced each other; one neat and bare and one with a telephone and a computer on it. A freestanding bookcase held a couple of ledgers and some office supplies. Max opened one of the ledgers and found a series of entries in some kind of code. "Look at this."

Rhonda took the book and read for a moment. "Whatever this is I think it would hurt these guys if the code were broken. It looks like deliveries and dates. There's also some numbers in the back. Maybe phone numbers."

"Let's take it." Max walked to the back of the room to a wall holding an impressive array of small arms and automatic weapons. "Danny would sure like this."

"Should we take him a gift?" Rhonda picked up an exotic looking autoloading shotgun. It was an eight-shot Benelli Super 90 with a pistol grip. "I don't remember seeing one of these at Danny's."

"Why not? What else is here?"

Rhonda leaned the shotgun against the wall and

turned on the computer. She found a stack of floppy disks in the top drawer. "I think I'll see what's on these."

"Let's look at the other room first."

They went to the other door and opened it. "Holy shit!" Max looked at the twelve by twenty room with three tall bins of Plexiglas going from floor to ceiling. Each one was four foot square and vented with small holes drilled at regular intervals. Two of the bins were empty. The other one they walked up to and circled. It was filled with money. Banded and stacked with silica packs every third row to stop mildew or mold. An air conditioner clicked on and startled the three of them. They laughed nervously.

"How much is there?" Rhonda asked of Jessica.

"Beats me. I've never been in here. He had no idea that I knew this was here. I figured it had to be good. I was too scared to come in here when he was alive."

"Well, Jessica, I think that, if you want to you can afford to go to school and become a nurse or, if you want, you could buy a hospital." Max tried to calculate how much money was here but it would not compute. "If they were pissed because we took a few million from them I don't want to think what losing this would do to their attitudes."

"What are you saying?" Rhonda looked at him. "Do you not want to take it?"

"Shit. I just wish I could see their faces when they find it's gone." Max pulled up a chair to the bin. "Help me up." Rhonda and Jessica helped him onto the chair and Max painfully reached up to feel along the top of the bin. "I want to check for any booby traps or alarms first."

He ran his finger along the top row of banded stacks till he struck a small wire. "I thought so."

"What?" Jessica watched in fascination.

"Yeah, that's how I'd of done it too." The girls helped him back down. "This is going to take a little time. Maybe thirty minutes. I need a few hand tools.

Are there any here?"

"Sure. In the barn upstairs. There's a toolbox. I'll go get it."

Rhonda looked at her watch. "I'm going to try to get into their computer files while you do that." She went back to the other room.

Jessica returned shortly with the toolbox and Max went to work. He carefully removed the lead wires from the stack of bills and with Jessica's help began to retrace them to whatever was supposed to be triggered.

Rhonda worked her way through the files in the computer. They were not hidden at all and were easy to read. First she ran a check to see if there were any hidden files by noting the space used by existing files and the space available. Whoever had set them up had just a basic working knowledge of computers. Good. She could hear Max and Jessica in the other room. She felt Jessica was a good person. Although, this was not a likely spot to find one; in this den of murderers and drug lords. She heard a scraping sound, not from the other room. She froze. Looking at the door she thought she saw movement, a shadow. The hair on her neck stood up. She crouched down and moved behind the bookcase.

The shadow stopped in the doorway. Boyle stepped in the room. Rhonda recognized him as the man on the dock at Lake Tahoe. Her heart pounded. She didn't move. Hell, she couldn't move. She felt her bowels loosen. Surely he could hear her breathing.

Boyle moved through the room, noticing the computer screen. He walked within two feet of Rhonda. She bit her lip, expecting to be discovered at any minute. Boyle never saw her. He went through the door and entered the other room. He watched the man and the girl work at pulling wires from an enormous tower of money. He smiled. The fee on this was going to be enough to never have to work again the rest of his life. From now on he would only do his work when it pleased him.

"Good evening folks."

Max turned and looked at the man in the doorway holding a wicked looking semi-automatic pistol. His first thought was for Rhonda. He must not have seen her.

"Could you please step down from the chair?"

Max let go of the wires and slowly got down off the chair. He glanced at the Automag on the floor.

"Don't even think about it . . . you." He pointed to Jessica. "Kick that gun over here."

She did as she was told. She started to shake violently. "Come over here."

Jessica walked toward Boyle. Boyle motioned her to stay to the right so he could keep the gun trained on Max. "Nothing funny, girl, or I'll end your life right now."

Max tested his leg a bit. Pain shot up through his leg and he stumbled. Boyle tensed on the trigger. Max froze.

"Sit down in the chair. Real slow."

Once Max sat down, Boyle took out a couple of nylon locking straps. "Now pay close attention, girl. Watch how this is done as if your life depends on it, because it does." He showed her how to pull the end through the opening to tighten the loop. "Now go over and tie your friend's hands behind his back."

After she finished he motioned her to walk back to him. "Turn around." He used another nylon loop and tied her hands. Then he pushed her down to the floor. Walking over to Max he pulled the end of the strap till there was no circulation in Max's hands and they began to turn blue. He stood back and looked at Max. "You look like shit. Do you know that?"

"It hasn't been one of my better days."

Boyle prodded Max's shoulder, watched him grimace, poked the barrel of his gun at Max's thigh and was rewarded with a sharp intake of breath from Max. "Oh my, you've already been softened up, haven't you?"

Max saw the excitement in Boyle's eyes. Jesus. This guy was getting off on this shit. Boyle took a leather jeweler's pouch from his jacket. "I want you to know something, pal. Can I call you that?" He didn't wait for an answer. "I'm going to ask you some questions and you're going to answer them quickly and honestly. If you don't, I will kill you in the slowest possible way."

"Are there any other options? Like a second choice?"

Boyle moved to him like a man on drugs. He held a short bladed scalpel; Max pulled back, remembering Shawn and Nolan. Boyle brought the blade in a sweeping arch to Max's face and stopped. "Your friends died much too fast. They hardly got to watch what happened to them." Boyle moved the blade to Max's midsection. "Where's the money?" He held the blade against Max's stomach, just enough pressure to break the skin.

Max started talking. "It's in a locker in Reno out on Virginia Street." He tried to look totally terrified. It was easy. In fact he felt pretty sure he could conjure up a bowel movement.

Boyle pulled the blade across Max's midsection, cutting through his shirt and drawing blood. "And?"

"And the address and key are in the truck." Boyle drew almost the same circle he had on Shawn and Nolan except he applied no pressure on the blade. It cut through the shirt Max wore but barely broke the skin. Max wondered where Rhonda was. Boyle finished cutting away Max's shirt and part of his pants in a large circle. He stepped away from Max.

"You're in luck. I believe you." He pulled Jessica to her feet, and shoved her down between Max's knees. "I'm going to kill you quick." He was so excited now he giggled. Sweat formed on his upper lip. He licked it away.

Max caught a movement near the door. He willed himself to not look. Instead he kept the look of terror on his face.

Boyle reached down and ripped away the cloth from Max's pants. "I'm even going to let you have some fun on the way to Hell. Both of you." Jessica was shaking and sobbing. "This young whore will take you in her mouth . . ." Boyle yanked Jessica's hair, pulling her head back. She cried out in pain. "Won't you?"

He nodded her head for her. "And when she does, or while she's doing her work . . ." Boyle was oblivious to everything except this macabre scene he had created. He didn't notice Rhonda enter the room. "I will mercifully send you . . ." Rhonda raised the shotgun to her shoulder. ". . . to the Hell you will be right at home in."

Max needed to keep Boyle's attention for just another moment. Rhonda needed to get to the side of Boyle or she might kill all three of them. He looked down at Jessica. "Don't be afraid, honey. Go ahead. It'll be okay."

Jessica lowered her head to Max's lap. Boyle moved closer so he could watch Jessica's face, keeping the gun aimed at them. Rhonda had moved also. Now she had a clear shot at Boyle but Max wanted Boyle to quit aiming at them. He didn't want to be shot by the nerve reactions of a dead man. He knew Boyle was aroused, his sick mind playing some kind of fantasy out, so Max moaned as if in pleasure and pain.

Boyle took the barrel of the gun and touched himself, rubbed the sight up his fly. "You disgust me." He curled his upper lip and made ready to spit on Max and Jessica.

The blast took most of his face and sprayed it across the wall. Jessica jerked, thinking she was shot. Max wondered how many years of therapy it would take to work through this one. Max watched as Rhonda moved toward Boyle. "This one's for Shawn." She leveled the shotgun to Boyle's chest and pulled the trigger. Boyle had just come to rest when the blast took nearly half his chest and tore a hole the size of a logging boot in it. Boyle's body jumped as the buckshot went through his lungs to the floor and brought his body back up with the ricochet. She brought the shotgun up again. “This is for Nolan.” She shot him in the stomach, braced herself and fired a round at his right knee, nearly separating the leg, causing the foot and calf to end up pointing up at Boyle’s head. She stepped to forward. “And this is for Tawna, you fucker . . . you!” She shot the other knee, moved the barrel up, centered it on Boyle’s groin, and sent that part to Hell. Rhonda fired the last three rounds into Boyle’s chest and neck and separated what was left of his head from what was left of his body. She kept pointing the shotgun and pulling the trigger even though nothing happened. Finally she could hear Max calling to her. She slumped to the floor and fainted.

Max surveyed the wreckage. This looked like a scene from a Fellini movie. Jessica sat back and stared blankly at the mess that used to be a man. Rhonda lay a few feet away in a dead faint, the empty shotgun next to her. Max sat in the chair. His ears rang from the shots in the closed room. No, it wasn’t a ringing. It was a high pitched keening sound that would make a dog howl.

“Jessica.” She didn’t respond. “Jessica.” He nearly shouted. Jessica jerked her head around and looked at him. “We’ve got to get out of here. Can you get the knife over there?” He nodded to where Boyle’s blade had landed next to one of the empty money bins.

She got the knife and, after a lot of effort and cutting Max twice, he was freed. He quickly cut Jessica’s bonds and together they got Rhonda to the bottom of the stairs away from her handy work in the vault.

Jessica got wet rags and Rhonda came back around in a few minutes.

“What happened?”

“Don’t you remember?” Max looked at her. He searched her eyes. “Good. Let’s just say you took care of our friend and evened the score with these assholes.”

“Oh God.” He could tell it was coming back to her. “What have I done?”

Max put his arms around her while Jessica held her hands. After just minutes Max helped her to her feet. "We'll have time to sort through this later. Right now we have work to do. Let's leave a little token of our esteem for these guys."

CHAPTER TWENTY-FOUR

Rhonda drove the truck and U-Haul while Max sat at the passenger side trying to read the map. Each bump brought pain and discomfort to Max. His right arm and his hip and leg where the dog had mauled him throbbed in spite of the pain pills he had taken earlier. His jaw had been reset in Reno and was swollen and discolored.

Jessica sat in the seat between them. Her head rested on Max's shoulder, mouth open in a deep sleep. She looked thirteen again. Only a thirteen year old could look angelic snoring with her mouth open. If a grown up did that it wouldn't work. She stirred as Rhonda turned the truck off the main road, the U-Haul bouncing behind them. She turned to Max's chest without waking up. The morning sun reflected off the windows of the few houses and pickups lining the road leading up the side of the hill. The Rockies loomed over them, growing larger as they drove on, hiding the sun, making it seem as if the sun were setting instead of rising.

Max looked from the map to the road again. "This is it here."

They turned on to a paved road that changed to gravel in short order, finally twisting up to a house sitting atop a rise, looking down on the valley floor below. Two large dogs, of the mutt variety, barked and ran at the truck, wagging their tails furiously, followed by five kids all shouting at the dogs and each other. Marlene came out of the front door, letting it slam behind her. Max imagined the infinite number of times the door must do that in a family house like this. The truck stopped alongside Marlene's big white Blazer, still with the Nevada plates on it. Rhonda leaped out with a yell and hugged Marlene, dancing in a circle, crying, laughing, stepping back to take each other in, hugging again.

Jessica watched from the front seat. Nothing could stop the smile that held her face hostage. Where had she seen this kind of happiness? Only here and maybe on TV. She climbed down from the truck and stretched. Max got out slowly, limped over to Marlene and took his share of affection.

Rhonda went to Jessica's side, took her by the hand and pulled her over with the others. "This is Jessica, the girl I told you about on the phone. Jessica, this is Marlene."

Marlene hugged Jessica. "Anyone who saves Rhonda's life is a friend of mine. Come on in. You must be beat."

"Okay," said Max as they went inside, kids and dogs milling about them, "but be easy. I've had all the beatings I can stand, believe me."

Inside the huge kitchen, smells of pancakes, bacon and eggs assaulted them.

"You're just in time for breakfast. How 'bout we eat first then you can catch me up on the details. It must really be over or you wouldn't be here."

They sat at a long redwood picnic table with chairs at each end. Max thought this table would be at home in any beer garden in Munich. Kids ran back and forth, all talking at once. "Okay kids, let's eat." Like a miracle each kid took a seat and waited quietly while Marlene, with the help of one of the older girls, brought the serving plates of bacon, toast, pancakes, scrambled eggs, and pitchers of orange juice and milk. None of them touched their food except one little girl at the end of the table who fidgeted with the bacon and was shushed by those around her. Marlene sat with them and looked at one of the boys. "Your turn, Nathan."

Nathan looked nervously at the three guest and bowed his head. "Our Father . . ." The others joined in.

When the meal was finished, three of the children met a school bus at the bottom of the hill; half a mile away. Max thought it looked animated. Each color stark and pure as the bright yellow bus stopped to pick them up, each one sporting bright colored book bags or sweaters. The bus continued down the winding road, coming in and out of view from behind houses, trees and grassy knolls, finally disappearing into the valley.

Rhonda, Marlene, and Jessica finished in the kitchen with the non-help of the two smaller children not yet in school. Afterward they sat in the living room, the huge picture window showing the valley below and the two youngsters playing in the front of the house.

Marlene took a sip of coffee. "I thought I had hid out pretty good. It was a surprise when you called here. All you told me was that this guy Boyle was dead and he's the one who killed Shawn. So, tell me how you found me."

"You won't be happy." Max sat his cup down on the thick wood plank that did duty as a coffee table. He reached in his shirt pocket, took out a small photograph and handed it to her. "We found the picture of you and Shawn in what was left of Boyle's wallet. Sorry about the condition. We also found this address and directions on how to get here, your cousin and her husband's name, what they do for a living, and the names of all these kids."

Rhonda looked at the picture of her and Shawn on the beach. She felt her heart would break. She wasn't ashamed of the tears that fell. It was good to feel. Shawn would always be a part of her. She held the picture in her lap and looked at Max. "I gather, since you're all here, that this thing is over for good. That man Boyle is really dead?"

Jessica shuddered. Max answered her. "Yeah. He is really dead."

"How do you know the others won't follow?"

"We don't. But we left a little surprise that may discourage them. It looks like you've been doing okay here."

Marlene laughed. "I've been Mamma Warbucks here. Randy and Alice keep telling me to slow down. I think we've got the best dressed foster kids on the planet. They made me stop buying clothes for the kids when they started to look too much like Beverly Hills instead of urban Colorado."

Smiling, Marlene continued. "I told Alice that since all these kids look so different it would be a good idea to buy them all matching outfits so they would look more like a family. That was my last clothes shopping day." Sipping from her coffee cup she looked at Max and Rhonda. "How long can you stay?"

"We can't," Rhonda said. "Max knows a spot with lots of peace, quiet, and wide open spaces . . . says you can see trouble coming twenty minutes before it gets to you." She rested her hand on Max's knee like they had been together forever. They had been through more than most couples go through in a lifetime. "When we're settled in we can come back and visit for longer."

Marlene set her coffee down and took Rhonda's hand. "Come on, I'll give you the nickel tour."

The two of them walked up the hill behind the house. Jessica went out the front door and sat with the two younger kids who began to use her like a human jungle gym. She laughed with them in obvious pleasure. Max wondered how she would handle all that had happened to her. She seemed to be bouncing back with the resilience of a child. Maybe now she could live a normal life again. Max remembered Jessica calling her father to tell him she was going away with Armando for a while. When she told Max and Rhonda of the arrangement her family had made with Armando they decided to bring her along. Hell, what's one more felony? Anyway, her family would never do anything about it as long as she called from time to time.

Max's favorite task was the phone call to Drew. He had caught the detective at home again and told him who Boyle was, his many aliases and not to bother looking for him among the living. He asked for Drew's mailing address and assured him that Christmas was coming early in the form of some great, anonymous evidence; computer disks, log books and stuff pertaining to a drug and crime cartel. Maybe Drew should be a captain or something like that. He also let him know that there would probably be some news in the next few days that should close the books. Max promised to send Drew a statement in a week or two, unsigned, just to tie up the loose ends. Then he thanked him for the help and hung up before any trace could be made.

He called Jim in the middle of the night to let him know they were safe and that they might even register the Blazers someday. They sent a message to Danny in the desert telling him to keep the "package" they left with him. He smiled at the thought of Danny trying to figure out what to do with all that money.

The next call had been here, to Marlene. It was frightening to think of what would have happened had Boyle decided to come here first instead of going to Armando's to drop off the money he had taken from Shawn and Nolan. Maybe they were just plain lucky. He had kept the phone conversation with Marlene short, just to say that the danger was over and they were coming out to see her. He figured giving her

Boyle's name would allow her to better deal with what had happened.

It felt right to be starting a life with Rhonda. They had yet to make love, at least in the physical sense, but they had formed bonds far stronger than those he had managed in past relationships by being good in bed. He couldn't wait for the opportunity to lay with her and discover all the things that would please her. The energy between them now had built to the bursting point. He smiled and hoped they didn't hurt each other when the flood gates opened.

Marlene and Rhonda walked up the path leading to a rise behind the house. "This is what the kids call the secret place. You can't see the house from here and if you look that way . . ." she pointed to the south west, "you can't see any sign of people. The kids pretend they just discovered this valley. Like the first settlers or something." They looked down the valley. "You have to ignore the contrails of the jets from Denver though."

"Maybe they pretend that they're just real straight clouds?"

"Maybe." She paused for a moment. "You look good with Max. I always thought that. Are you two okay with how this worked out?"

"I work on just being with him instead of trying to figure this out. You know . . . if someone had told us that we would be here and all this would have happened . . . just a couple of weeks ago we were waiting for the boys to get back from their hike. I was finally beginning to heal from the loss of Tawna and was starting to get on with my life. Now we're millionaires, living somewhere else, with someone else . . . I killed someone. I don't remember all of it, but I'm afraid someday I will." They were both crying now. "I think having Jessica with us is kidnapping or something, I don't know, and I don't care."

"Does this mean you're quitting the Real Estate business?"

They laughed and the dam broke. They laughed and cried and hugged each other and began the process of healing. On the way back down to the house Marlene stopped. "Oh, I forgot to mention. We made another withdrawal from those assholes. You know what? I think that the war on drugs is financially motivated. I mean we've only been fighting it as mercenaries for a short time. We have so damn much money we have to weigh it." She grinned at Marlene. "Anyway, we have a box for you. Don't insult us by arguing about it. Just put it to good use."

"No problem girl. I'll just build a shopping mall here in the valley, right next to the feed store. That ought to go over good with the locals."

They came in, arm in arm, and Max watched the weight of the past few days begin to fall from Rhonda's shoulders. The three of them sat down in the living room. Max and Rhonda filled her in on what had happened since they left Placerville. When they finished, Marlene looked at Max. "So what was the surprise you left for the bad guys?"

CHAPTER TWENTY-FIVE

It was the same sunrise that greeted Uncle Lucho, sitting in the back of the black Buick sedan as it came to a stop behind the compound in Bieber. They sat waiting for someone to come from the house. Nothing moved except the dogs that stood watching them from under the trees where they were chained. They looked well fed.

After several minutes Lucho cleared his throat. "Well, we can't learn anything sitting in the car. Let's go." They got out of the car. Luis and Raul, Lucho's men, were jumpy enough to reach for their guns as a man walked around the corner of the house. He was carrying a large bag of dog food and a pail of water. He stopped short when he saw the three men. Seeing they were Hispanic he smiled.

"Hi there. I'm Don." He waited for the reply that didn't come. "I live next door. I was told to keep the dogs fed and that someone would be by to take care of me." He grinned at them.

"Who told you this?" Lucho asked.

"My daughter, Jessica, said they had to go somewhere, Armando and her, and that I was supposed to keep feeding the dogs. Damned things were always too hungry if you ask me. Got much better dispositions now. Not nearly so ornery. Know what I mean?"

"How long ago did your daughter tell you this?"

"Well, let's see. Was day before yesterday I think. No, day 'fore that. Yeah. So's you the one s'posed to take care of me?"

Lucho took a clip of money from an inside pocket. He toyed with it. "Did they say where they were going?"

"Nope." Don eyed the money clip.

"Got any ideas?" Lucho peeled off a fifty, then another one.

Yeah, Don thought. *I think you should fuckin' pay me and quit making me out to be a fuckin' hired hand. Greasy fucker.* He kept the smile on his face. Nice and respectful like. "No. They didn't make me privy to what they had on their minds. Know what I mean?"

"Sure do." Lucho handed him the hundred. "Why don't you leave us alone here for a while." He took another fifty and gave him that one too. "We will need to talk to you again about staying on and maybe making more of this?" He indicated the money clip.

Don smiled bigger. "You sure got the language down good. I live next door there."

Next door was not even visible through the trees but Lucho smiled with him. He wanted to slap the smile from his face and tell this ignorant piece of shit to learn to speak English too. "We'll stop by in a little while and make arrangements for what we're going to need and, of course, your pay."

"Course." Don sat the dog food and water on the porch and walked off into the woods.

Lucho looked to the sky. "Gracias." He began to walk to the porch. "Is this place perfect or what?" Raul and Luis laughed.

Lucho and his henchmen walked to the back porch. Lucho nodded and the shorter man, Luis, stepped up on the porch and tried the back door. It was locked. Lucho took out a ring of keys, selected one and gave it to him. Once open, the kitchen assaulted them with the smell of death. Flies could be heard in the house. On the kitchen floor was dried blood and evidence of a struggle that didn't turn out good for someone. Lucho took in the chair on its side, the bloody rope, and knew someone had told their life's story here. He pointed down the hall and Luis led the way.

A loud buzzing could be heard. It came from the first door down the hall. Both of Lucho's men took out guns and stepped back against the wall opposite the door. One nodded and they kicked the door off its hinges. The door flew into the bathroom, twisted against the toilet, bounced off the shower curtain rod, and came to rest after shattering the mirrored medicine chest. In the tub lay the dog, legs sticking straight out from its body like a piñata; its stomach bloated to bursting with gasses, eyes open, flies swarming on the head and maggots moving where it had been shot.

The taller man, Raul, swallowed hard to keep from vomiting. Luis looked at him and smiled. "We got to stop to eat after this." He said it low so Lucho couldn't hear. It had the desired effect. Raul couldn't hold back and vomited into the toilet. Luis looked disgusted at him and Lucho walked down the hall. Luis mentally notched another rung in his climb to take Armando's place. Luis knew Armando had to be dead. Either he or Raul would be taking his place. He smiled.

The rest of the house revealed only dust and evidence that no one had been here for days. "Let's go."

Lucho walked out the back door and headed for the barn. He could see the black Bronco there, covered in a thin layer of dust. A bug of some kind had left a meandering set of tracks across the hood like a miniature horse. Lucho pointed at the Bronco's door and Luis opened it. The buzzer came on indicating the keys were still in the ignition. Lucho turned away and looked to the rear of the barn. “In here.”

Lucho walked to the back room and pulled the lever opening the vault. The smell was not as strong here, but since the temperature in the vault stayed the same all the time that didn’t mean much. Luis moved to go down the steps and Raul held back. Once at the bottom of the steps Luis looked in the computer room first. It seemed untouched. Then he looked at the other room. When he saw the money he was glad that he would take Armando’s place. No one knew this place existed except Armando and Lucho. That meant that those who had helped build it were busy decomposing now and Raul would soon join them. “Come on down.”

Lucho and Raul came to the doorway. The body of Armando lay face down, head turned and staring at them with sightless eyes. Lucho looked at the bin and realized it was still full. Why hadn’t they taken the money? He looked at the mess spread across the far wall and the small piles scattered nearby. At first his mind did not accept what his eyes told him. This used to be a man. He made out a hand, bits of clothing, and worst of all an eye setting in maybe the left side of a head. Raul began to gag again.

Lucho caught Luis’ eye and nodded. Luis snorted, turned to him with his gun drawn. Raul, a trusted soldier of Lucho for six loyal years. Lucho moved to the side as Luis shot Raul below the right ear, removing most of his brains and depositing them against the entryway wall, thus insuring Luis as Armando’s replacement.

Luis turned and moved to the body of Armando. Lucho walked over next to Luis and looked down at his nephew. “I wonder if we’ll ever know what happened here?” He reached down and turned the body over.

“What’s this?” Luis pointed to the remote control. It was his first and last official act as banker of the Lucho Compound.

Max had spent a year mining underground for a small outfit up near Coeur d'Alene, Idaho. A real small outfit. All underground mining, with a tunnel small as could be and still get equipment through. He got to do the drilling, lugging the Jackleg up to the new face after it had been cleared away, or "mucked" as they said. Then he would position neatly spaced, six foot deep, drill holes into which he'd place one stick of dynamite with a fuse and primer. After all the holes had been done he would fill them with the nitrogen pellets the miners called Prel. Cheap way to get more bang for the buck. Once the dynamite went off, so did the prel.

He always wondered if he was actually helping the forest nearby to grow . . . with all that fertilizer blown to hell and gone and spreading over the countryside. Maybe that made up for the big hole he was digging in Mother Earth's mountain.

Never thought that training would pay off so well.

With Jessica and Rhonda supplying the labor, they had emptied the money out of the Plexiglas bin, stacking most of it in boxes Jessica found in the barn.

Max figured he needed a six-percent solution of number-two diesel fuel added to the ammonium nitrate. Diesel weighs about seven pounds per gallon so starting with three hundred pounds of the prel he added a little less than three gallons of the diesel. This was high-density ammonium nitrate so it wouldn't work quite as well as industrial grade but it would still make one hell of an explosion. Then they took a plastic garbage bag and filled it with nitrogen pellets. They stacked up a single row of banded hundreds against the outside of the bin, and put the tightly packed bag of nitrogen pellets in the center. Inside each bag was a dog collar attached to makeshift primers made from shotgun shells.

To make the primer Max had emptied out a dozen shotgun shells and packed the powder into a short piece of PVC pipe he found in the barn. Into one end he jammed a shotgun shell with the shot pellets removed. These were set to be triggered by the remote collars.

By repeating this process they used all three hundred pounds of explosives and had built a tower surrounded with one single row of banded hundred dollar bills. After they finished the job it looked like what it had been before they started; a Plexiglas tower full of money. In fact, it could be the world's largest firecracker.

Max checked the remote receivers from the dog collars. These would be triggered by the remote control under Armando's body when he was turned over and the pressure was taken off the button. Three hundred pounds of Prel. Man. Max really wished he could be here to see it. Anyone who knew how to get down here was one of the Bad guys. He only hoped it was *the bad guy*. If nothing else it would cover their trail.

The bad guy was busy being vaporized at that moment. By turning Armando over, Luis released the trigger on the remote. It took seconds to set off the Prel. Lucho and Luis were looking straight at the bin when it exploded. The row of money concealing the explosive and the Plexiglas outer shell passed right through them, became fused with them, joined them on the short trip to the wall.

The flesh, muscle, organs and fluids separated from the bone first, like the skin of buildings set up real close to ground zero to test the effect of an Atomic blast. Then the rest of what remained smashed against the wall. The blast was contained by the thick concrete walls, very nearly atomizing what was in the room at the time.

There would be no identification of the bodies. Hell, there would be no body count. Even with the right equipment it would be hard to tell what had been in the room. Only Raul could be identified as human at one time; partly shielded from the blast by conveniently being dead in the entryway.

Oddly, the blast made little noise above ground. More of a "whump" sound accompanied by the ground shaking beneath his feet as Jessica's father stepped up on his back porch.

Charles L. Hill

CHAPTER TWENTY-SIX

One year later . . .

Barry had been running the streets forever. At least forever as far as someone sixteen cared. Why not? School sucked. That was for sure. There were no heroes that he could see anywhere on campus. The spell of education had worn off around grade six. That's when he had first tried it. Just a little smoke. That's all. Man. Everything got okay in a hurry. Music got real. Seemed like the ones singing the songs were talking to him alone. Food was good. Got home late but could not wait. Tore the fridge up. Tuna sandwich, chips, Coke, Mom yelling about how that shit had to last for all of us to the end of the month. Didn't he know that?

Right. Till the end of the month cause that was when the checks came in. State and Fed. Maybe if dear old Dad showed up there'd be extra.

Heroes. The ones who had the money in this neighborhood were barely older than he was. Shit. What did they know? They knew if you sold three or four, you kept one. After that was gravy. Get some clothes. Lame fuckers that couldn't dress just didn't know what was what. Needed to be in school. That was the market place. Kids from the real homes, the Cosby show homes, the Brady Bunchers, brought him the cash. Brought him more than that later. Young honeys brought the leg. Easier than cash. All he could stand.

So now what? Some dude gets caught with a stash and has to plead his case to Mom and Dad. Then off to the school. Do you know where our little Jimmy got this stuff? Do you Mr. Barton? Boys' counselor of the world? Boys' counselor of the ones named Aaron through Lynch? This has got to stop.

No shit. Here it comes. We got to talk to you. No sweat. Just like getting busted. Old home week in the holding cell. Cool. Now what. Probation? Yeah. Sorry Mom. It was just some kid had to pin his shit on some beaner that looks guilty just standing there. You'll see.

Report once a week for a month or so. Got to go to the classes and get the teachers to sign off. Shit. Half of them wish I would never show up. Suit them just fine if I never came back. Stuff like this works good. Now I'm dealing to the kids in high school. Off campus of course. Can't get on. Booted me out now almost two semesters. Mom wants me to get some job that buys a meal.

In the cop shop. There's someone who thinks he can work with you. Okay, Mom. I do love you. Got to love your Mom right?

Here I sit. Waiting for the man as usual. What does he know?

"Barry?"

Barry looks up to watch the man walk over and offer his hand. He ignores it. It doesn't seem to bother the cop. He just holds it out there in space for a while, then sits down on the edge of the desk. "I'm Captain Drew. I've been asked to talk to you on behalf of your probation officer, Mr. Daniels. It seems you sold drugs to a kid that goes by the name of Spider."

Barry sat up. Sure he did. It was his main outlet to the school. "Don't know him."

Drew looked at him and smiled. A little one that made his lips turn up only slightly. "Too bad. He turned on you. Couldn't say enough about you. Do you know what the word 'habitual' means?" He didn't wait for the answer. "It means someone keeps doing the same crime over and over again. Same shit. Again and again. Gets old for us here in law enforcement." He sighed, put down the folder he had been reading, pinched the bridge of his nose and squinted. "Repeat offender. Career criminal. Drug dealer. That's all you know, isn't it?"

"So? Is there a point to all this?"

"Maybe there isn't one this time. I'm going to let you make a choice here today. It's all yours. Whatever you choose is okay by me. I'm not all that sure this kind of thing works anyway. Here's the deal. You like deals don't you?"

He got up and walked around the desk and sat on the edge facing Barry. "You got a case coming down on you right now. We got the pictures, the statements, the dope; it's all set. We get to take advantage of the fact that, this being an election year, the politicians are hot to look like real live heroes in the war on drugs. You get to take a fall as a habitual drug dealer under a new law that says we get to try you as an adult. Body slam you with the full weight of the law. We get to make an example of you. When you get out, if I'm not retired by then . . ." Drew put on a real smile this time. "Well, I'm going to make you my personal project to step on at every turn."

"Gee, sounds like a great deal to me, boss."

"How do you like it so far?"

"I was kind'a hopin' for something like you would say . . . on the other hand . . . an alternate thing."

"Okay. Barry. On the other hand, instead of sending you somewhere for a few years where your young ass may come out the size of a number ten tomato can, we might send you on a vacation . . . to a ranch . . . with real horses, wide open spaces, no bars."

"No bars?"

"No bars. Except if you walk off you get to come back and finish up here."

Barry figured he knew what that meant. "For how long?"

"One year. After that, it's up to you and the ranch as to what happens. You might get to stay longer, but at the end of a year you don't owe us squat unless you come back and run up another tab by going back to the same old game, which is the ending I envision."

Barry considered this new gig. Sounded like a YMCA camp. "How about my Mom? Does she know about this?"

"She's one of the reasons you're being considered for this. She really pitched hard for you. I think she cares more for your life than you do." He paused and stretched his back. "It's up to you. Tell me now because I got room for only three and there's other candidates."

"Sure. I'll go. When do I leave?"

Quick action. Two days later, sign some forms. Say goodbye and off to the races. Couple days of bus ride after that and Barry could no longer stand the two traveling companions. Just from different gangs but the further they got from Sacramento the less that seemed to matter. Now they are not only a long way from home but maybe on a different planet. Miles between towns. Only Hispanics he could see now were doing low life manual labor. Not too many of them either. Just for fun he signed one, made a circle with his thumb and fore finger and spread the other three, kind of a backwards OK sign. Back home that would get him an answer sign from a fellow member or a bullet maybe if they weren't. Got him nothing here but the finger. Not any members here. He should recruit. Maybe he could make that extended middle finger their sign.

Now. Finally. Off the fucking bus. This ain't really a town. Barely room for the city limit sign. All three of them standing around, profiling for the locals, uncomfortable as hell. This place looks all white.

"Okay, boys. Show me the papers and we can get on the road."

Barry took out the forms the detective had given him. This woman was a looker. Dark hair, olive skin, great body. Must feel pretty sure of herself, picking up three home boys all by her lonesome. Maybe she's packing. Don't see where in those Levi's and red flannel work shirt. Shit. That color shirt would get you cut in half on his street back home.

She shows them to this white Blazer with a picture of a brand on the side in offset letters . . . TH. They pile in. After about half an hour down a main paved road they turn off and head toward rolling hills that probably pass for mountains here. Bouncing around in the back seat. The three of them. Her all alone in the front seat, a couple of boxes next to her.

"How soon are we going to get there?"

"We've been on the Ranch for the last twenty minutes."

Barry looked for a building of some kind. This place was huge. That detective had said it wasn't State or Fed. This place was private. What was their gig here? "You got cows here?"

"Some."

Real talkative.

The road went between two outcroppings and below them was the ranch. It had a main house of stone and wood, a large barn and several out buildings. Two good sized barracks buildings sat at opposite ends of the main house. "That building on the left is for the boys."

That could only mean that the other one was for the girls. Barry thought he might like the place.

"There's where you eat." She pointed to a building with a sign over the double wood plank doors that said Mess Hall. Nice name for a place to eat.

She brought the Blazer to a stop in front of the boy's barracks. As they got out two people waited for them. The welcoming committee. Both wore red flannel work shirts. Must be the uniform here.

The man spoke first. Old guy but didn't look like someone to fool with. "Welcome. I'm Max. This is a working ranch. You're a long way from home but if you want to go back just say the word. You'll leave immediately." He paused for effect. "This building behind me is your home for the next year. The building over there . . ." He pointed to the other large building, "is the girl's barracks. If you go near it without one of the cadre, you go home. If you use any drugs here, you go home. If you don't know for sure what is expected of you, read the sheets posted in the barracks. Did you all understand that?"

They nodded in unison. "You are here because someone thinks there's a chance you can get off drugs and live a better life. Several have come here and accomplished just that. There are letters from some of them posted in the barracks. Sometimes they come back to visit. One of them is visiting here next week. There are two others who have stayed on here. You will meet them later this evening. Ask them whatever you please, they'll be more than happy to talk to you."

The girl next to him was not any older than Barry but wore the cadre shirt. Barry wondered what her story was. He started to feel something new. He couldn't identify it. This looked better than the street where he came from. Unfamiliar. New. He started to smile, then stopped himself. He postured like he was still on his corner. It didn't carry as well here. He would hold his own till he figured what did fit.

The one named Max motioned to them to follow. They passed under a wooden arch with a sign. It showed the TH brand. There . . . painted in white letters was the name of the ranch.

"Tawna's Hope"

FROM THE AUTHOR

The Hike was written while living in Auburn, California in the foothills of the Sierra Nevada Mountains. The storyline was conceived while hiking the Pacific Crest Trail.

Some of what you read comes from my personal experiences . . . except the parts about Boyle, of course.

Irene Parker's parents were in the Civil Air Patrol and lived near Lake Lahontan in Nevada.

I, myself, have a private pilot's license and worked for two years drilling and blasting for gold in the Sawtooth Mountains of Idaho.

The excerpt from Daylight Pass that has been included here begins at The Exchange Club in Beatty, Nevada. During the 1980's and 90's this small town casino was owned and operated by my parents, Murphy & Maxine Breedlove.

DAYLIGHT PASS

CHAPTER ONE

Don sat on the back porch of his ten-year old double-wide mobile home enjoying the last few drags of his twentieth cigarette and the glass of Courvoisier he used to celebrate any day kept within the one pack limit. The sky changed from the star speckled shades of indigo to pale lavender and finally surrendering to the sliver of sun now coming up over the desert mountains to the east. Daylight was coming to Beatty, Nevada. It was time for Don to hit the sack.

Sleeping during the day when others were fighting to stay comfortable in one-hundred degree plus, asphalt softening heat was something he considered a bonus to working the graveyard shift at the Exchange Club. There were other benefits. No gung-ho bosses would work graveyard. Not enough exposure. Swing shift was for the social climbers. Graveyard was for the coasters. Peaceful. Many times there were fewer customers in the place than employees. The joke went around that if a fight ever broke out between the tourists and the employees during the graveyard shift the employees would be heavy favorites.

A butterfly the size, shape and color of a well-used dime landed on the sage brush by the porch and spread it's wings to the rising sun. Sand and sage was the landscape around Don's mobile. So was all the other landscape for about a hundred miles in any direction. Sage, sand and a desert floor of sun cooked rocks the texture of a well-travelled but poorly maintained road. The big difference here was the arrangement of cantaloupe-sized, white washed rocks Don used to line the driveway. His faded, silver, not quite old enough to be deemed a "classic" Thunderbird took up most of the drive.

Of course there were disadvantages to working graveyard. His sleep patterns were certainly out of kilter. He wore a watch and constantly checked it during the day. His mind conversations went like this . . . Let's see . . . it's eight in the morning . . . if I go to sleep now I might wake up too early . . . then I'd be ready to go back to sleep about the time I have to go to work . . . but if I wait, I might not be able to sleep . . . maybe I'll just run a couple of errands. Oh great. Now it's seven at night and I can't sleep simply because I have to . . . now I won't be able to wake up when the alarms go off, etc.

The sound of the vacuum cleaner, a constant companion on the latter parts of the graveyard shift, was a bit maddening. He developed a theory that the easiest way for graveyard shift workers to sleep was to run a vacuum cleaner in their bedroom.

The temperature rose quickly. The smell of sage baking and sand warming. The sound of a car driving down the highway from Death Valley, slowing as it came into the small desert town. He could hear the hum of the tires change to the distinct crunch of individual bits of gravel as the car paused at the only stop light in town. The only stop light between Tonopah, ninety miles to the north, and Indian Springs, ninety miles to the south, unless you counted the one at Lathrop Wells which was not really a stoplight but just there to let everyone know the house of ill repute was, indeed, open.

He tossed the remaining brandy at the base of the sage brush sculpting a small crimson replica of a wave cresting and changing from deep red to pastel pink as the brandy soaked through. The sand here was finer and lighter than the beaches of Texas where he'd grown up.

The tiny butterfly moved on in search of a quieter bush . . . much like he had done in leaving Patty.

Morning activity started up. His nearest neighbor lived in a powder blue mobile home half a block up the hill and slightly newer than his. Oleander bushes, five feet high, five feet wide and alternating between red and white flowers, were planted around the mobile and had grown together to form a wall against the wind except where the driveway was supposed to be. He couldn't see the front door as it opened and closed with a muted metallic clang. He could, however, see the end of the porch where a big yellow dog of the mutt variety stood, stretched, shook and lay back down.

I'm with you pal, Don thought as he stood, stretched and went inside. Time for sleep before I get drawn into a real day with real people. I'll just make sure I'm asleep before this day gets up a good head of steam.

He drew the kitchen blinds, cutting out most of the sunlight. The remaining windows had heavy drapes to keep out the heat and light. All the drapes had velcro fasteners sewn onto the leading edges. When they were pulled together the effect was of being hermetically sealed from the sunlight. This increased his chances of getting enough sleep to make the night shift more comfortable. He had bought the Velcro for all the windows after a month of trying unsuccessfully to sleep during the day. It had gotten old real quick, waking up to tape aluminum foil to the windows and stacking whatever was handy on the curtains to try to keep out the sunlight that intruded into a daytime sleeper's very heart with irritating, flash-bulb intensity from the smallest pin hole.

Nothing was worse after a day of no sleep than a night of no customers, standing at an empty twenty-one table, trying to stay awake. Nothing. It had to be a piece of hell. Slamming down as much coffee as possible during the twenty minute break, even washing his face with ice water. Going back to the table to pull his next hour and spending it not quite awake but nervous and needing to pee. It was a time when he prayed for a customer. Even a customer who wanted to start a beef was better than struggling with fatigue, listening to the Muzak tape playing songs it's embarrassing to admit you know the words to, through the same speakers used to summon a porter to mop up some drunk's last meal. Of course the whole mindless experience would be played out to the steady drone of a vacuum cleaner.

After rinsing out the brandy glass and putting it upside down on the sink edge, where it would be in the morning to use again, he ran cold water and prepared the makings for a pot of coffee. The coffee maker used a timer which he set to start ten minutes before the alarm would go off that evening. Waking up to the smell of fresh coffee was nice. He would sometimes lay in bed for awhile after the alarm went off and imagine someone was about to bring it in to him.

He switched on the power to the VCR. Another timer. This one set to record the basketball game between the L.A. Lakers and the Phoenix Suns later in the day so he could watch it before his shift started. He turned off the phone ringer, switched on the answering machine, and walked down the hall to the bedroom.

Halfway down the hall he paused and looked into the room kept made up for his son's infrequent visits. Empty. At least it wasn't dusty.

Once, two years ago after one too many brandies, he had paused to look at this room on his way to bed and noticed a film of dust over everything in the room. Why not? No one had been in it since Mark had gone back home to Patty's for the school year two months before. He had felt a great sense of loss in that moment.

Mark's room had been covered with dust as if he would never come back. This room suddenly became a reminder of his loneliness. The room might just as well be used for something else. Put in a couple of mounted bass or trout and call it a den. He started to cry silently without noticing at first until the warm tears worked their way down the bottom edge of his nose. He went into the kitchen and took out the vacuum cleaner and the feather duster. When he finished with the room it looked fresh and that had been the last time the room ever looked abandoned or unused.

It was that incident which made him realize what he had become. He was no longer a father to Mark. He had become an uncle. By having Mark live here in the summer he could try to demonstrate good character, but when it came right down to it, during the school year, for the major decisions in Mark's life, it would rest on the shoulders of Patty and that asshole Bob.

Bob.

Bob, his old boss and almost business partner. Heady associates in a new venture that just might bring Patty and himself a better lifestyle than they ever enjoyed before. After starting out small with just he and Bob running a two man security company and skip tracing operation they had built it up to a prosperous enterprise with almost a dozen employees if you counted the bookkeeper.

That had been Patty.

Someone had warned him about couples working together. He thought it would help them to stay close. Maybe it would keep the job from interfering with the marriage.

Coming home early from a trip to Las Vegas, after signing up the largest account to date, there Patty was, asleep, her head resting on Bob's chest, smiling.

Don called Beatty "home" a week later.

Going from Las Vegas to Reno for more of the same revelry he hoped would ease the bonds constricting his emotions, the icy fingers around his heart like a tangible force. He sat in the coffee shop of the Exchange Club at three in the morning, graveyard shift, and fell into a conversation with Vern, the shift boss for the non-shift--the head coaster of the on-till-dawn crew. He went to work the next day, or morning, on a temporary basis. That was five years ago this August.

The dog next door began to bark. Three short barks, another short and another short. Three shorts, a short and a short.

In Morse code it read "see, see."

See what?

Don drifted into sleep.

Alissa reached over and shut off the alarm. It had to be the middle of the night. Sitting on the edge of the bed she stretched, yawned and stood facing a large bay window where light from the early morning filtered through the shear drapes. Before her body could overrule her head she reached as far as she could toward the ceiling. Her morning ritual began. She twisted in place, feeling her abdominals begin to respond. Twenty, twenty-one, twenty-two. She was tall. Five foot ten. Athletic like her Dad.

Her height had done well by her, opening the door to University of California, Davis, for a sports scholarship in Volleyball. Now touching the floor with her palms, heels flat, legs straight, ten, eleven, twelve. Perspiration began to dampen the lightweight cotton sweat suit she favored for night wear. She lay on her back, legs pointed to the ceiling, hands clasped behind her head, crunching her stomach as she touched first one elbow to the opposite knee, then the other, fifteen, sixteen, seventeen. The room was flooded in morning light by the time she finished. She picked the towel up off the window seat, left there to remind her not to miss this self-imposed morning ritual, and walked to the white tiled bathroom.

She turned the hot water on in the shower before looking at her reflection in the triple mirrors above the two marble sinks. Living here in these rich surroundings, a rent-free benefit of her parent's heroism and her own dedication, had a lot of pluses. Waiting for the water to get hot wasn't one of them. Since this room, where she lived for thirteen years now, was quite a distance from the utility room and the water heater, she had to wait several minutes for the hot water to reach this part of the sprawling home.

After the shower she dressed comfortably in a white cotton blouse, faded blue denim jeans and white tennis shoes. She tossed a couple of articles she had used to get ready into a suitcase packed the night before, closed it and walked to the main house.

She went to the kitchen and poured herself a mug of hot coffee, a vice she didn't intend to give up, and sat at the table near the walk-in pantry reserved for the

"Help". She preferred it to the huge slab of mahogany in the dining area.

"Morning Delores."

"Good morning, Alissa." Delores sat the plate of scrambled eggs, sausage, cantaloupe, toast and strawberry jelly in front of Alissa. "I've baked some sweet-rolls . . . Cinnamon . . . they'll be ready about the time you're done with this."

"Great." It was being able to eat whatever she wanted to that motivated her exercise routine. "Is Tommy up yet?"

"Oh, he certainly is. He's been up and fidgeting for the last hour. I think he slept in his clothes." Delores brushed the front of her crisp, starched white uniform. "He is really excited to be going on this trip with you. He is treating it like a real adventure." She moved through the kitchen with the grace of a woman maybe a hundred pounds lighter. Delores had been here longer than Alissa. Her easy manner and constant good humor had filled this room for as long as Alissa could remember.

Alissa ate her food. Never one to pick at her plate she worked on it with enthusiasm.

Tommy burst through the kitchen door with all the energy of a healthy seven year old. His freckled face beamed at Alissa. "How soon are we going? Are you all ready to go? Can I help? Are we gonna' stop in Dead Valley?" All this came out in one long breath. He stood with both arms resting on the table looking at Alissa through bright green eyes, an unruly shock of red hair dropping down over one eye. He brushed the hair back with one hand, never letting go of the two toy action figures he clutched. The hair fell again.

Alissa beamed back at him. "Soon, almost, yes and I don't see why not." She brushed the same shock of hair out of his eyes. "How about you? Are you really ready?"

Somehow, he beamed even more. "I was ready last night. Delores even packed my stuff in the car."

Delores wiped her hands on her apron. "I had too. He would have never quit pestering me otherwise." She rubbed his head playfully. The shock of hair fell again.

Alissa finished the last of her cantaloupe and took her dishes to the sink. "Did you say goodbye to your dad?"

"Yes. He came in and kissed me before he went to the airport. He said by the time you get up he's gonna' be half way to English."

"England." Alissa lifted the lid on the picnic basket Delores held out to her. "Do you really think we'll eat all this?"

Delores laughed and all her parts moved like firm pudding. "It's just in case. I already called up Giesla at the Sun Valley house and told her I wanted you two back in the same condition you're leaving here in."

Alissa rolled her eyes. "You're like a mother hen. We're going to miss you." She hugged Delores. Tommy ran up and did the same. Delores' eyes filled with tears. "Come on now . . . it's only for the summer. We'll be back before you know it. Anyway," Alissa escaped the embrace and took the basket, "we will call you as soon as we get there."

"Promise?"

"Promise." Alissa walked out the side door into the garage area. She pushed the button to raise the automatic doors, moved past a Mercedes 500 sedan, a 735i BMW and a Mercedes wagon to a 1979 Volvo Coupe. It was the oldest car in the garage and Alissa's personal favorite. She had argued successfully to keep it from being traded and it was considered her's by everyone working here.

Delores waved to them as the car drove past the

entrance to the main house, around the tree lined curving drive and through the open automatic gates at the stone entrance to the Bruener Mansion. Alissa and Tommy waved back and disappeared down the road into the valley below.

She drove with the windows down, the crisp morning air filled the car with smells of the baking soil getting ready for new growth and a hot summer. Not for her and Tommy. The house in Sun Valley Idaho enjoyed summer temperatures way up around a scorching seventy five or eighty degrees. Coats at night were the rule. She drove onto Highway Five, through San Diego proper. Looking to the west they could see a collection of small sailboats jockeying for position around a series of brightly painted buoys. Tommy fiddled with the radio dial until he got a country and western station. He listened for a moment, tapping his hand on the door in time to the music--a mirror image of the way his dad listened to music. Same music. Alissa smiled.

"How long before we get there?" he asked.

That question didn't take long. "We won't be in Sun Valley until tomorrow. It's just a little too far to make in one day.

"How long can we stay in Dead Valley?"

"You mean Death Valley. We should drive through it and see what's there, right? I got brochures from a place called *The Inn*. We should see that and Scotty's Castle."

"How come they call it Death Valley?"

"I don't know. Should we ask them?"

"Sounds kinda' scary to me. Like a spook house. It won't scare me though cause I'm seven now."

Alissa smiled but refrained from laughing. "Yep, almost a week now." The birthday party had been another display of the real reason Alissa stayed on.

She adored Tommy and cringed inside when Mona, Tommy's mother, finally had enough to drink and passed out on a lawn chair by the pool. Most of the kids ignored her but a few went over to stare at her like she was some beached whale.

Even with all the money Karl Bruener had, and all the fancy drying out farms and psychotherapy he could buy, Mona still drank like a fish. She had even tried Alcoholics Anonymous but the first meeting she went to, disguised with sunglasses and coat, she had seen her gardener there and bolted.

They were driving through the picturesque town of Fallbrook when Tommy mentioned the inevitable. "I need to go to the bathroom."

Alissa pulled in at a combination fruit stand and convenience store. A hand painted sign indicated the restrooms were "around back" and were for customers only. Alissa sighed, got out, and went in to buy some gum while Tommy took the key, attached to a brightly painted, two foot two-by-four with a length of chain, and went to use the restroom.

Alissa waited back in the car for Tommy. She was the only car in the gravel parking lot with the exception of a late model, black Dodge van with windows tinted till you couldn't see inside. She didn't remember it being parked there when she drove in. All she could see of the driver was a meaty arm resting on the outside mirror with a cigarette held idly between fingers sporting heavy gold rings. She never smoked but was intrigued by the mechanics of it all; the lighting up, the holding and flipping. She once tried to write a paper on personality types and smoking styles. Her professor at the time, a three pack a day, down to the hot nub, non-filter kind of guy, discouraged it to the point where she opted to pass on the project and get a possibly higher grade with a less antagonistic subject.

Psychology was her major but she didn't need a degree to know a smoker resented helpful advice from a non-smoker. It only prompted irritation and the possibility of open hostility. The smoker in the van was a filter smoking, let it cool between drags and toss it while it's still got life in it kind of guy. A thinker with imagined self- control. Sure enough. The arm disappeared in the window, a stream of smoke drifted out of the window and traveled along the black roof of the van, suddenly whipped away by a breath of wind, a casual replacing of the hand on the mirror.

Tommy came bounding back from the store and climbed into the front seat. "Okay, here we go." Alissa backed up the Volvo, checked the rearview mirror and pulled onto the main road. "That bathroom needs a cleaning. Pheweeu."

"That's why they are so careful about the key." Alissa and Tommy laughed as she ran the Volvo through the gears, up to cruising speed, enjoying the tight feel of a well-built machine handling curves as though the car was just dying to be driven.

The man in the dark Dodge van took one last short drag, let the cigarette fall from his fingers, started the engine and pulled after the Volvo.

CPSIA information can be obtained at www.ICGtesting.com
Printed in the USA
LVOW08s1705270814

401204LV00017B/962/P

9 780990 523215